The Midwife

Pegg Thomas

Spinner of Yarns
PUBLISHING, LLC

S PINNER OF YARNS PUBLISHING, LLC
Sault Ste. Marie, Michigan

Copyright @2026 by Pegg Thomas
https://peggthomas.com/
Published in the United States of America
ISBN: 979-8-9929079-5-7
Cover Design by Pegg Thomas – *(Elements of this cover were created using AI technology)*
Cover Art Copyright by Spinner of Yarns Publishing, LLC

This is a work of fiction. Names, characters, and incidents in this book are products of the author's imagination or are used in a fictitious situation with the exception of characters listed in the Author's Notes. Any resemblances to actual events, locations, organizations, incidents, or persons – living or dead – are coincidental and beyond the intent of the author with the exception of those listed in the Author's Notes.

In this series are many actual historical figures. The author has used her imagination to flesh the characters out for the purposes of the series. While using the known facts of the characters, they are not intended to be historically accurate in every detail.

Join Pegg's Newsletter
writing updates – sneak peeks – fiber arts updates – personal content
https://www.subscribepage.com/PeggThomas

Salem Village
Fictional Characters

Puritans

Verity Manton
Mary Scudder
Becky Simpson
Joseph Tripp
John Biddle
Jane Biddle

Quakers

Hester Fuller
David O'Sullivan
Isobel O'Sullivan
& O'Sullivan children
Elias Barwick
Arthur Stokes
Phoebe Stokes
Stephen Draper

Salem Village
Historical Characters

Puritans

Thomas Buffington
Sarah Buffington
& Buffington children
Rev. Samuel Parris
Elizabeth Parris
Betty Parris
Abigail Williams
Dr. William Griggs
Rachel Griggs
Elizabeth Hubbard
John Indian
Tituba Indian
William Good
Sarah Good
Alexander Osborne
Sarah Osborne
Rebecca Nurse
Mary Sibley

George Corwin
Lydia Corwin
Ezekiel Cheever
Rev. Increase Mather
Rev. Cotton Mather
John Hathorne
Jonathon Corwin

Quakers

Caleb Buffum
Hannah Buffum
& Buffum children

In an age where our national birthrate is plummeting, while we have every convenience at our fingertips and all that modern medicine can do for us, delving into the world of Colonial American midwives was an eye-opening experience. So I wish to dedicate this book to the brave women who literally gave birth to a nation under hardships and dangers we can barely imagine. Without them—we wouldn't be here.

Chapter 1

❝❞ TIS A FALSE ALARM, but thy aunt was right to fetch me." Hester Fuller patted the back of Jane Biddle's hand. "There may be a few of them before the day is to come. I should think the babe will remain where it is for at least another fortnight."

The brown-haired woman on the bed gave her a weary smile. "I told my aunt 'twas too soon, but she worries so."

As well she should, but Hester wasn't about to admit it and upset the mother-to-be. This was Jane's fourth child, and as such, should have been less complicated. But she'd become pregnant on the heels of her last babe, a little girl who had turned a year old last week. She'd not given herself proper time to rest in between. Hester firmly believed that two or three years between births was best for both the mother and the infant.

The aunt, Sarah Cloyce, sat on a chair on the other side of Jane's bed. "I am sorry for bringing you out for no cause."

"'Tis no bother." It never failed to amaze Hester that a woman could give birth—nine times in Sarah's case—and fail to remember the details of the experience. Once the babe was in her arms, all thought of the process seemed to slip away. Perhaps it was God's blessing. "Do not hesitate to call me back if thee are unsure. A fourth child can make a surprisingly fast appearance."

Sarah sighed. "I remember my fourth. Such a winsome child."

"I should be on my way." Hester lifted her basket and strode to the door before Sarah could launch into her memories of all nine of her birthings. "Do not hesitate to fetch me again. 'Tis only a short walk down the street." She slipped out the door and down the stairs.

"Midwife?" Jane's husband stopped his pacing in the parlor as Hester entered.

"'Twas a false alarm."

The air seemed to melt out of the tall man. Thin to the point of skinny, he bent forward, hand to his forehead, the faint light of morning filtering through the window behind him, dimming the light of the single lit candle on the side table. "Does it never get easier?"

Hester refrained from chuckling. Husbands came in two varieties, it seemed, those who suffered along with their wives, albeit from a distance, and those who regarded childbirth a woman's responsibility, and therefore of little concern to themselves. Hester much preferred John Biddle's sort. It was her high success rate for assisting with live births—something she took pains not to be proud of—that made her popular with her Puritan neighbors, but any birth had its inherent dangers. It did the man credit that he cared so much for the woman upstairs and their unborn child.

"Each babe will come into the world in his or her own way, some easier than others." Even though Hester had never given birth herself, she'd assisted well over a hundred women between helping her physician father, and then becoming a midwife after the death of her intended. That had caused a bit of a stir, even among the Friends, to have an unmarried woman as midwife. But there had been few options at the time, and her training had been exemplary. It hadn't taken long before she was accepted by both Friends and Puritans alike.

She wished John Biddle a good day, and then stepped out into the fresh air of an early April morning. Smoke drifted from the chimneys in town, hanging low with the promise of rain to come. *Sweet April showers, doth spring May flowers.* The old poem, as appropriate that morning as when Thomas Tusser had penned it some hundred years past, was one of her favorites.

If only the village were as peaceful as it seemed. If only a good spring rain could wash away the taint that hung over it.

Hester was the only Friend living within the village limits, which had a statute that restricted property ownership to members of the Puritan church. She rented a humble cottage from the innkeeper, Nathaniel Ingersoll, and the village elders permitted it because their women wanted a midwife they could count on nearby. Even though they had a new, rather elderly, physician in town, the women were generally more comfortable with a woman assisting in childbirth.

Which had suited Hester just fine until the accusations of witchcraft had begun.

Everyone knew that the first execution of a witch in the American colonies had been Margaret Jones, a midwife, back in '48. A shiver crept up Hester's back. Margaret Jones had been a Puritan among Puritans. How much more vulnerable was Hester as a Friend living among Puritans? Several of the families among their Friends had offered her a place in their homes, but she'd resisted. Partly because she enjoyed her independence, and partly because she feared that the Puritan women—or their husbands—wouldn't fetch her from a Friend's farm when their time came. As accepting as they were of her, that might be too much for them. They were a stiff-necked lot, even if, taken one at a time, most were agreeable to be around.

She reached her cottage and entered through the back door, wiping her feet on a colorful rug one of the Puritan ladies had gifted to her after the birth of her child. None of the Friends would have created something so vibrant, preferring the somber, plain hues of soft grays, blues, browns, and greens. But it made Hester smile when it greeted her upon her return, and so she'd kept it.

Pushing aside the makings of another basket, Hester put her midwife's basket on the table. She stretched and yawned. No sense in going back to bed, as morning was already breaking. She'd mix herself a bit of porridge and then hunt in the forest for more basket-making materials. Spring was a good time to gather red-twig dogwood shoots, river willow withies, and woodbine vines. Selling her baskets in the village and in Salem Town, along with her midwife fees, allowed her to stay in the cottage. The income supplied the independence she enjoyed.

Perhaps a little too much.

The alternative was to live as a spinster aunt with one of her brothers, which she did not favor. Her sister would take her in, of course, but Emily lived in Connecticut Colony, so far away. Hester had turned down the matrimonial offers of several widowers with children in need of a mother. Not that she didn't love children, she did, but to be married to a man other than Timothy Newman? That she couldn't do. There'd only been one Timothy, and God had called him home far too soon. Far too young.

Perhaps it was knowing she'd never have children of her own that made Hester so passionate about the babes and mothers she assisted. Timothy's death had changed everything for her, and perhaps for those children she'd successfully ushered into the world. It was good to think that God was working out His plan, that Timothy's death had been just a senseless farming accident.

It was still early enough in the year to let the cream rise in the cool of the dairy. Hannah Buffum, Jr., poured fresh milk into wooden troughs on her workbench. In another week or two, she'd need to haul the buckets to the spring house to keep the milk cool from the fresh water that flowed through the trough Father had built there. With the cows out on pasture and grazing the early greens, their milk was thick and rich with cream. It was the best time of year to make her hard cheeses, which needed to cure for several months.

Hannah Jr. enjoyed the process of cheesemaking. It gave her a purpose beyond helping her mother with the house and the children. The eldest of originally six children—now eight counting the two orphans currently living with them—she split her time between the dairy and the house. She was also training her sister Tamson to work in the dairy, along with Verity, the orphan who had been given into their family by the Puritan elder, Thomas Buffington, just the past week. Hannah Jr. couldn't help but be happy at the thought of having another sister in a family so full of brothers.

The door separating the dairy from the main part of the barn banged open. Joseph, the boy living with them until the situation in the village changed, poked his head inside, straw-colored hair disheveled and gap-toothed grin wide. "Old Buttercup is calving right now. Come and see." He disappeared as suddenly as he'd arrived.

The boy had been going on and on about witnessing a cow give birth for the first time. Hannah Jr. and her siblings were used to the rhythm of farm life—birth and death, planting and harvest. They took everything in its season. But to Joseph, a boy orphaned very young and shuffled from one house to another, it was all new. And very exciting.

Since the cream would rise without her watching it, Hannah Jr. slipped off her dairy apron and hung it on its peg before following the lad through the barn, past the area that still smelled faintly of smoke from the fire last winter, and on to the cows' pen. Buttercup, their poorly named cantankerous cow, let out a raucous bellow as they approached. She was alone, the other cows having gone outside to graze after milking.

Robert and Caleb Jr. were already watching. Nobody would approach Buttercup unless they had to. While some of their cows were docile and allowed themselves to be handled even in labor, old Buttercup was against any human interference in the birthing process. Strenuously against it. Once, she'd even tossed Father over the top rail of the cow pen.

Another long and loud bellow brought Father out of his carpentry shop. He rested his forearms on the top of the gate. He wore just his waistcoat in such fine weather, curls of wood from his current project clinging to his shirtsleeves. He was working hard to finish the large order for the new doctor in the village.

Hannah Jr. stifled the sensation in her middle at the thought of that order. Not the order, exactly, but the man who might come to collect it for the doctor—Benjamin Buffington. She shouldn't be thinking of him at all, but she couldn't help it. He was the only young man who had caught her eye. Three years her junior, he was two years from majority age, but that wasn't the real issue.

Benjamin was a Puritan.

The Society of Friends didn't intermarry with Puritans, and the Puritans would reject the possibility even more forcibly. The last thing Hannah Jr. needed was to replay some tragic version of *Romeo and Juliet*. She shouldn't even have known about that play of William Shakespeare's, but her friend Mary O'Sullivan had somehow gotten a copy of it and had shared it with Hannah Jr. Guilt still pinched her over reading such a worldly story, and that'd been several years past, when she'd been a youth.

Buttercup gave a mighty push, and the tips of the calf's front hooves poked out, and then disappeared again.

"I do not favor the look of that," Father said.

Tamson and Verity arrived with the little boys, Benji and Jonathan. "Why, Father?" Tamson, Hannah Jr.'s twelve-year-old sister, climbed onto the gate until her head was level with Father's.

"Because there was no nose showing with the hooves." It was Caleb Jr. who answered. At eighteen years old, he was the eldest of the brothers and four years younger than Hannah Jr., who answered.

"Is that bad?" Joseph's brow wrinkled.

Father put his hand on the boy's shoulder. "It can be. We shall have to wait and see."

"Will she die?" Tenderhearted, nine-year-old Verity had never witnessed a cow giving birth either.

"Death is as much a part of life as birth is." Hannah Jr. drew the girl to her side. "'Tis one of the things we learn early on the farm."

"I know about death." Verity's arms came around Hannah Jr.'s waist. "But I wanted to see a birth."

The words hit Hannah Jr. hard. This child had suffered so much loss. Was it too much to ask that she be able to witness a happy occasion in the barn?

Buttercup sank to her knees, then groaned and rolled onto her side, her tail cocked as she heaved against another contraction. The hooves appeared again, even further this time—but still no nose.

Father rolled his sleeve up well past his elbow and took a stout piece of tree limb with a curve to it from its storage place near the pen. Caleb Jr. fetched a length of rope. Robert ran for a bucket of water. Hannah Jr. and Tamson kept the young boys out of the way. They'd all done this before, more than once.

Not always successfully.

"What is happening?" Joseph asked.

"They must assist Buttercup. 'Tis most likely that the calf's head is turned back."

"What will they do?" There was a tremor in Verity's voice.

Hannah Jr. squatted to her level. "They must turn the calf's head around so that it can come out of Buttercup."

Jonathan started to whimper, so Hannah Jr. scooped him into her arms. At just three, he hadn't seen this happen before either. Most birthings occurred in the barn or out on pasture without any assistance.

Father and Caleb Jr. entered the pen first, the limb held between them. They waited for Buttercup to give another mighty push, then rushed forward, pressing the limb against her neck, right behind her ears, pinning her to the barn floor. Robert left the bucket of water near her tail, then took Father's place holding one end of the limb.

Buttercup bellowed and kicked, but the boys and Father knew how to stay out of harm's way. Father wetted his arm, waited until after the next push, then grabbed the hooves with the rope in his hand. When the hooves disappeared again, Father's hand, arm, and the rope went with them.

Verity turned her face into Hannah Jr.'s petticoats, while Joseph let out a loud, "Ugh."

Robert, almost sitting on his end of the limb near her back, spoke in a soothing tone to Buttercup.

Caleb Jr. kept both hands on his end, being careful not to cut off the cow's breathing by keeping the limb's curve up as he knelt near her throat. He was doing a good job of it, judging by the increased volume of her bellowing.

The straw around Father's feet was mussed as he strained to reach the calf's head, groaning against the cow's next contraction. "I have the rope in its mouth." The words came through gritted teeth. "Now to get it around the bottom jaw."

Verity peeked from Hannah Jr.'s petticoats while still clinging to them.

Joseph had climbed to the top rail of the pen, where he sat open-mouthed.

Father groaned again as Buttercup bore down, but as soon as she ended the push, he dug his toes in and pushed back almost to his shoulder, his other hand keeping the rope taut. "'Tis turned." Father pulled his arm out. It was covered in slime and blood enough to make Verity blanch. He got to his feet. "Let her up, boys, and get out of here."

Caleb Jr. and Robert dropped the limb and ran for the gate, Father not a full step behind.

Buttercup lurched to her feet with the closest thing to a roar that a cow could manage and turned to face them, the calf's front legs and nose swinging out behind her.

Father got the gate shut and the latch thrown across a breath before the cow smacked into it.

The cow's anger reverberated on the pen's boards, and Joseph teetered, nearly losing his balance.

Caleb Jr. grabbed him before he tumbled into the pen with the irate bovine.

After another smack against the gate, Buttercup returned to the far side of the pen and bellowed, nose in the air. Behind her, the wet calf slid onto the straw with a frightful thud.

Hannah Jr. held her breath until the calf raised its head and shook, wet ears slapping against its neck.

"Look at that!" Joseph pointed.

Buttercup ignored her babe and charged the bucket in the middle of the pen, driving her head into it. The sharp crack of sturdy oak seeming to satisfy her. She returned to the calf, muttering to it as she licked it dry.

The calf shook its head again, mouth opening and closing as it spat out the loop of rope that had guided its nose around.

"Ungrateful old beast." Chuckling, Father dried off his arm on a piece of sacking. "If she did not produce such fine milking heifers..." He let his threat remain unspoken.

"Will the calf be all right?" Verity asked.

Robert answered, "It should be right as raindrops now." Even as he spoke, the calf struggled to rise.

"She did it again." Father rested his forearms on the top rail. "Another heifer."

"May I name her?" Verity asked.

Father smiled at her. "And what would thee name her?"

Verity clasped her hands beneath her chin. "Buttercup Jr."

The boys groaned, but Father nodded his approval, so Buttercup Jr. it was, and the rule was, a named calf stayed on the farm.

Which meant another good milk producer for their herd. Hannah Jr. set Jonathan down and picked Verity up, giving her a squeeze and enjoying the girl's squeal of delight. The live calf meant so much to her, who had lost so many. Hannah Jr. had never suffered as Verity had. She'd never gone without her needs met by her parents, had never lost anyone she was close to.

What right had she to pine over some young man who was beyond her reach?

It was time to put thoughts of Benjamin Buffington aside, and concentrate on being the best dairymaid she could be. The best daughter and big sister too. She who had known only blessings needed to concentrate on being a blessing to others. That was a noble life for anyone, and honoring to God.

The empty feeling in her middle would surely lessen with time.

Chapter 2

April 5

T HE POUNDING ON HER door jerked Hester awake. The world was pitch dark outside her window as she rose and pulled on her wrapper. Hopefully, this was another false alarm. It was too early for Jane Biddle's babe to come into the world yet. Thankful for a one-story cottage where she didn't need to manage stairs when summoned from her bed, Hester hurried to the door and pulled it open.

It wasn't John Biddle on the other side.

A strapping boy of perhaps fourteen years strangled a knitted cap between his hands. "Can you come quick, ma'am? Ma is in a bad way with the new babe."

"Of course." Hester stepped back and gestured to a chair. "Have a seat while I dress." She didn't wait to see if he complied but rushed back into her room and slipped into her clothes. She didn't bother with her hair, just pinned her braid up under her linen cap. After pulling a clean apron over everything, she stepped into her shoes and buckled them, then rejoined the boy.

"What is thy name?"

"Me?" He looked confused for a moment, his distracted concern filling Hester with dread over what she might find when they arrived at his home. "Sammy, ma'am. Sammy Tolbert."

"Very good." She put her midwife basket over her arm, grabbed her canvas sack, and headed for the door. "Let us be off, Sammy."

The lad had a wagon out front with two lathered horses hitched to it. He awkwardly handed Hester up to the high seat, then climbed aboard, untied the lines from the brake handle, and unlocked the brake. Before Hester could straighten her petticoats, the wagon was in motion. The horses were in a full gallop by the time they reached the edge of the village.

"Is it safe to run the horses in the dark?" Hester gripped the edge of the seat with one hand and secured her supplies with the other.

"Ma is in a really bad way, ma'am." He shook the reins again, urging even more speed.

"We will do her no good if we crash the wagon into a ditch or a tree." That seemed to get through to him, and he slowed the team to a canter.

Hester led out a breath of relief. "Where is thy home?"

"Just this side of Salem Town. Pa's farm backs up to the river."

Almost three miles away. Hester issued a silent prayer for the woman awaiting her. When the wagon increased speed again, she added another prayer for their safe arrival.

"Thank thee, Stephen." Hannah Jr. tucked the forged hoe heads into her basket. "These will make our work go much faster, will it not, Tamson?" Her sister gave a half-hearted shrug as Hannah Jr. passed over the coins Father had given her to pay the blacksmith.

"The fire was a terrible thing. 'Tis good that the Lord provided for thy father to replace the things that were burned." Stephen had been one of the Friends to stand alongside Father when he'd bucked against the decree prohibiting doing commerce with the Puritans by filling the Puritan doctor's furniture order. "Let him know that the rest will be done by next week's end." The large man grinned. "Just in time for spring planting."

"He will be so relieved. Good day to thee." With a wave, they left the smithy.

Hannah Jr. nudged Tamson with her elbow as they walked. "Thee are awfully silent."

Another half-hearted shrug was her only reply.

Stopping, Hannah Jr. faced her sister. "Tell me what is troubling thee."

"Why must something be troubling me?" Tamson huffed out a breath and marched forward.

"Because thee have said barely ten words this morning, and that is not my little sister." Hannah Jr. hurried to catch up, the hoe heads clanking in her basket.

Tamson thrust out her arms in a dramatic gesture, turned and walked backward, facing Hannah Jr. "Just because I have nothing to say does not mean there is anything wrong."

"Of course it does. Thee are always full of words." Hannah Jr. gave her a cheery smile. "That is one of the things I love most about thee." Which was true. As a quiet person herself, she admired her sister's zest for life, her active imagination, and the way she forged ahead for what she desired. "Now, will thee tell me what is on thy mind? 'Bear ye one another's burdens, and so fulfill the Law of Christ.'"

"Oh, quote not scripture to me this morning." Tamson whirled and marched forward again. "I am not in the mood for it."

Not in the mood for scripture? That didn't sound good. But obviously her sister wouldn't be jollied out of her grumpiness. She grabbed Tamson's sleeve and stopped her, searching her face.

"Now thee have me worried, indeed. What is wrong?"

"I do not wish to be like thee and Mother." Tamson crossed her arms, a mulish set to her mouth. "Having babies and tending a garden"—she jabbed a finger at the hoe heads in the basket—"and never having any adventures."

As if raising a houseful of children, keeping them all fed and clothed and healthy, were not an adventure in itself. A very rewarding adventure, one Hannah Jr. might never know for herself. But she pushed away that thought to concentrate on Tamson.

"What type of adventures do thee wish to have?"

Her sister uncrossed her arms and let them flap to her sides. The girl would have been good on the stage, but that would have scandalized their Society of Friends to no end. "I know not. Perhaps venturing farther north to the great river and beyond, or west to the mountains, or south to where it never snows. Perhaps to sail on a ship with three masts and yards and yards of canvas flapping against the sky."

As if a woman could do such things without a man to accompany her, but pointing that out to her sister would only send her back into her ill humor. "What would thee do in such places?"

"*See* them. Breathe their air." Tamson flung her arms out and twirled, face to the sky. "'Twould be a glorious thing."

Hannah Jr. had no wish to squash her sister's overly dramatic flights of fancy, but neither did she share any such thirst for adventure. A safe home with Friends nearby, a family who loved her, enough food and clothing to be comfortable. That was the ideal life for her.

"I know 'tis not what thee would do, if thee could have thy dearest wish." Tamson walked on, but cast a glance back at Hannah Jr. "Thee would marry Benjamin Buffington and have a brood of children."

"Do not speak such nonsense." Hannah Jr.'s words were sharper than she'd intended, so she moderated her tone. "Thee know perfectly well that he is quite unsuitable."

Tamson blew a rude snort. "We already have two Puritans living under our roof. How much different could that be from marrying one?"

How much different? As different as a shrew from a snake. "Joseph is only with us until 'tis safe for him to return to the brewery. Verity is a Puritan by birth, that is true, but in all the ways that matter, she has embraced the way of the Friends. Why, just last week she told Mother that she had accepted the Light of Christ. That makes her far more Friend than Puritan now."

"Benjamin could do the same, could he not?"

"'Tis an entirely different situation."

With a slant-eyed glance, Tamson demanded, "Tell me how."

"For one thing, his family is very much alive, unlike Verity's. His father is an elder in their church. Do thee think Thomas Buffington would take kindly to one of his sons leaving that same church to attend meeting with the Friends? Thee know they consider us heretics."

"He has been very kind to our family, taking Robert in as an apprentice, and siding with Father and Mother to allow Verity to stay." She frowned at Hannah Jr. "'Twas he who made sure she could stay with us. I like him."

Hannah Jr. pinched the bridge of her nose. The girl was too starry-eyed by half. How to get through to her? "I like him too. But can thee imagine Father and Mother giving their blessing for me to attend the Puritan church?"

That brought a sharp gasp from her sister. "Of course not."

"'Twould be equally unbelievable for Benjamin's family to give their blessing for him to leave their church and join the Society of Friends. Do thee not see that?" And could they please speak of something—anything—else?

Tamson tucked her arms across her chest again, the mulish set returned to her mouth. "I think we should be free to make our own choices."

"Indeed, as do I." Hannah Jr. sighed. Would her words get through to her sometimes willful and stubborn sister? "I choose to honor our father and mother and live according to the teaching of scripture. 'Tis the best way to prosper. Following one's own heart, if thy heart aligns not with the truth, is the way to grief."

Another halfhearted shrug, but at least Tamson didn't argue. Even better, she fell silent again. This time, Hannah Jr. had no desire to change that.

Goodie Tolbert's labor was long and difficult, draining the woman to an alarming extent. Hester would advise her against trying for any more children after this one. If, indeed, she could conceive again, her being well into her forties. The child had been turned when Hester arrived. It had taken all her skill to get the babe presented properly for delivery. Even then, it was midway into the afternoon before the child was born.

A girl, red and wrinkled and crying lustily from her first breath.

"'Tis another girl, Ma." One of the woman's adult daughters, who had a babe of her own in a basket near the wall, leaned over Goodie Tolbert.

The weary woman sighed. "Your father will be disappointed."

Hester clamped her lips shut as she finished her administrations with the babe. She'd come to understand that Sammy was the lone male offspring in the family of eleven—now twelve—children. A farmer needed helping hands, but surely the girls could do much of the work. Still, many men had the same reaction to daughters. Disappointment. It wasn't fair, but little in life was.

The babe cleaned and wrapped, Hester handed her over to Goodie Tolbert. "She is perfect in every way."

"Thank you, Midwife." The woman unwrapped the child and examined her as if to reassure herself, then looked up at Hester. "I am so relieved. I had feared the babe might be born with a mark." She lowered her voice. "The magistrates are checking for those, you know."

A witch's mark.

Hester held her tongue. It was not her place to disagree with the Puritan magistrates. However, she'd seen plenty of babes arrive with marks on them, innocent marks that ranged from a birthing trauma or simple moles or even red patches. None of them had been evil in any way.

But saying so would only draw attention Hester didn't want, and under the circumstances, attention she might not survive.

An experienced mother, Goodie Tolbert nursed the child and snuggled her close until she slept, while Hester and the daughters changed the sheets and cleaned the room. The husband was out in the fields, but one of the daughters dispatched a younger sister to take him the news.

"She is a beautiful girl." Hester touched the dark downy fuzz covering the sleeping babe's head. "But I believe she should be thy last. Thy body is tired, as it should be from bringing so many children into thy family. Thee have done thy duty well."

Goodie Tolbert's blue eyes filmed over with tears. "If the Lord wills, but my husband would like at least one more son." She closed her eyes and succumbed to much-needed sleep.

So it would go, and nothing Hester could say would change it. She turned to the three adult daughters. "Make sure she drinks plenty of water for the next few days, and fix a nourishing broth. Older women sometimes struggle to produce enough milk. Keep her abed as much as possible for the next week. Two would be better. Thy mother is truly worn out, from the pregnancy as well as the labor." She packed up her basket. "If she bleeds more than she should, fetch me back."

"Thank you, Goodwife." One of the girls brought coins from her pocket and handed them over. "Sammy is in the fields with the team so—"

Hester stopped her with a raised hand. "Worry not. The walk home will do me good." And she had no desire to be bounced around on that wagon again.

The three miles passed pleasantly beneath the early April sun. The grass was so green it almost hurt the eye, bursting with growth and goodness. Birds sung to each other from the budding trees. A deer paused at the forest's edge and stared at her before bounding away, its tail waving like a white flag. It should have been an enjoyable stroll, but Hester couldn't get the woman's words out of her head.

I had feared the babe might be born with a mark.

If she had been, would Hester have been blamed? Should she consider limiting her services to only the Friends until this witch madness was gone from their county? They had a doctor now, a man well able to deliver the babies of the Puritans. She'd met him briefly and found him to be a gentle soul, and had heard no bad report against him.

Hester didn't doubt that her calling was to administer to the women of county. To turn her back on those in need, no matter their beliefs, was something she didn't want to do. At least not yet. If things turned worse, if they starting hanging—the Lord forbid—those women who stood accused of witchcraft and jailed in Salem Town, then she might have no choice.

Where would that leave her? Would she have enough income from her basket sales and births of the Friends to make her rent payment? Or would she be forced to move, to live with one of her brothers or another of the Friends, or even travel to her sister's place? It wasn't right or fair that her life hung suspended by the actions and wrong-headed beliefs of others. But it did.

And she was powerless to change it.

Chapter 3

O N A BREEZY FRIDAY morning, almost a week since her disturbing conversation with Tamson, Hannah Jr. helped Mother hang their laundry over the rope strung between the house and a stout pole with a crossbar that Father had planted nearby. The sheets snapped as the wind caught them, making the rope dance. Hannah Jr. caught hold of it and folded damp toweling across it.

"It might be safer to spread the smaller pieces on the bushes today." She wrestled another piece of toweling in place.

"Thee are right." Mother took the basket of stockings, smallclothes, and hand rags to the nearby hedge of red-twig dogwoods they kept trimmed for that purpose. She spread out the pieces so they were caught on the twigs and wouldn't blow away, then came back to help Hannah Jr. get the last sheet across the moving rope. "There. They should dry in no time at all today."

"Then I shall work in the dairy for an hour or so." Hannah Jr. picked up her basket, but before she could take a step, Mother took her by the arm.

"I would have a word with thee while there is just the two of us." About something serious, by the troubled look in her blue eyes.

"As thee wish."

"Things have been quiet of late, as far as news from the village." Mother's lips quirked in a half-smile. "David has not visited in more than a fortnight."

Their friend, David O'Sullivan, was the local gunsmith. As such, he worked for many of the Puritans and generally knew everything that was going on throughout the county, details of which he was well known for sharing.

"We should have them to supper again," Hannah Jr. said.

"Indeed. I will mention that to thy father this evening." Mother paused and glanced toward the barn.

"But that is not what thee wished to speak with me about."

"Nay." Mother took a deep breath and faced her. "'Tis about Benjamin Buffington."

A rock rolled into the pit of Hannah Jr.'s stomach. "There is nothing to discuss."

"When he comes to collect the doctor's furniture, I cannot help but notice that thee are gathered around him with the children." It wasn't a question, but there was a question in the midst of it.

Hannah Jr. picked at a stray thread caught on her basket while she gathered her thoughts. "I will make a point not to do so anymore."

"I also cannot help but notice how thy face illuminates when he is here."

"Mother, I—"

"I am not accusing thee of anything. But I cannot miss how much his presence brings thee joy."

Joy. After a fashion, it did. Like looking at the dresses in the window of the seamstress shop in Salem Town, even when she knew there were no pennies to spare on such luxuries as a dress made by someone else. Those were intended for women with far more money than simple farmers. As Benjamin was intended for a Puritan woman, not a simple Friend.

"Why do thee bring this up?" Hannah Jr. tried to keep the hurt from her voice. "I do enjoy seeing him, but I know my place is here at the farm and among the Friends."

"Because I worry over thee, my dear." Mother squeezed Hannah Jr.'s arm. "I want thee to be happy. I want thee to have a full life, with a husband and children. Thee were made for that."

"First Tamson, and now thee." Hannah Jr. stepped away, needing more space to keep her emotions under control. "I love my life here. I love my family, the farm, the dairy, all of it." But she had to struggle to keep her voice even. To keep her treacherous thoughts—longings—at bay. "'Tis best if we do not discuss this again." She took the basket to the house without a backward glance, and then fled to the dairy.

Denying herself a possibility with Benjamin was hard enough without her family bringing it up to her. Who would be next, Father? Nay. That she couldn't face. She would need to stay away the next time Benjamin came to the farm.

Then he would have no opportunity to pass her another note to add to the small stash secreted away in her trunk.

Determined to make more baskets to sell, and thus lessen her dependency on the midwife fees, Hester spent the breezy morning in the forest gathering last fall's long pine needles, surrounded by their spicy scent. It was a tedious task to gather them, clean them of any debris, remove the damaged needles, and then pack them into her gathering basket. She should have been in the forest sooner, before the new spring growth had broken through their layer beneath the stately trees.

Pine needle baskets were popular since they were tightly coiled and stitched together with waxed linen thread, leaving no cracks for even the smallest particles to fall through. They were also time-consuming and messy. Her fingers would be left sticky and smelling of pine for several days until the worst of it wore off.

Hester climbed to her feet and shook the dirt and clinging vegetation from her apron and petticoats. Basket full and belly growling, she headed for the road and home. She'd gone no more than a few steps when a team pulling a wagon rounded the bend behind her.

"Hester." David O'Sullivan pulled his horses to a halt beside her. "Are thee heading to the village? I can offer thee a ride."

"I should decline and make my own way." She cocked her head and returned his grin. "But I thank thee and will take thee up on thy kind offer."

He started to set the brake and tie off the reins.

"No need. I can climb onto the seat myself. Just take my basket, if thee would." She handed it up, then climbed the wheel and settled beside him. One advantage of being the midwife was that no one looked scandalously at her for being with other women's husbands. They were often dispatched to transport her. She took her basket back and nodded to him. "All set."

"Thee have been industrious this day." David tipped his chin toward the basket. "I daresay, my Isobel could use another good pine-needle basket. Those are her favorite, and thy work is the best."

"I shall let her know when they are ready." A sale before she'd even started was a good sign. "Tell me, what news do thee have to share today?"

He planted a hand in the middle of his chest. "Do I look like a courier or town crier to thee?"

"Indeed, the best in these parts." Theirs was the banter of old friends, as it should be. After all, she'd delivered his three youngest children.

"In truth, I have not been to Salem Town in quite a while." His voice lost its jovial tone. "We Friends thought to limit our interactions with the village, but I tell thee, 'tis Salem Town we need to avoid now."

Hester clutched her gathering basket tighter. "Is it truly that bad?" Would she lose the ability to sell her baskets there? It was her best market.

"I fear 'tis." He rubbed his chin. "Their jail is filling up with the accused." Even David, for all his cockiness, refrained from using the word *witch* out loud. "I hear conditions there are bad, that the women are kept in the cellar where 'tis damp and cold."

"Where they might die of illness before they can be sentenced to..." She let that thought trail off, as reluctant to voice the possible outcome as he'd been to name anyone a witch.

"These are tryin' times in which we live." He slowed the horses as they entered the town, then pulled them to a stop outside her cottage.

She turned to him on the seat. "Have a care. Thee see more people than most of us, many of them Puritans. I would hate for anything to happen to thee."

His face pulled into sober lines. "I will say the same to thee. Both of us have more interactions with the Puritans than most in our community." He scanned the street, the few people walking along it, and houses around them. "It makes us more of a target for their distrust."

"I know. I cannot say it does not worry me."

"If thee ever have the need, there be room for thee in our home." He meant it, but he also stretched the truth. With eight children, none of them young anymore, the O'Sullivans barely had room to turn around in their house.

"I will keep that in mind." She climbed down and took her basket from him. "Tell Isobel we need a good, long visit soon."

"That I will." He clicked to the horses. "Hup, Izzy. Hup, Bella."

Hester waited until he'd driven out of sight, then walked around to the back of her cottage. She had a lot of work ahead to fashion the pine needles into baskets. A lot of work—and perhaps little market. But at least it would keep her fingers busy, keep her from thinking about babes with marks and where that could lead.

Hannah Jr. finished setting the table for their supper as Father entered the kitchen, the aroma of ham gravy and butter biscuits making him pause and sniff. The other girls were scrubbing the garden dirt from their hands and helping the younger boys clean up as well. The three older boys were seated at the table, and Mother was slicing bread. It was a typical family evening, but their conversation over the laundry still had Hannah Jr. on edge.

"I am finished with the doctor's furniture." Father whisked his hat off and hung it on its peg.

"Wonderful." Mother smiled at him. "In time to plant the fields."

"God provided exactly what we needed, exactly when we needed it." Father waited while Verity and Tamson helped the little boys dry their hands before he washed his. "Caleb Jr. and I shall begin in the fields on Monday, if the Lord wills and it does not rain."

Some of the tension she'd been carrying eased from Hannah Jr. While her parents had assured her—several times—that last winter's fire hadn't been her fault, she'd still felt responsible since it had been a spark from her worn-out lantern that had caused the blaze. Knowing

Father had replaced all the lost equipment, thanks to the money collected from his work for the doctor, comforted her.

Once all were in their places, the silent prayer over, and everyone's plates filled with warm biscuits topped with ham gravy, dried green beans that had been soaked and boiled, slices of fresh bread, and applesauce so thick it could be eaten with a fork, all were free to speak about their days.

"Will Benjamin come tomorrow to collect the doctor's furniture?" Robert asked.

Hannah Jr. kept her attention on her plate, even though she could sense Mother looking at her.

"I shall let the doctor know 'tis ready tomorrow when I go into the village. I should think one of Thomas's boys will collect the pieces on Monday or Tuesday."

One of the boys, so it could be Thomas Jr. and not Benjamin. A thought that curled through Hannah Jr. with a mixture of relief and disappointment. To her shame, mostly disappointment. But she'd told Mother she would stay away, and she would.

Caleb Jr. set down his fork. "I have news to share." When Father nodded to him, he continued, "As thee know, I went hunting this afternoon." He pointed to the brace of turkeys hanging over the kitchen work table, waiting for Hannah Jr. to finish preparing them for the next day's supper. "And I came across Mark doing the same."

Mark, David's second son, was the same age as Caleb Jr. and had inherited his father's ability and willingness to tell a story, so Hannah Jr. anticipated a good tale.

"Did he get a pair of turkeys as well?" Mother asked.

"He got three, all toms the same as me. We left the hens to sit on their eggs."

"Good thinking, son." Father helped himself to another slice of bread. "What news did Mark have to share?"

"Nothing good, I fear." He looked around the table. "More people have been arrested and taken to Salem Town. They are keeping them in the jail, in the cellar of the jail where it is cold, dark, and damp."

"Oh, my." Mother put her hand to her throat. "Those poor women."

"Not just women." Caleb Jr.'s words brought a hush to the room. "The Puritan farmer, John Proctor, has also been accused."

Father put his slice of bread on his plate and looked across the table at Mother. "I had heard that John Proctor has spoken out against what is happening in the village, denying that the accused women are actually witches."

Mother's face lost some of its color. "Do thee think him falsely accused because of that?"

"'Tis possible," Father said.

"'Tis likely." Joseph looked from Father to Mother and back again. "He is not well thought of by some in the village."

"As the first women accused were also looked down upon." Hannah Jr.'s words slipped out before she'd considered them. But they chilled her, mainly because the Friends were also not well liked by many there.

Father sat back in his chair and surveyed those at the table. "I believe we should all restrict ourselves to the farm or the forest until...well, until we know more, at least."

They finished the rest of the meal without much more said, except from young Jonathan, who babbled about a fascinating rock he'd discovered on the edge of the garden.

Afterward, while Tamson and Verity cleaned the dishes, Hannah Jr. plucked and prepared the brace of turkeys, getting them ready to plunge into a brine. Next week would be the last pickup of furniture, the last temptation to see Benjamin on the farm, and then her life could get back to its familiar and satisfying routine.

Perhaps.

Or perhaps, the accusation of witchcraft would be cast onto one of the Friends. And if that happened, they might have to grab what they could carry and flee the area. They had the canvas travel sacks ready, but Father seemed less likely to run now than he had been a couple of months back. Not that he'd fight, of course. The Friends were pacifists. But he seemed determined to stay and face whatever might come.

Worrying over Benjamin was a luxury she couldn't afford if her family was in danger. That helped put the situation in perspective for Hannah Jr. Helped make her decision to avoid him easier to accept. A little, at least.

Chapter 4

W ITH THE MONDAY-MORNING WASH drying on the rope, Hannah Jr. was on her way to the dairy when a heavy wagon pulled by a matched team decked out with jingle bells came up their farm lane. The Buffington Brewery wagon. Caught halfway between the house and the barn, she couldn't very well walk on as if she hadn't seen it. There was no excuse for being that rude. Mother would agree.

Tamson and Verity charged out of the house at the jingle of the bells, the barefoot Benji and Jonathan not far behind. Caleb Jr. was in the field with Father, but Robert and Joseph set aside their pitchforks and waited to greet their friend.

How Hannah Jr. envied them for being able to call Benjamin a friend. Of course, she wouldn't know if it was Benjamin, and not Thomas Jr., until the wagon stopped. The twins were almost impossible to tell apart if one didn't know them. But only Benjamin looked at her with a gleam in his eye that she couldn't misinterpret.

She continued on her way to the barn at a dignified pace that brought her to the wagon after her siblings had it surrounded. The warm brown eyes and polite nod that greeted her were not those of Benjamin. Again, she fought the conflicting emotions of disappointment and relief, but at least she didn't have to excuse herself and move on to the dairy.

"How are things in the village?" Joseph asked before Thomas Jr. could dismount from the wagon.

"Much as it has been," the young man said. "The hubbub about who is accusing whom has become almost commonplace, I fear."

Hannah Jr.'s heart dropped. "None in thy family, I hope."

"Nay. We are all fine." He shot her a look she couldn't interpret. Had Benjamin confided in his brother? Hannah Jr. turned her face away before anyone noticed the blush burning its way across her cheeks.

"Do you have the latest names?" Joseph liked knowing the details, perhaps more than was good for him, but it took attention away from her and gave her face a moment to cool.

Thomas Jr. leaned back against the wagon and hooked his thumbs in the waistband of his breeches. "Sunday service was a sight, I can tell you that." He launched into a vivid description of several girls accusing Sarah Cloyce—one of Hannah Jr.'s former butter and cheese customers—of witchcraft. Their pastor had lost all control of the meeting, people yelling, fingers pointing, and Thomas Jr. told it almost as well as David could have done.

"Are they really witches?" Benji's eyes were wide and round as he stared at the tall young Puritan man.

Thomas Jr. squatted to Benji's level. "There are some who believe 'tis true, but I do not. I believe things in the village have gotten quite out of hand. You stay here on your father's farm, and all should be well." He ruffled the boy's already unruly hair and got a grin in return.

As he stood, his eyes caught Hannah Jr.'s again. She gave him a smile and nod, thanking him for his gentle way of handling her little brother's fears.

He clapped his hands together. "Shall we load the good doctor's furnishings?"

Robert and Joseph started for the door to the carpentry, but Thomas Jr. stopped and turned to Hannah Jr. again. "I almost forgot. Mother asked me to fetch back an order from your dairy. Here is her list." He handed over a thick scrap of paper and then grabbed a basket from the wagon and gave it to her.

"I shall fill this for thee." Hannah Jr. hurried to the dairy where she opened the note. Another paper, folded much smaller, fell out of it. The larger one had Sarah Buffington's order written on it. She unfolded the smaller note to read the familiar script.

Hannah Jr.,
I have only a moment before my brother leaves to fetch
the doctor's furnishings. It saddens me greatly that Fa-
ther assigned the task to him. I had hoped to see you this
morning. Perhaps next week.

She pulled in a steadying breath and pressed a hand to her chest.
To read words that echoed the feelings of her own heart put an ache
there.

I know I have no right to ask, and you have been careful
to give me no encouragement, which I understand under
our circumstances. I must, however, write that of which
I cannot speak in person at this time.

In but two years I will be old enough to strike out on
my own. 'Tis my heartfelt wish to become a farmer in
the manner of your father, with a dairy of goats as well
as cows and a large apple orchard. Working hard, and
with the money I have saved from working alongside my
father, I should be able to sustain myself and take a wife
two years after that.

If this appeals to you at all, indeed, if I appeal to you
at all, would you wait for me? Would you find a way to
let me know one way or the other? Because if you are
willing, we will bridge our differences, that I promise
you.

Your humble servant and willing to be forever yours,
Benjamin Buffington

Hannah Jr. let the note settle on the work table. Tears gathered
at the back of her throat, threatening to choke her. How could she
answer, except to deny him? That was the right and proper thing to do.

It's what she had told Mother she'd do—deny herself and thus deny him.

So why did the ache intensify? Why did she feel as if all hope were being sucked from her soul? She carefully refolded the note along its original crease lines and tucked it into her apron pocket.

She was being overly dramatic, much more like Tamson than herself. Benjamin was a dear young man, she could admit to that, and he had sparked an interest in her that no other young man had, but it didn't mean he was—or ever could be—a husband to her. He might promise to overcome their differences, as he had put it, but their fathers would never allow it. And by the time he was ready for a wife, she would be six and twenty, well on her way to spinsterhood.

A future to which she would reconcile herself, yet again.

Laughter from those loading the wagon reached her and spurred her into action, filling Sarah Buffington's basket with the large order on her list. Then she turned the list over. With the sharpened piece of charcoal she kept in the dairy for noting the dates on the cheeses, she wrote to Sarah:

> *Sarah,*
> *If thee can spare one of thy sons the time to fetch them,*
> *I would be pleased to continue to fill thy butter and*
> *cheese orders, as well as orders for thy friends and*
> *neighbors, until such time as I can resume my normal*
> *delivery rounds. Mondays would be best, as I will be*
> *well-stocked on those days.*
> *Respectfully,*
> *Hannah Jr.*

Would Benjamin think that her wish to retain his mother's business was some sort of encouragement to him? She had no desire to play false with his heart—or her own. Yet it wasn't as if she could send him a denial note back in his brother's hand. That would have to wait until, Lord willing, she and her family were allowed to enter the village again. And who knew when that might be?

Babies rarely made their arrivals in the light of day, so Hester was surprised when young Becky Simpson, the orphan girl living with the Biddles, approached her in her garden in the middle of the afternoon.

"Midwife Fuller?" The girl bobbed a curtsy, fingers fidgeting with the edge of her apron.

"Becky." Hester rose and dusted off her knees. "Does Jane require my services?"

"I think so." The girl glanced over her shoulder and then back again, obviously nervous. "She is having pains again."

Hester didn't like the sound of that. It was still too soon. "Come into the cottage with me while I wash my hands."

"I should get straight back to the children." She glanced toward the Biddle house again.

"Of course, I should have remembered. Tell Jane I shall be there directly."

Becky bolted like a startled horse, all but running out of Hester's garden.

Hester washed the garden dirt away, changed into a clean apron, gathered her midwife basket and canvas sack, and left the cottage.

Becky was hovering by the door when she arrived at the Biddle house, two Biddle boys half hidden behind her petticoats, a sleeping girl in her arms.

"Go right on up," Becky whispered. "Goody Biddle is expecting you."

Two stairs squeaked when she stepped upon them, giving Jane plenty of advance notice of her arrival, but Hester called out anyway. "Jane?"

"Do come in, Hester." A low groan followed as Hester stepped into the room. It was dark and stuffy with the curtains drawn.

"Let me open the room for thee." Without waiting for permission, Hester opened the curtains and the windows, letting in the cool mid-April breeze as well as the light.

"Thank you. I should have done that but—" Jane's words cut off with another groan, her arms going around her middle.

"Relax now." Hester hurried to her side, where a chair already waited. Becky had no doubt anticipated the need. The orphan was a Godsend to the family. "When did the pains begin?"

"My back ached something fierce this morning, but I thought 'twould pass. I returned to bed after dinner and slept for a short time. Then the pains started, but they have been very sporadic."

Sporadic was good. Hester would breathe easier if the babe would stay put for another fortnight. It could probably survive if born now, but was bound to have problems. She fussed over the woman, putting pillows under her and talking to her, hoping to get her to relax even more.

"Young Becky seems a big help to thee."

"Oh, my. I should say so. I know not what I would have done without her."

"Thee have blessed her as well, giving her a home here."

"I hope so." Jane pulled breath through her teeth in a gentle hiss. "That one was not as strong."

"Good. Allow me to roll thee onto thy side." Hester did that and massaged the woman's back where the pains had started. "What do thee know of Becky's family?"

"She said her mother died in childbirth."

Hester winced. Perhaps they needed a different topic, but Jane continued.

"Perhaps that is why she loves the children so, her mother having died along with the babe Becky never got to know."

That could explain the girl's nervousness as well. "She does seem taken with thy children, and they with her."

Jane issued another moan, but this one softer, more as if she appreciated the massage than felt pain. "I should say so. The boys look to her before me these days, and not because she spoils them. That girl is a taskmaster, but fair and gentle as well. She would make a good schoolteacher, I should think, to run a dame school."

A perfectly respectable occupation for an unmarried woman. Becky having no family—therefore no dowry—would need to find a way to support herself, or marry whomever would support her whether she favored him or not. Women had so few choices.

They continued to chat for several minutes, and then Jane rolled onto her back. "The pains are gone."

Hester sat back and folded her hands. "That is good. I do not think thy babe is ready to be born just yet."

"By my calculations, the second week of May." Jane adjusted her pillows so that she could sit up.

Hester rested her hand on the woman's shoulder. "I would rather thee stay abed as much as thee are able."

"Stay abed?" Jane's voice rose in surprise. "With three little children to care for?"

"Were thee not just now singing the praises of young Becky?"

"Of course, but I cannot expect a girl of just three and ten years to run a household."

"The household will wait. She can tend the children, make meals, and deal with the laundry. Thy husband can tend to the garden. And thee"—she gave Jane a very pointed look—"can rest and await the next Biddle's arrival."

With a sigh, Jane slumped against the pillows. "I know you are right. I can feel it"—she pressed her hand to her rounded abdomen—"here."

"Then listen to what thy body is telling thee." Hester rose. "And send Becky to fetch me the moment it tells thee to."

"I will. Thank you, Hester." She took Hester's hand. "I know not what I would do without you."

"Thee would call on the new doctor."

Jane made a face and shook her head. "A man, deliver my babe? 'Tisn't decent." She voiced the opinion held by many of the village women, if not women all through the colonies. They put their trust in the midwife, calling a doctor only if something went terribly wrong, often far too late for the poor man to change the outcome, which was why doctors didn't have a good reputation for live births.

Hester bid the woman a good day, then went down to the kitchen, where Becky was stirring a pot near the hearth, the one-year-old girl now awake and attached to her hip, while the boys rolled a leather ball back and forth across the room, giggling when one of them missed the target of the other's cupped hands.

"Thee are doing a wonderful job here," Hester said. "I know I am leaving Jane in the best of hands."

The girl flushed at her praise.

"She will require bed rest now as much as possible." At the girl's stricken look, Hester shook her head. "Worry not, 'tis almost the babe's time, but if 'twill sit still for another fortnight, all the better." That didn't seem to erase Becky's anxiety, so Hester approached and took the babe—Patsy, if she remembered correctly—and enjoyed the moment of holding her. "Jane is strong and healthy, just tired. With enough good rest, she and the babe should be fine."

"'Tis said that you are the best midwife in the colonies." Becky swung the pot a little closer to the fire, then turned back and took Patsy, who was beginning to fuss in the arms of a stranger.

"In the end, 'tis all in the Lord's hands. Keep Jane and the babe in thy prayers."

"I will."

"So shall I. Fetch me as soon as she tells thee, any time of night or day."

With the girl's affirming nod, Hester let herself out of the house and walked back to her cottage.

Please, Lord, let it be as uneventful of a birthing as ever I have attended. For Jane, for the babe, and for young Becky.

While she didn't often ask for too much for herself, with the threat of being labeled a witch never far from her thoughts, Hester whispered aloud, "And for me, too."

Chapter 5

W HEN HER GENTLE TAP on the back door brought a faint invitation to enter, Hannah Jr. pushed open the door of the midwife's cottage. While they were all to avoid the village, there was a well-worn path through the woods that led straight to Hester's backyard. Most of the Friends used that path when they visited her and had done so, even before the witch scare had descended on the village.

The kitchen was empty but smelled of freshly baked bread. The table was strewn with the makings of a new basket that added a tang of pine to the air. "'Tis Hannah Jr. with thy butter and cheese."

"What wonderful timing." Hester entered the room, her dark hair in a simple braid that hung over her shoulder, and held up a ball of linen thread. "I knew I had another ball somewhere, but it took me a minute to locate it."

"Is that for thy basket?" Hannah Jr. pointed to the rows of loose pine needles and the stitched coil of them that would form the bottom.

"Indeed, and I should have been unhappy had I run out of the thread and needed to take the time to spin more." She pointed to the workbench, where three small loaves of bread cooled. "Would thee put the butter and cheese over there? I shall clear off a spot on the table and we can sample the butter on some of that bread."

"I would not wish to disturb thy work."

"But I should like nothing better." Hester swept the basket materials from one side of the table to the other. "I have had quite enough of my own company for a while. Do sit and visit." She glanced at Hannah Jr. "If thee can spare the time?"

Hannah Jr. had already delivered the orders to her Friends customers, so she took a seat at the table. "I have plenty of time. Mother will not need my help with supper tonight. Tamson and Verity will assist her."

"Speaking of Verity, I have gotten to know the other orphan girl from Widow Scudder's care. Becky is her name." Hester sliced the bread and plated it, then added a block of butter and a knife to the plate. She filled two cups with water from a pitcher before joining Hannah Jr. at the table. "She lives with the Biddles now and is a great help to Sarah with the children."

"Verity and Joseph have remained fast friends, but she never mentions Becky."

"The girl is quite a bit older, so perhaps that is why." Hester buttered a slice of bread and passed it over to Hannah Jr. "They must be five or six years apart in age, and to children, 'tis a lifetime."

Five years was Benji's entire lifetime, and Jonathan was only three, so that made sense.

"Are thee keeping busy in the dairy without thy regular Puritan customers?" Hester asked before taking a bite of her bread.

"'Tis a good time for teaching Tamson and Verity how to make cheese." Hannah Jr. covered her smile with her fingers. She shouldn't find humor in the girls' first attempts. "When things go wrong, no one is left without cheese for their order."

"I suppose one cannot learn any craft without making mistakes." Hester pointed to her basket materials. "I cannot tell thee how many pine needle baskets I ruined in my quest to master them."

"And yet, thee support thyself with basketmaking and midwifery. 'Tis no small thing for a woman."

"Thee are right, 'tis an accomplishment." But the look Hester gave her was troubled. "Yet always there is the chance that I might not earn enough to cover my food, clothing, and shelter."

Hannah Jr. set down her half-eaten piece of bread. "Things a husband should provide."

"And what of thee?" Hester asked. "Are thee interested in any young man among our Friends?"

In the space of nine days, everyone seemed to be poking into her private concerns. She stared at her clasped hands on the table.

"Pray, pardon me." Hester covered Hannah Jr.'s hands with one of hers. "I did not mean to pry."

And for that, Hannah Jr. was grateful. But who better to understand her position than another woman who had chosen not to marry? She must have chosen, for she was a comely woman and easy to be with. Men surely had taken notice of her over the years. Talking with Hester felt... safe. Being ten years Hannah Jr.'s senior and more experienced, it wouldn't hurt to ask the questions that niggled at her.

"Did thee never wish to marry?"

"Ah." Hester sat back in her chair. "I had forgotten. Thy family moved into the community the year after Timothy died. Thee never met him."

"Who was Timothy?"

"Timothy Newman was the love of my life." Hester looked out the window, but Hannah Jr. was pretty sure she didn't see anything through the glass. "He was a farmer, a few years older than I, and had worked his own land for nearly three years. We were to be married, but after the first reading of the bans, he was kicked by a mule. At first, we thought it simply a setback. My father was still alive then. As our doctor, he did all he could, but Timothy seemed to slip a little farther away each day. By the time the bruising spread across his body, 'twas clear there was nothing Father could do. Something had been broken inside of Timothy. He passed six days later."

It wasn't any more her business why Hester hadn't married than it was anyone else's business why Hannah Jr. hadn't. "I am so sorry, I should not have asked such a personal question."

Hester waved her apology away. "'Tis all right. 'Tis good to speak of Timothy sometimes, to remember him." She gave Hannah Jr. a rather sad smile. "To introduce him, in a way, to someone who knew him not."

"Then, is there anything else thee would like to tell me about him?"

"Where to start?" Hester looked up at the rafters, took a deep breath, then met Hannah Jr.'s eyes again "He was handsome, maybe not in the traditional way, but one of his glances would set my heart aflutter. And he had the gruffiest voice, which would make me laugh sometimes, because it hid such a tender heart. He was good with animals, often taking the time to nurse one through an illness or injury when another farmer might have chosen to simply put the beast down." Her lips twitched, but not into a smile exactly. "In fact, he made his father promise not to put down the mule that kicked him. He claimed it had been his own fault—not the mule's—and killing the beast would not repair the damage done."

In the pause that followed, Hannah Jr. asked, "Did his father honor that request?"

"He did. That mule died in the pasture on the farm of old age just a couple of years ago. Timothy's father died the following year, but his brots with the farm. 'Tis near Ispwich."

Before Hannah Jr. found a way to word her next question, Hester said, "Thee are probably wondering why I did not marry another."

Hannah Jr. nodded.

"Because I knew I could never love another as I had loved Timothy." Hester shrugged. "It seemed not fair to saddle a man with a wife who would forever find him wanting by comparison."

Plenty of women married for reasons other than love. It wouldn't surprise Hannah Jr. if at least half of them did. After all, how many single women could a community support? There was only so much need for the professions a woman could hold, like Hester as the midwife. Without a father or brother to support her, a woman had very few choices. Hannah Jr. was blessed to have not only Father, but a passel of brothers who would make sure she never wanted for life's necessities.

She understood what Hester meant about the feelings a man could disturb within her. Even though she and Benjamin had very little time together, no other young man had ever—how had Hester put it?—set her heart aflutter. That was exactly the reaction she had whenever Benjamin looked her way.

"Are thee happy as an unmarried woman?" That was what Hannah Jr. really needed to know. "Even with the responsibility of earning thy own way in the world?"

"Happy?" Hester nodded. "Happiness is a choice, thee know. As a Friend—as a Christian—I have no reason to be unhappy. While I have lost my earthly father and Timothy, my heavenly Father provides for my needs." She shrugged. "Even though at times I need to remind myself of that."

"Remind thyself?"

"Aye, when I begin to worry over this and that"—she pointed to the partially constructed basket—"I need to remind myself that 'tis the Lord who provides. I provide nothing."

"And yet, thee work hard to make the baskets, walk them to Salem Town, and then all the nights thee are called away to attend birthings." How could Hester think she did nothing to provide for herself?

"True, but who grew the pine trees the needles fell from? Who grew the flax plants that provided the linen for thread? And who knew the babes in their mother's wombs before ever I saw them guided into the world?"

Of course, Hannah Jr. should have understood. "The Lord."

"He will take care of thee as well." Hester chuckled. "Perhaps He already has, with a houseful of brothers."

They shared a comfortable silence while they finished the bread and butter. Then Hannah Jr. said, "To answer thy question, none of the young men of the Friends has caused my heart to flutter."

"Then my advice is this"—Hester leaned forward—"if thee are happy with thy family, do not feel pressured to marry anyone just to be married." She sat back again. "I would love to be married to Timothy and have a house filled with children, but this life God has given me is a good life. A worthy life."

"Thee bring life into the world with thy work."

"I am doing the work He has given me, which is why I choose to be happy."

Hannah Jr. walked home shortly after that exchange, her mind whirling with everything Hester had shared. Oddly enough, what comforted her most was knowing that someone else had loved and lost and overcome. Not that Benjamin had died, but the chasm between the Friends and Puritans was as insurmountable as overcoming death.

It was helpful to know that in spite of all of that, she could still choose happiness.

After Hannah Jr. left, Hester picked up her needle and threaded it with the length of the waxed linen thread. Using a small cone of birchbark held in shape by dried leather wrappings, she fed a handful of the long pine needles into the larger end, keeping them aligned, and shook some of them out of the smaller end. Once she merged them with the needles at the end of the coil she was working on, she began lacing them together. It was tedious work, but it gave her plenty of time to reflect on her conversation with Hannah Jr.

She needed to take her own advice and rely on God to provide for her needs. Worry about the rent wouldn't change it. She would make her baskets and trust in the Lord to provide the buyers at the right time. His time—not hers. As she'd told Hannah Jr., choosing happiness was a lifetime commitment.

Speaking of Timothy, something she didn't do often anymore, had both comforted her and renewed her sense of loss. He'd be five and thirty now, and they would have had at least four or five children, Lord willing. One boy with Timothy's reddish-brown hair and hazel eyes, and perhaps a daughter with his coloring.

The empty cottage was quiet except for the occasional clomping of horse hooves, voices from those who walked along the street, and the bark of a dog somewhere in the distance. No happy chatter of children here. As much as she missed Timothy, she also missed the children they'd never had. Several men near Ipswich had approached her after Timothy's death, all of them widowers with small children in need of a mother. But Hester hadn't wanted just anyone's child. She wanted—and could never have—Timothy's. And so she'd taken on the position of midwife when the previous woman had moved away. Daughter of the doctor, she'd been welcomed by this community in spite of her unmarried state.

She paused stitching and let her hands rest on the tabletop. Could she have loved those other children enough to make up for being married to their fathers? At the time, in her grief, she hadn't thought she could. Years later, years more mature, having held countless babes as they drew their first breaths, she knew she could have. At two and thirty, she could certainly marry a widower, but the community saw her as what she was, an aging spinster. And even though at times she pondered over how her life would be had she made another choice, in the end, she was happy. Lonely sometimes, of course, but even then, not unhappy.

Had she given her best advice to Hannah Jr.? Perhaps not, but the Lord seemed to have His hand on that young woman, and He would guide her better than Hester could ever hope to.

As Thee have guided me, Lord, and as it pleases Thee, guide Hannah Jr. into the life Thee have for her. And for me, thank Thee for being my provider, and forgive me when I slip into worry instead of worship.

Humming one of her favorite tunes, a lullaby Mother had hummed to her from infancy, Hester resumed her basketmaking, content that she had done her best by Hannah Jr., and that the Lord would provide for them both.

Chapter 6

A TTACKING THE HARD SOIL in her garden to ready it for spring plant- ing, Hester almost missed the women's voices carrying from her neighbors' garden just out of sight. She paused her hoe and wiped a film of sweat from her brow with the hem of her apron.

"And so I tell you, 'tis because he stood up for his goodwife, and for no other reason."

"Giles Corey is a good man. I cannot believe anyone thinks him guilty of..."

The second voice dropped too low for Hester to hear the next word, but there was no need.

Witchcraft.

Hester had heard of Giles Corey, but she'd never met him. Every- thing she'd heard, however, had been complimentary to the gentle- man.

"Have I not known the man my whole life?" The first speaker's voice rose. "I cannot believe 'tis true. Not a word of it."

"I agree. He has been an upstanding member of the church for as long as I have been here, and that nearly twenty years. He may have married his last wife in haste, but at their ages, 'tisn't truly scandalous."

Hester didn't know her neighbors well. She wasn't shunned because her occupation made her a necessity in the village, but neither was she accepted. Tolerated would be a better word. She wouldn't be that if she were caught eavesdropping on their conversation. But before she could step away, the next sentence stopped her in her tracks.

"They say all of them are being checked for a witch's mark." The second woman's voice dropped again, so Hester held her breath and waited to hear the rest. "They shave them—every inch—the women as well as men are looked over in an undressed state."

The first woman gasped, and Hester had to fight the urge to join her. When would the madness end?

"Though they do say that if the mark bleeds, then 'tisn't a witch's mark at all. That is why they prod the spots with a pin."

Hester couldn't listen to any more. Nonsense, all of it. She tiptoed away from her garden, away from the gossiping women. She was hot and sweaty, but that wasn't what made her go the basin, pour fresh water from the pitcher, and scrub herself clean.

She felt dirty from listening to such gossip.

What if a babe she delivered had a mole or a birthmark of some sort? Or even a normal birthing bruise? Would it be subject to poking and prodding and bleeding to make the Puritans of the village happy?

Hands still in the water, she pondered. What could she do to protect the babes she helped usher into the world? To speak out against the practice would almost assure she would be the next one accused of witchcraft. Never had she felt so helpless.

It was Saturday evening, and the daily chores were done. The little boys were abed, and the girls were in their room. Hannah Jr. relaxed in the parlor with a small pile of mending in her lap, Mother in the chair opposite her with a similar pile, while Father dozed in front of the fire. A light rain spattered against the windows when the wind gusted. It was a good evening to stay indoors and listen to the fire crackling in the fireplace.

The back door banged open, jerking Father awake with a snort.

Robert raced into the room, heavy boots still on, water pooling on the floorboards. "'Tis her time."

"Dolly?" Father was already on his feet.

Hannah Jr. rose. "The young ones will wish to see."

Father waved a hand at her as he headed for the door. "Leave them sleep for now. It could be hours yet since 'tis her first foal."

"I think not, Father," Robert said. "The hooves are already showing. She must have been laboring for a while and doing it quietly."

Mother set aside her mending, and Hannah Jr. did the same. Tamson and Verity met them at the bottom of the stairs.

"What is it? What has happened?" Tamson's eyes were wide and Verity's frightened.

"'Tis a good thing happening in the barn." Hannah Jr. waited for their expressions to change, indicating they had figured it out. "Dress warmly and bring the little boys out with thee."

Soon, the family gathered around the roomy box stall her brothers had built weeks ago, lighted by three oil lanterns hung along its front. Those gave Hannah Jr. a moment of worry, remembering the fire of last winter, but they were newer lanterns without holes from which to throw a spark.

Dolly, her sorrel hide damp despite the cool mid-April evening, circled the pen, pawing the straw bedding, sniffing it, then moving on and did the same in another spot. From beneath her cocked tail hung a long wet string, the remains of the broken water sack that had protected the foal these past months, and at the top of that, the tips of two hooves.

Hannah Jr. enjoyed the excitement, the anticipation of another birth. Was this how Hester felt when she attended a human birthing? How fulfilling that must be.

Rags and Button, the two farm dogs, barked outside before the jingle of harness reached them in the barn.

Who would be visiting so late in the evening? And in such weather? Hannah Jr. exchanged a worried glance with Mother as Father headed to the door.

"Ho there!"

Tension eased from Hannah Jr. as David's hardy greeting carried into the barn.

"I saw the light here and bypassed the house," he said as he came through the door.

"We are awaiting Dolly's foal," Father replied. "Join us."

Any birth was an event to be celebrated, but a new foal was special. Father hadn't bred Dolly before, partly because he wanted her fully mature before she gave birth, and partly because he'd needed her to work the fields. This spring, he'd been able to borrow an old gelding from a neighbor to hitch with Dandy and work the ground, leaving Dolly free to produce the farm's next work horse.

David shook the rain from his hat, but there was something a little off about their usual good-natured friend, although Hannah Jr. couldn't quite put her finger on it.

Father got right to the point. "What brings thee out on such a dreary evening?"

"Giles Corey." The way David said the Puritan's name sent a chill through Hannah Jr. Giles' wife, Martha, had been accused of witchcraft.

"Giles Corey must be all of seventy years old." Mother gripped her shawl at her throat. "Tell me not that they have accused him."

"Aye, that they have." David put his hat back on. "'Tis my belief—without proof mind thee—that protesting his wife's being accused put him on the list."

"The list?" Father asked.

David shrugged. "Not an actual list, but among those who will be named as witches solely because they have spoken out against what is happening."

"David"—Mother took a step toward him—"thee are being careful, are thee not?"

He grinned at her, but it seemed forced. "Isobel would have my head on a platter were I to run my mouth off to the wrong people. Have no fear. I am as tight-lipped as an oyster these days when I am out and about."

"Glad I am to hear that." Father cast a glance at Dolly's progress, then turned back to his friend. "How did thee hear about Giles?"

"A Puritan from the village came to collect his repaired musket and told me about it. I grunted and nodded as it seemed appropriate, then hurried him from my shop since it was nearly suppertime, and my goodwife had sent one of the children to remind me. Now, after a fine meal, I am on my way to let our elders know. I thought to tell thee as well, since thy farm is on the way."

"'Tis probably for the best to restrict the news to just those people." Father addressed them all. "Thee heard what was said, but it goes no farther than this barn." He jabbed a finger at the wooden floorboards. "Not a one of thee is to repeat so much as the name Giles Corey, do thee understand?"

Hannah Jr. nodded, as did the rest, except for little Jonathan who had surrendered to sleep in her arms, his warm body keeping the chill away.

"If speaking out against the witch trials can see one accused, we shall go above and beyond and not speak of the witch trials at all from here on out." Father paused, making eye contact with each one of them in turn. If he lingered a bit on Joseph, Hannah Jr. couldn't blame him. That boy had a quick tongue and was not always the most circumspect. He was a Puritan, but so were all those being accused. Perhaps he'd be safer if he were a Friend, as odd as that thought was.

"Pa, look!" Robert pointed into the box stall as Dolly sank to her knees with a groan.

"Good girl." Father leaned against the top rail of the stall. Mother stood on one side of him and David on the other. The rest of them squeezed in where they could.

"Wake up, Jonathan, lest thee miss the birth." Hannah Jr. jiggled the boy in her arms. "Wake up."

Her littlest brother arched his back, yawned, and flopped against her again, eyes shut, his breath against her neck deep and even.

"Let him sleep," Mother said. "He is too young to remember it anyway. Dolly will have another foal for him to witness."

"I will remember." Benji rubbed his eyes. "I am a big boy now."

Hannah Jr. chuckled and ruffled his unruly hair. "Thee are getting bigger every day."

Dolly groaned again, a more intense sound than before. After a long session of pushing and resting and pushing again, a dark, wet foal lay on the straw. Dolly nickered to it. The mare stood and shook, then nosed the foal, which flopped over onto its side.

"'Tis a filly." Caleb Jr.'s voice was hushed, almost reverent. "'Tis a filly, Pa."

Father grabbed his shoulder and gave it a shake. "A fine start to thy team, I would say."

They watched until the foal had stood and nursed. By then it was fully dark. David excused himself and drove away to continue his errand. Robert toted Benji—who had succumbed to sleep—to the house, and Hannah Jr. followed with Jonathan. She gazed at the stars twinkling above.

The world was full of hardships, even dangers, but Hester was right. One could still choose to be happy. As with Buttercup's calf, witnessing the foal's birth ushered in a sense of joy. Hannah Jr. would hold on to that.

With just a wrapper over her shift, Hester lifted the candle and opened the door a crack in answer to the knocking that had awakened her. Becky Simpson stared back, eyes as round as teacups.

"The pains are back then?"

"Aye, Midwife, worse than before."

"Hurry home, heat plenty of water for me, and place the clean baby wrappings Jane has ready near the fire to keep them warm. I shall be along as soon as I dress."

Becky whirled away and was gone before Hester had finished her thought.

Yawning, Hester hurried to her room, where she dressed. Her basket and canvas bag were always packed with the necessities, so she scooped them up and headed outside. The air was cold, not a cloud in the sky to keep in any warmth. The scent of woodsmoke lingered in the air even though most fireplaces would have been banked by now since it must be well past midnight. The stars shone brightly, lighting her path more than the sliver of a moon.

It was good to soak in the calm of the night after the unsettling gossip she'd overheard from her neighbors that morning.

At the Biddle house, Hester didn't bother to knock. Becky had the cloths heating and a large pot over the fire in the hearth. The girl turned from her work, and Hester nodded to her as she went up the stairs.

John Biddle shot out of the bedside chair when Hester reached the doorway. "Praise God you have arrived. She awoke in such pain." He hadn't kept his voice down, and a child cried.

"Why do thee not deal with that"—Hester pointed to the closed door across the hallway from where the crying issued—"and I shall take over here with Jane." She all but shoved him from the room, eased the door closed, and then turned to her patient. The woman was bathed in sweat, even though the room had no fire and was quite cool. "'Twould appear this is no false alarm."

"I think not." Jane gritted her teeth and sucked in a hissing breath against the pain, then relaxed. "I know 'tis not. But I am frightened, Midwife. 'Tis too soon."

"Not by much." Three weeks, if the woman had calculated correctly. Hester set out the things she'd need on the bedside table. "Some babes arrive earlier than others." Despite her words, she sent up a silent prayer. *Lord, if it pleases Thee, let this babe arrive healthy and let this mother recover quickly. Amen. Oh, and Lord, please let there be no marks on the babe's skin for anyone to poke with a pin.* The neighbor women's comments that afternoon wouldn't let her be, a consequence of listening to gossip.

"This one"—Jane ran her hands over her bulging middle—"has been by far more worrisome than the other three. Do you think that might mean something is wrong with the babe?" Panic slipped into the woman's voice.

"Nay, I do not." Hester used her most soothing tone. "Thee have three children and no two are alike, is that not true?" She waited for Jane to nod in reply. "This one will be its own self as well. Perhaps giving thee issues early will mean the babe will not do so later in childhood."

"Would that not be nice?" Jane's smile turned into a grimace when another contraction arrived.

"Is thy aunt not coming to attend to thee?" Sarah Cloyce had arrived before Hester for the first false alarm. Most women had a family member present to help and encourage.

A stuttering sob came through Jane's clenched teeth. "She has been accused." Tears leaked from the corners of her eyes.

Hester did her best not to react to the news. The last thing Jane needed was to think about something so horrible. Indeed, the shock of her aunt's accusation may have caused her early labor. Hester had seen worry and tragedy impact pregnant women before.

"Then we shall have to welcome the babe ourselves, just the two of us." Hester put every ounce of positivity in her voice that she could muster, even while she wished she could heap her opinion of the whole witchcraft nastiness upon those ruining lives in the village. "Since we have both done this before, I am sure we shall do just fine."

The contraction ended, and Jane wiped away her tears. "Of course."

Hester rolled up her sleeves and washed her hands at the basin on the bedside table. "Let us see how far along thee are, shall we?" The child was turned correctly, but Jane had a lot of work to do before it could be born. And she was already tired, worn out from the pregnancy.

It was going to be a long night.

Chapter 7

S UNDAY MEETING WENT LONGER than usual. It seemed as if everyone had a word from the Lord to share. When it was finally over, Hannah Jr. climbed into the wagon, hitched to Dandy and the borrowed gelding. She settled herself by the tailgate and then took Jonathan from Caleb Jr.'s arms. The little boy curled into her lap, head resting against her shoulder.

Across the meetinghouse yard, Isaac Kerley made eye contact with her and held it. Hannah Jr. had known Isaac from a distance her whole life, but lately, he'd been watching her. She lowered her eyes to the brother on her lap, smoothing his hair away from his forehead. Perhaps if she ignored Isaac, he'd keep his distance.

The wagon rocked as Father took his seat and unwound the reins from the brake handle. "Everyone ready?"

Mother turned and counted heads. "All accounted for."

"Hup, Dandy. Hup, Scout." The leather reins slapped against the broad rumps, and the horses leaned into their harnesses.

After the first lurch of the wagon, Hannah Jr. peeked out the back. Isaac had closed the distance between where he'd stood and their wagon, but now watched them drive away. Relief flooded her. Not that Isaac wasn't a good man. As far as she knew, he was. But the way he'd been watching her these past weeks—before, after, and even sometimes during meeting—was unsettling. She blew out a slow breath.

"What has thee so melancholy?" Caleb Jr. leaned close and kept his voice low, under the volume of Benji, who was describing the toad he'd discovered near the bushes beside the meetinghouse. "Did it have anything to do with Isaac heading our way?"

Her brother's eyes were far too sharp. "I have given him no encouragement."

"I do not believe he needs any." Caleb Jr. turned his head, his voice barely a whisper. "I happen to know he would have thee for a wife, should thee show the slightest favor upon him."

"I shall not." Hannah Jr. matched his low tone, and even she was surprised at the fierceness of her response.

Her brother's eyebrow hiked almost to his hairline.

"What is so interesting between thee two?" asked Tamson.

Caleb Jr. shot Hannah Jr. an uncertain look, then turned to their younger sister. "Things of which thee are too young to understand." There was teasing in his voice, and Tamson began to debate him on her age and what she should be privy to.

Hannah Jr. ignored them, watching out the back of the wagon. When they passed the brewery, Benjamin was outside, leaning against the building. Like Isaac, he was watching for her. Unlike Isaac, she couldn't pull her eyes away from his. It was wrong, so very wrong, to encourage the young man. Yet at the sight of him, her heart fluttered. He didn't move and neither did she, until the wagon angled away and he was out of sight.

If only Isaac's glances brought the kind of response that Benjamin's did, how easy her life would be then. Father and Mother would approve of the match. They were not close neighbors, but the Kerley family was well respected among the Friends. Isaac farmed alongside his father, and she'd heard he'd bought the acreage adjoining his father's farm. And even more importantly...

Isaac Kerley wasn't a Puritan.

The babe squalled before Hester even had him fully in hand. A little on the small side due to his early arrival, he was making up in noise for what he lacked in size.

"Thee have another son, Jane."

"Praise God." Jane's voice was thin and reedy, and her face lined with more than just her well-earned fatigue. "Is he"—she struggled to see the babe in Hester's arms—"is he perfect?"

"I should say so." Hester wiped his skin free of the birthing fluids. "A handsome one too."

"But there are no spots? Thee would tell me if there were?" Again, the edge of panic crept into Jane's voice.

Hester took a moment to thoroughly examine the squalling infant as she dried him off, then placed him in a clean receiving cloth, wrapped him snuggly, and handed him over to Jane. "Not a mark anywhere."

Jane took the child and wept, pressing her face against the downy hair on his head that already promised to be as blond as his father's. When she raised her face to Hester again, the worry lines were erased, and the smile—despite the weariness—was genuine. "I have been so afraid. They say some of the women who have been accused were born with marks, you know."

Had it not been the pregnancy itself but this nagging fear spilling over from the witch nonsense that had made Jane's pregnancy so difficult? Had it robbed her of sleep and rest? How had Hester missed that? How many other expectant mothers were facing the same fear? She again squashed the urge to march into the street and tell the whole village what poison they were fomenting with their witch hunt. But that would only result in Hester's being accused and arrested.

A door opened below, and then footsteps rushed up the stairs. John Biddle arrived at the bedroom in his Sunday-best suit looking rather disheveled, as some expectant husbands did. The good ones, in Hester's opinion. His attention was captured by the wrapped babe who had settled quietly in his mother's arms. "All is well?"

"All is well." Jane's voice was clearer and stronger. "Come, John, and meet your new son."

"Just a peek," Hester said. "Then we have the finishing-up to do."

"Of course, Midwife." The man crept into the room as if making noise were a crime and looked into the face of his child.

Hester swallowed back the emotions that tugged at her as the tall man fell in love with his newborn son. There was no other way to describe it, and it touched her deeply. John Biddle was a man to be admired. If there were more like him, perhaps even she would be tempted to reconsider marriage.

"Off thee go, now, and see thy other children fed." Hester shooed him toward the door. "When we are finished, thee can bring the children up to see him and their mother."

"Of course."

How he managed to say the words around his wide grin, Hester couldn't imagine. She turned her attention back to Jane and the finishing work they needed to do.

An hour later, in her bed with the curtains drawn against the bright sun, Hester mulled over the emotional reactions around the birth of baby Biddle. Despite John's obvious adoration of both his new son and his wife, what would his reaction have been should the boy have been marked at birth? What would Jane's reaction have been?

If a mark had been on an unseen part of the boy's body, such as an armpit, they could have hidden it. But what if it had been on the boy's face or neck? Then what would they have done?

The story of Moses was perhaps the best example. Jochebed had kept her baby boy completely hidden from Pharaoh, who had ordered all the Israeli boys to be killed. At great risk to herself and her other children, she'd defied Pharaoh's order. The Lord had ordained the outcome, of course, but Jochebed had carried it out.

Would any of Hester's Puritan neighbors—or even one of the Friends—have to make a choice like that in the days, weeks, or months to come? Would they have to hide a child to save its life?

The witchcraft craze that had taken over the village and spilled into Salem Town as well as the surrounding villages might call for that level of sacrifice. In their fear and ignorance, the people of the area, who were normally a pious and hardworking people, could be put to the test.

It remained to be seen if any in their communities could rise to the level of a Jochebed.

Hannah Jr. had excused herself for a walk after dinner to enjoy the warm spring day. Also to escape Caleb Jr.'s irritating grin and Tamson's knowing looks. There were times when being part of a big family was overwhelming. The peace and quiet would do her good. She strolled along the wooded edge of their property where small white flowers with pinkish veins in their five petals were welcoming the new season.

Rags and Button trotted ahead of her, until Button stopped and faced the house, ears perked. So much for being alone. She did her best not to groan as Mother came toward her, shawl wrapped around her shoulders against the light breeze.

"Thee had a good idea," Mother said. "'Tis a fine day for a walk. Spring is truly here at last."

It wasn't often that Mother had a moment away from the little boys and the house, so Hannah Jr. had no business being selfish with her longed-for time alone.

"We should plant the garden's root crops soon." Hannah Jr. pointed to the little flowers. "See, the fairy potatoes are blooming."

"They are lovely. We could mark the spot and send the boys to dig some of their tubers in a couple of weeks."

The wildflower's tubers were a spring favorite, first boiled and then fried in butter. Hannah Jr. broke a dead branch off a nearby tree, pushed it into the ground to mark the spot, and tied her hair ribbon around it. "There. That should do it."

"Thank thee." Mother crossed her arms and looked back at the house. "I could not help but notice Isaac Kerley's interest in thee again today. He seems to be a well-liked young man."

Since walking off would be rude, Hannah Jr. settled for as bland of a reply as she could think of. "So I have heard."

"Have thee not spoke with him?"

"Never."

"I believe he would have approached thee today had thy father not been in a hurry to get home."

"Perhaps."

Mother hiked a brow. "From thy one-word answers, I take it thee have no interest in this topic of discussion."

"I do not." There. She'd just said it plainly. Now maybe they could leave it alone.

Mother took her arm and turned them toward the pond at the far corner of the cleared property. "Then let us continue with our walk and enjoy it, shall we?"

"May I ask thee something first?" Hannah Jr. might as well get everything out in the open.

"Of course, my dear."

"Are thee and Father disappointed in me?"

"What?" Shock colored Mother's tone and showed in her expression. "Thee could never be a disappointment to us. If we have given thee reason to think that is so"—Mother gripped Hannah Jr.'s arm tighter—"I am sorry."

"Nay, 'tisn't anything thee have said or done." Hannah Jr. started them walking toward the pond. "'Tis just that I know thee would like me to be settled with a husband, house, and family of my own. Thee has said as much before." They had discussed it back about the time Verity came to live with them.

"I just want thee to be happy, to be fulfilled and blessed."

"Hester is all of those things, and she has no husband or children."

"She is a very special woman, for sure." Mother shook her head. "Most women in her position would have chosen another for a husband after Timothy died."

"I spoke with her on Tuesday when I delivered her dairy order. She told me about him, and how he died so young."

"A very sad story, to be sure, but thee are not mourning a death as she was and is still. And thee are at least ten years her junior." Mother sighed. "I hope thee will not close thyself off to other opportunities of marriage and family."

"Other than with Benjamin." Saying his name was almost painful, as if cutting into her heart. How could she be so taken with a young man—a Puritan, no less—with whom she had exchanged so few words, even though they'd known each other for years? It made no sense. But that didn't make it any less real.

"I wish I could tell thee that all this will pass away." There was regret in Mother's voice. "But I know not. I pray for thee every night, as I do for all my children. The Lord will have to do the rest."

The Lord would have to work on Hannah Jr.'s heart. First, that she not lose patience with her brothers and sister, and second, that she would wish only to follow His leading. And she did honestly wish to do that. But knowing what was His leading and what were her own desires...

That was where things got muddled.

Chapter 8

I T'D BEEN TWO WEEKS since Hannah Jr. had written the note to Sarah Buffington when Thomas Jr. had picked up the last of the doctor's furniture. It was Monday again, the final one in April. Would Sarah send Benjamin—or Thomas Jr.—after an order of butter and cheese? Hannah Jr. pulled in a long breath, the air tangy with the aroma of aging cheeses. At least on a Monday, she could keep busy in the dairy, packing for her Tuesday deliveries to the Friends, her nerves not on display for all the family to witness.

Yesterday's display had been enough. After Sunday meeting, she'd had to finagle a way into the wagon without drawing attention from Isaac. Caleb Jr. had played his role, keeping the young man talking by the meetinghouse steps while she made her escape. Tamson, of course, had teased her about it. Two weeks in a row of avoiding Isaac. Would he get the message and turn his attentions elsewhere? Or should she speak with him and get it over with? That seemed the more direct route, but everything in her balked at confrontation.

Tamson would wade in and tell the young man her thoughts with no ifs, ands, or buts. But Hannah Jr. wasn't Tamson. If she were, she wouldn't be pacing the dairy and worrying over whether or not Benjamin would come. No, Tamson would be out on the road, walking to meeting him, and if he didn't appear, she'd walk all the way to the brewery to make her wishes known.

Mother and Father should hope that girl didn't find herself attracted to a Puritan young man.

Pacing wasn't getting her work done, and neither was mulling over her actions versus her sister's, so she set up the butter churn and poured the separated cream into it. She had enough for tomorrow's deliveries to her Friends customers, but if one of the Buffington sons came, she'd need more. And she needed to keep her hands busy.

She'd no more than fallen into the rhythm of the churn when the dogs barked. Of course, it could be anyone come to see Father, although most would know he'd be out in the fields on such a fine morning. It could be someone come to visit Mother, yet most women stayed home and did laundry on Mondays. It could even be one of David and Isobel's sons looking for her brothers to go fishing or hunting.

But none of those options included bells dancing on a pair of harnesses.

"Benjamin!" Robert's cry outside rose above the swish and thump of the churn.

Hannah Jr. let go of the churn's handle and buried her face in her hands. She needed to find the strength to be more like Tamson. Not in going after what she wanted, but finding the strength to say what needed to be said.

The hum of male voices went on for a long time, while Hannah Jr. collected her thoughts, her resolve, and her courage. Then came the knock on the dairy's door.

"Enter." Her voice was calm and composed and nothing like the tempest inside of her.

Benjamin entered by himself, a basket in one hand. "Hello."

Hannah Jr. rose. "Hello."

They stared at each other for far too long, and then she reached for the basket. "Thee have brought thy mother's basket for me to fill." She almost cringed at stating the obvious.

"Indeed. She was happy to get your note." He shifted his feet, looking down and then back at her, his expression hopeful. "As was I."

"Thee mustn't—" Hannah Jr. pressed her fingers to her lips, to stop her outburst and started over. "Thee must know that I appreciate thy mother's continued patronage of my dairy."

Benjamin took a step back, scanning the dairy and looking at anything but her. "Are you saying that I should not have interpreted that note as a way for us to meet again?"

Was she? Of course she was. Only that wasn't true. Not completely. Hannah Jr. had known that as she'd written it. But it had brought them together, and now she needed to be truthful with him.

"I cannot in any way encourage thy interest in meeting with me." She gripped the basket's handle in both hands, staring at it. "'Twould be to no end, as we both know."

"Nay, I do not accept that." His voice was low and intense, and she raised her face to him.

Benjamin's dark hair, as curly as his father's, had escaped his queue and framed his face. His deep brown eyes were penetrating, as if he willed her to listen to him. Normally creased with humor, his face was serious, mouth a slash above a chin that dimpled at the bottom. His widely spaced brows were drawn inward.

Hester's description of *aflutter* hardly began to describe what was happening inside of Hannah Jr.

"Our parents would never allow us to be..." She could not presume the rest. After all, he'd not actually declared his interest in her.

Benjamin had no problem voicing it. "A courting couple?"

She forced herself to relax her grip on the basket's handle before she damaged it. "Aye."

He took a step closer. "You are already of age, and I have but two years to wait. Then we shall not require anyone's permission."

" nor my community of Friends would accept us." He must be able to see that. "Even if we defied our families and courted, we could never..." She couldn't finish the sentence.

Once again, he filled it in. "Marry each other." He shook his head, the curls dancing in the sunlight pouring through the dairy's two windows. "Not by the reverend from my church or by one of your elders, of course, but there are other ways."

Married by a magistrate? "Not for me. If ever I marry, 'twill be in front of God and witnesses."

"If?" Benjamin's brows lifted. "Does that mean no Quaker man holds your heart?"

The conversation was frustrating her. It was time to put an end to it. "I must fill thy mother's basket, and then thee should leave. Next time, perhaps 'tis best if Thomas Jr. comes to fetch her order." She turned her back on him, unfolded the note, and stuffed the requested items into the basket, taking little care how they landed. When she turned around, she named the amount due without meeting his eyes.

Benjamin handed over the coins, his fingertips touching her palm and lingering a moment too long.

She met his glance then.

"I shall return, Hannah Buffum, Jr. I shall not be put off so easily." He chuckled. Chuckled, as if he found humor in the situation.

Indignation flared inside of her, pushing the flutter out of the way. "Thee should listen to me."

"I have. Do you know what I heard?"

She shook her head, miffed at the wry smile he gave her.

"I heard that you have no other suitor and that you have no plans to marry. Say what you wish"—he pressed a fist to his chest—"that gives me hope."

"Did thee also hear that we cannot..." She stopped when he raised a hand.

"I heard." A shake of his curly head, along with his grin, made him frustratingly appealing. "But I am not convinced. Nor will I be until you have accepted the troth of another man." He took the basket from her and left the dairy without another word or backward glance.

Hannah Jr. collapsed onto the stool. What had she done wrong? Instead of warning him away, she'd encouraged him. The whole experience had exhausted her.

But that didn't explain the flicker of hope burning deep inside of her.

Basket filled with more of the long pine needles, Hester returned to the village. These were the last she'd collect this spring, as the new foliage pushing up from the forest floor was making it too difficult to harvest them. Next she would gather grape and woodbine vines before they leafed out, and then perhaps talk one of the young men among the Friends into cutting her a length of cedar trunk for the long strips she would hammer and pull to use in her baskets. There was also birchbark and come fall, plenty of different varieties of reeds to cut.

Even if her sales slowed due to the circumstances of Salem Town and the village, she would have plenty of baskets made and ready to sell when things got back to normal. Other villages and towns had gone through similar witch trials and survived. There was no reason to doubt that Salem Village would too.

How unscathed they remained, however, no one could foresee.

She nodded to her gossipy neighbor, who was shaking a rug at her front door, then turned the corner of the cottage and walked into her back yard. A basket sat by the door, one she'd made, her distinctive yet plain embellishments clear even from a distance. Probably someone needed it repaired. From the cloth bunched over the top and tucked into it, they'd left her some sort of payment as well. Hopefully bread, as she hadn't set any batter to rise last evening, so couldn't bake until tomorrow.

The cloth covering the basket's contents moved, and she paused. There wasn't a whiff of breeze. What on earth? Hester put her basket of pine needles down and peeled back the other basket's cover to expose—

A babe.

Not just a babe, a newborn not even properly cleaned, it couldn't be more than a few hours old.

She glanced around to see if anyone was watching, but she was alone. Hester picked up the babe, basket and all, and took he or she into the cottage. Who would leave a newborn infant on her back porch? And why? The babe was content, so couldn't have been on the porch for very long.

Hester hadn't helped deliver a babe since Jane Biddle's, and that more than two weeks past. This little one couldn't be Jane's. She pulled away the wrappings to see if the babe was a girl or a boy.

She gasped, hand over her mouth.

On the child's stomach, over a clumsily tied clout, was a large red mark. Not a bruise—a birthmark. Hester had seen the like before, but never so large. It covered almost all of the babe's stomach, its irregular edges jagged against the pale of the rest of the skin. Hester lifted her, a little girl, and turned her over. Her back was free of the strawberry-red splotching. But her front...

This was no ordinary foundling, which happened from time to time. Often they were babes born to unmarried women or someone unable to care for the child. They were usually left at an elder's house among the Friends, or at the Puritan church. But this child, without a shred of doubt, had been left a foundling because of that mark.

A witch's mark.

Not that Hester believed in that. She cuddled the babe to her shoulder. Since the little girl was both dry and content, whoever had left her couldn't have been gone long, or been from far away. But who?

Did it matter? They clearly didn't want the marked babe, and yet, they wished to give her a chance with someone, and probably thought, being a midwife, Hester could settle her with a good family.

Hester reached back into the basket and pulled out a dozen or so clouts for the babe's use, as well as an extra blanket. Someone had known she wouldn't have these things on hand. They hadn't been folded and laid inside, but stuffed around where the babe had laid, as if whoever had done so had been in a hurry.

The cloth was neither poor nor fine, just the sort any goodwife would use, lovingly stitched by the expectant mother, or perhaps an older sibling. The blankets, however, were too fancy for one of the Friends to have made, with bright colorful stripes along their edges.

She must be a Puritan babe.

A chill crept over Hester. Why would a Puritan have left the babe with a Friend?

She sank into her rocking chair and hummed to the child. What would she feed her? A memory niggled from long ago of an old auntie who had sworn by stewed and strained oats for a colicky child. She'd said the broth from the oats was as good as milk for seeing a child grow.

Once the babe was asleep, Hester settled her in the basket and filled a small kettle with water, then dumped in a handful of oats. How much was the right amount? Since she could always thin it if needed, she added another handful and swung the kettle over the fireplace, poked the flames back to life, and added another log.

While that came to a boil, she pulled out a length of linen fabric and cut off six small squares slightly larger than her hand. With the babe asleep and the oats boiling, she stitched a hem around the first two squares. She'd finish the rest later. With a much larger square of the same cloth, she lined a bowl and then poured the boiled oats into it. Pulling up the edges of the cloth and tying them with string, she hung the boiled oats over the bowl. A thin, steady stream of cloudy liquid pooled into the bowl.

The babe awoke with a mewl, her tiny legs thrashing against the basket.

"There, there, my sweet." Hester lifted the girl, who was in need of one of those dry clouts. It took only a moment to tie on a fresh one. She dropped the soiled one into a bucket, and poured half of her fresh water over the top. She'd meant to draw more at the well after gathering the pine needles.

How was she to do that now without someone seeing her with a child?

She couldn't very well leave the infant alone in the house while she walked to the center of the village and back. What if the girl awoke and cried? Someone would hear and come to investigate, since her neighbors knew she had no child. But children cried, and sooner or later, someone was bound to hear.

Hester pulled her rocking chair beside the table where she could reach the bowl of oat broth. She settled the babe in her arms and took one of the hemmed squares of linen. Dipping it in the broth, she brought it to the babe's mouth. It took a few tries, but the little girl caught on, and soon, Hester could barely supply the liquid fast enough. By the time the babe was satisfied, they were both dotted with the thick broth.

What should Hester do next? Logic said to take the child to the Puritan church, as she had come from a Puritan family. But they would see the mark and... and what? Would the babe be pricked with a pin? Put into prison? Surely not. Yet people were accusing others of witchcraft on far less than a bright red mark on the body.

Or would they accuse Hester of having put a hex on the child and blame her for the mark?

No, she couldn't take the babe there.

What about one of the families among the Friends? Several would accept the babe without question, mark or not. Isobel O'Sullivan for sure, Hannah Buffum, and at least half a dozen others.

Hester burped the babe, and then washed her, removing the last of the dried birth fluids. The little girl, clean and dry, fed and comfortable, drifted off to sleep in her arms. The child who'd been left for her to take care of.

For her to protect.

The thought of turning the babe over to anyone else had lost all its appeal. But how could she, a single woman barely getting by, manage to raise a child on her own? A child with a secret to be kept.

Chapter 9

S TILL STEWING OVER BENJAMIN'S refusal to accept her arguments against his interest in her the day before, Hannah Jr. was more than happy to take the back path to Hester's cottage, and thus avoid the main street and the brewery's front windows. She'd saved Hester's delivery for last. Despite the separation in their ages, she felt drawn to the midwife who was bravely living her life by herself among the Puritans.

Hannah Jr. tapped on the door.

"Enter."

Hester stood in front of her table, hands folded in front of her. "Oh, 'tis thee." She closed her eyes and puffed out a breath. "I forgot 'tis Tuesday and thee would be here." Her words came fast and clipped.

"Is anything amiss?"

"Indeed, I should say so." Hester stepped to the side, exposing a basket with a babe in it.

Hannah Jr. set Hester's order on the workbench, and came to look at the child. "Whose babe is this?" The murky blue-gray eyes of a newborn peered up at her, a cloud of fine dark hair showing above them.

"I know not."

"What?" Hannah Jr. stepped back and met Hester's eyes. "What do thee mean?"

"The girl is a foundling. She was left on my back porch sometime yesterday in the forenoon."

"Why would? Who would?" Hannah Jr. stumbled to finish a sentence. "Thee have no idea who it could be?"

"Nay. The child is newly born, and none of our Friends was expecting at this time. I have two Puritan women I am waiting to deliver, but neither before the middle of next month. This little girl was not born early. She is as plump as a partridge, a clear sign that she was a full-term babe."

"A little girl?" Hannah Jr. bent over the basket again. "May I hold her?"

Hester appeared to hesitate before nodding.

Hannah Jr. gathered the child in her arms. How good it felt to hold a newborn again. She breathed in her scent, that intoxicating aroma of newborn and fresh linen and something herbal Hester must have used to wash her. Babe to her shoulder, she faced Hester. "What will thee do with her?"

The midwife pointed to the rocking chair by the table. "Have a seat. I shall prepare us some tea." She bustled around the room while Hannah Jr. rocked the child, the creak of the rocker against the floorboards nearly lulling her to sleep along with the babe.

"Here." Hester placed a cup of tea on the table near Hannah Jr., then took the chair on the other side of the table and cradled her cup between her palms. "In answer to thy question, I know not. 'Tis in me to decide to keep her for myself, but I wonder if that would be the best for her. A child should have a mother and a father." She tilted her head and looked squarely at Hannah Jr. "Do thee not think so?"

"'Tis the best arrangement, I believe," Hannah Jr. gathered her thoughts as she spoke. "Yet there are plenty of children raised by just a mother or a father when the other passes on to glory."

"I have no idea what happened to this girl's parents." Hester took a sip of her tea. "Nor why whoever left her on my porch chose me." She pointed to the babe. "See the blanket she is wrapped in? 'Tis too fancy for a Friend."

"A Puritan babe?" Shock rippled through Hannah Jr. After all the uncertainty and fear her parents had endured to be able to keep

Verity—a Puritan orphan—with their family, it seemed unfair that this babe had been given to Hester.

"She must be."

"Why would a Puritan have left her with a Friend? Thee are too well known for it to have been a mistake."

"'Tis true." Hester set her cup aside, most of the tea untouched. "I believe they wished me to have her."

Gifting a child was not unheard of. There were times when a family simply couldn't afford to feed another, or if the mother died in childbirth and the father had no help to raise the babe, or if the child were born to an unmarried daughter. In those cases, he or she was given to a couple, often childless, who had the ability to care for and raise the babe. A couple—not an unmarried woman.

"How will thee be able to raise her and attend to thy midwife duties?" Hannah Jr. asked.

A long sigh followed. "I know not. 'Twill be difficult, of course."

"Thee would need someone to watch her while thee are gone." Hannah Jr. looked around the room. "How are thee even feeding her? Do thee have everything thee need to care for her?"

Hester detailed her use of stewed oats, and explained that the basket had contained clouts as well as a spare blanket. "But 'tis only enough to get by for a while. I shall need milk from thy dairy."

"The best for a newborn is goat's milk." Hannah Jr. had heard that said many times.

Hester nodded. "'Tis, but who would sell it to me? No one keeps a goat dairy in our community."

"Phoebe Stokes has a few goats, and I happen to know that one kidded this past week and is in full milk."

"I should approach her after Sunday meeting."

"I would be happy to speak with her before then, if thee like." Hannah Jr.'s mind jumped ahead to other needs. "I shall see if Caleb Jr. and Robert could come and build a shelter for the goat in thy back yard. Thy fence is in good condition and will keep it contained."

"I know not what to say." Hester blinked against a sheen of dampness. "Thee are so kind to offer thy help."

The babe took that moment to rouse, scrunching against her shoulder and emitting a cry.

Hester was on her feet and around the table before Hannah Jr. could reposition the babe. Taking the child, the expression that came over Hester's face—love and protectiveness and happiness all mixed and mingled—twisted something inside of Hannah Jr.

Jealousy? What a horrible feeling. She was happy for her friend, and happy for the babe who couldn't wish for a better mother. But that feeling, icky and dark, lurked somewhere deep inside her.

A moment of panic raced through Hester. The babe needed a dry clout, but how could Hester change her without Hannah Jr. seeing the mark? She could leave the room and change her in her bedroom, but that would only raise questions. She jiggled the babe in her arms while her mind raced, but the child's next cry was louder.

"Where are the clean clouts?" Hannah Jr. asked. "I will fetch one for thee."

Of course she'd offer. The eldest of a large family, the girl had probably been helping her mother with such things since she was a toddler.

Hester pointed to the dwindling stack on the shelf by the workbench. "I need to wash the rest this evening." She took the clout as the babe's cry became a full wail. Still, Hester hesitated.

"Is there anything else I can do?" Confusion colored Hannah Jr's voice.

Lord, give me the right words. Taking a deep breath, Hester looked the younger woman in the eye. "There is a reason the babe was left a foundling. I must ask thee to keep what thee are about to see a secret."

"A secret?" Hannah Jr.'s voice rose.

"Her life could depend upon it." Hester waited for Hannah Jr.'s nod, then placed the squalling infant on the spare blanket and unwrapped her from the one swaddling her.

Hannah Jr. gasped.

"'Tis a type of birthmark, not an uncommon one, but 'tis overly large." Hester kept her fingers busy making the child more comfortable. "But given the present climate of the village..." She left the rest unsaid.

"Thee are wise to keep her covered." Hannah Jr. took the wet clout and dropped it in the bucket already half full of them. "Some would be fearful. Whoever left her here trusted that thee would not."

Hester hadn't thought of it that way. "Thank thee for understanding."

"'Tis a difficult time we live in."

"Indeed." Hester handed the dry babe to Hannah Jr., who took her without any hesitation. "If thee would hold her while I get her oat broth."

"She is a comely babe, and that thing is not where anyone will see it unless they undress her." Hannah Jr. looked up at Hester. "When thee need to attend a birthing, tell whoever fetches thee that first thee must bring this one to our farm. Mother and I can attend to her, and neither of us will breathe a word of..." She tipped her chin toward the babe's belly.

Hester had the bowl of broth and a clean square of cloth ready, so she took the child from Hannah Jr. "Are thee sure?"

The younger girl nodded. "Mother would say the same."

"'Twould be a relief." She dipped the cloth and offered it to the babe, who slurped it dry, then repeated the process.

"While I am here on Tuesdays, I can do a few things to help thee." Hannah Jr. scanned the room, stopping at the empty bucket by the door. "I would be do the wash."

"I must fetch water first."

Hannah Jr. picked up the large empty kettle near the hearth. "I will fill this and the empty bucket, so thee will have plenty."

"I cannot thank thee enough. I was not sure how I could handle that on my own."

"'Tis nothing," Hannah Jr. said on her way out the door.

A weight eased from Hester's soul. "Bear ye one another's burden, and so fulfill the Law of Christ." She quoted the well-known verse to the babe. "How wise that verse is. How lucky we are that Hannah Jr. is our friend."

The local water supply was a well on the village green—on the opposite side of the brewery from Hester's cottage. Hannah Jr. could walk the back alleys, but that was too likely to raise questions. There was nothing for it. The safest thing to do to not raise eyebrows or suspicion was to simply walk down the street.

If she were lucky, Benjamin would be out on a delivery.

She smiled and nodded to several of her former dairy customers. Most responded in kind, but none spoke to her. The mood of the village was tense, even though most of the activity had been relocated to Salem Town. Father and Mother would not be happy that she'd walked about the village, but they would understand Hester's need.

Once she passed the brewery without incident, Hannah Jr. breathed easier. She filled the kettle first and then the bucket, drawing the water up with the help of the metal crank made by the village blacksmith a few years back. It was an improvement from the hand-over-hand method the villagers had used before.

How blessed they were at the farm to have their own fresh spring for water, with a spout Father had fashioned that they could pull out to redirect the water into their buckets, then push back into place to allow the water to go on its normal path through the springhouse and then back underground until it surfaced again near their pond.

Laden with the two heavy containers, back toward the midwife's cottage.

Footsteps hurried from behind her. "Allow me to carry those for you." Benjamin's voice flowed over her like warm honey, rich and low and entirely too enticing.

She had more than half a mind to tell him to be about his own business, but the handle to the kettle was biting into her grip, so she surrendered it to his care. "I can carry the bucket."

"Nonsense." He took hold of the handle.

Her choice was to argue with him in the street amid the growing foot traffic and interested onlookers, or to be gracious. "Thee are very kind." She let her voice carry for the benefit of those within listening distance. "Thee are the brewer's son, are thee not?" His startled expression nearly made her laugh, but she tilted her head as if requiring his answer.

"Indeed, I am." He sketched a short bow even encumbered with the two heavy containers. "Benjamin Buffington, at your service."

Hannah Jr. tipped her head, the extent of deference a Friend would show to another. "Hannah Buffum, Jr."

Their polite exchange seemed to erase anyone's interest in them, and people went about their own errands. It was good to see the villagers out and about again, but on the other hand, Hannah Jr. wouldn't have minded not being seen. Memories were long and tongues were longer.

"Where are you going with these?" Benjamin held both bucket and kettle out to his sides, as if they weighed practically nothing. Of course, he moved huge barrels while making deliveries for his father, so they must be light by comparison. "'Tis a lot of water."

"Hester Fuller has need of them. She will soon have a milk goat, and it must be watered."

"The Quaker midwife?"

Hannah Jr. pressed her lips into a firm line to stop from correcting him. *Quaker* was the term the Puritans used for the Friends. At first, it'd been meant as an insult to them and their manner of worship. Over the years, it had become simply a name. No reason to take offense.

"Indeed. Someone left a foundling on her porch." After all, the babe herself wasn't to be a secret, just the mark on her belly. "Hester needs the goat's milk to feed her."

Benjamin started down the street. "I have seen her walk to the well and back many times."

"Did thee offer to carry *her* buckets?" Hannah Jr. kept her face forward, resisting the urge to look at him for his reaction.

"Well, I..." He cleared his throat. "I have seen her while I have been working."

"Oh?" This time she did steal a peek at him. "Are thee not working today? Did thy father give thee leave to be a good Samaritan?"

His face flushed a handsome ruddy hue. "The day is approaching when I shall not be tied to the brewery, nor subject to my father's employ." He shot her a look that started the fluttering in her middle. "I hope to be more than a good Samaritan to you then."

In a voice barely above a whisper, she replied, "Nothing will change then except thy occupation. Thee will still be a Puritan and I a Friend. Two worlds that may exist near each other, but never together."

"As I have said before, I do not believe that."

Hannah Jr. stopped in front of the cottage. "Thank thee for thy kind assistance." She let her voice carry again, but then lowered it and added, "It matters not what thee believe. I will not distress my family by turning my back on them and leaving our faith."

"Nor would I ask that of you."

"But 'tis exactly what thee are asking. I cannot be a part of thy life, Benjamin. I have much to do, including enlisting my brothers to build a shelter and then fetching a milk goat for Hester. Thee must excuse me." She took the bucket and kettle. "Please let the matter drop." She walked away, but his soft words reached her.

"I cannot."

Chapter 10

A LONG-HAIRED BLACK DOG charged into the lane, barking and greeting Hannah Jr. with a display of teeth. She stopped and waited, letting the animal sniff her and walk around her. The dog's underside hung low, showing signs of her nursing a litter. Spring was the season of giving birth, for all God's creatures.

"Smokey!" Twelve-year-old Anna Stokes called from the front porch of the farmhouse. "Smokey, come here!" When the dog retreated, she waved. "Come on up, Hannah Jr., and welcome."

The dog wagged its tail as it stood beside Anna while Hannah Jr. approached.

"Sorry about Smokey, but she's a little protective because of her puppies right now." The girl was a good friend of Tamson's and nearly as chatty.

"How many does she have?"

"Six this time, and each as black as their momma. How can I help thee?"

"Is thy mother about?"

"Aye, in the garden." Anna sighed. "Where I best be getting myself off to as well. Come on."

Hannah Jr. followed her around the back of the house. The garden was large and orderly, with Phoebe right in the middle, wielding a hoe.

She stopped when she saw them, putting a hand to her lower back and straightening.

"Welcome, Hannah Jr." She came to the edge of the garden and handed the hoe to Anna with a look that said the girl was to take over the chore. "What can I do for thee this morning?"

"I have come to inquire about a goat."

Phoebe laughed. "Thee have? And thee with all those nice cows at thy dairy?"

"Not for me, for Hester Fuller."

Phoebe put her hands on her hips. "What use has the midwife for a goat?"

Since she had Hester's permission, she explained about the foundling girl.

"The poor dear, left on a doorstep." Phoebe *tsked*. "What is our world coming to, I ask thee? Follow me." She led Hannah Jr. to a lean-to off the side of the large barn beyond the garden and opened the top half of a door. Inside, a scraggly reddish-brown goat looked up at them, a newborn kid at her side. "This is Pumpkin and her babe. It was a twin, but the larger one died. She is left with the runt of the two. The little doe will not nurse too much and will keep Pumpkin from having to be milked at regular intervals in case Hester is called away to a birthing."

"'Tis the perfect solution. Hester will pay thee, of course, for—"

"'Tis no bother to loan her out. We have plenty. Perhaps the twin died for this very purpose, since it seemed the more likely to survive. Only the Lord knows. Hester can return them when she has no more need." Phoebe turned to Hannah Jr. "Does Hester have any shelter there? Pumpkin would be fine without, but the wee one should have some protection."

"My brothers will build her something this afternoon."

Phoebe unhooked the bottom of the door and slipped a rope from where it hung on a nail inside. "Come now, Pumpkin. Thee will have a new home for a while. 'Twill give thee and thy little one some privacy." She looked over her shoulder at Hannah Jr. "'Twill be good for her. I have her separated because the others in the flock might bully the runty kid. I did not want poor Pumpkin to lose both of her babes. She is a good old girl." Phoebe rubbed the reddish-brown neck, and the goat leaned against her.

"I know Hester will give her the best of care."

"If a midwife cannot look after a momma and babe, then who can?" Phoebe chuckled as she scooped up the tiny kid. "If thee carry this one, Pumpkin will follow. Good mother that she is, she will never leave her babe." A frown crossed her brow. "Unlike some human mothers. Imagine, leaving a child a foundling." She *tsked* again and handed over the kid.

The poor thing weighed less than one of Mother's five-pound sugar cones. She was a much darker brown than Pumpkin, with grayish hairs around her muzzle and feet. "What is her name?"

"The children said that since she was so small and came of out Pumpkin, that we should call her Seed. Hester can change that if she likes."

"I will let her know. And thank thee, 'tis most generous."

Hannah Jr. tucked the kid under her arm and took the goat's rope. With a gentle tug, Pumpkin followed her out of the farmyard. Smokey raised her head from a wooden box on the back porch, where she was probably nursing her puppies. A farm in spring was all about new birth and new growth, the rhythm of life Hannah Jr. enjoyed.

"Hester will be pleased to meet thee."

The goat ignored her, swiping a mouthful of grass along the side of the road, and the kid fell asleep against Hannah Jr.'s side.

It wasn't much over a mile from the Stokes' farm to the path leading to Hester's cottage, but it was slow going with Pumpkin stopping to grab a mouthful of whatever greenery she could find along the way. They reached the cottage, and Hannah Jr. let them into the fenced back yard through the rear gate.

Caleb Jr., Robert, and Joseph were already at work there. They'd erected a three-sided shelter the day before, and had returned to put the finishing touches on it that morning.

"About time thee arrived." Caleb Jr. wiped his brow. "'Tis nearly noon."

"And no doubt thee are hungry." She handed him the goat's rope, and then set the kid on its feet. It immediately searched out its mother's udder and, tail wagging furiously, enjoyed its own lunch. "Did thee bring the basket of food?"

"On the wagon." Robert pointed to where Dandy and the borrowed gelding were tied to a tree beside the cottage, resting in the shade.

Hannah Jr. retrieved her basket and took it inside the cottage. "Hester?"

"Coming." Hester entered the kitchen.

The dark circles under her eyes brought a pang of sympathy from Hannah Jr. "Did the babe keep thee awake through the night?"

"Much of it." The other woman rubbed her eyes with her free hand, the other keeping the babe securely at her shoulder. "She did not fall into a deep sleep until nearly dawn."

"Our Benji was that way. Some babes are." But Mother'd had both her and Tamson to assist and allow her to sleep when she needed it. Hester had no one.

The hammering from outside, as the boys pegged the last wall section into place, said otherwise.

Hannah Jr.'s family would help the midwife, and others in their community would too, like Phoebe Stokes. People pitched in when someone was in need. Caring for orphans and widows was part of their beliefs. The babe was as good as an orphan, and Hester almost a widow.

It was obvious the woman already loved the little girl in her arms. Dark circles or not, when she glanced at the sleeping babe, her face all but glowed with happiness. Hester may never have a husband, but there was no reason she couldn't have a daughter.

Protectiveness rose within Hannah Jr., and she silently pledged to do whatever she could to help Hester keep the little girl.

And to safeguard her secret.

Rocking the babe was lulling Hester to sleep along with the dry and fed infant. The gentle clatter of Hannah Jr. washing up after the meal she'd brought was a blessing almost as wonderful as the goat in its shelter near the back fence. The boys had brought hay to pile against the shelter for her to feed the animal for a couple of weeks while it got used to living in the village. Once it was content in its new surroundings, Hannah Jr. had assured her that she could let it graze in the back yard while she supervised and kept the beast out of her garden.

Hester had never cared for an animal before. Her father had raised their family in town. He'd kept a horse for the family buggy, but he had seen to its needs himself. They'd never even had a dog because her mother hadn't been fond of them. So the loan of Pumpkin was a blessing—and a challenge.

As if learning to be a mother wasn't a challenge enough by itself.

Mother. She lifted her head from the back of the rocker and gazed at the sleeping infant's face. Delicate lashes lay against her satiny cheeks, rose lips pursed in a bow, and a nose as delicate and straight as could be imagined. How could anyone have abandoned such a perfect example of the Lord's creation? All for a birthmark that meant nothing. Nothing to Hester, anyway.

"Shall I milk the goat for thee before I leave?" Hannah Jr. wiped her hands on a towel.

"Thee have done so much already."

"Milking the goat will not take long." The younger woman grinned. "Do thee know how to milk one?"

"Oh." Hester hadn't thought about that, but how difficult could it be? Farm children milked goats, so surely, as a grown woman, she could figure it out.

"While the babe sleeps, let me show thee how. 'Tis not difficult, but there is a knack to it."

Hester settled the babe in her basket, then walked across the yard with Hannah Jr., who had a piggin in one hand, the small bucket a perfect size for the goat's milk. She must have brought that, too, for Hester didn't own one.

"'Tis a good idea to give Pumpkin something to eat while thee does the milking. 'Twill keep her busy." The boys had built a rack on the inside wall of the shelter, into which Hannah Jr. pushed a small armful of hay. The goat stuck her head inside and munched. Hannah Jr. tied the goat with the rope as well, then knelt by her side and put the piggin underneath. "Thee want to squeeze, not pull, to strip the milk. Use thy finger and thumb to start, holding as close to the bag as possible, and then squeeze with thy remaining fingers in sequence." Milk shot into the bucket. "Thee can use both hands at once, and 'twill go faster." Hannah Jr. had two streams of milk squirting in rhythm, one side and then the other.

"I think I can manage that." When the younger woman moved out of the way, Hester knelt in the same place and put her hands on the goat. Something bumped into her elbow.

Hannah Jr. laughed and picked up the kid. "I shall keep Seed out of thy way."

Hester positioned her hands again, squeezing her first finger and thumb together. A tiny trickle of milk emerged, nowhere near the impressive stream Hannah Jr. had achieved.

"'Tis a good start. Now engage thy other fingers, like this." She mimicked the motion with her hands.

Taking her bottom lip between her teeth, Hester tried again.

The goat stomped her back foot, and Hester jumped. "What did I do wrong?"

"Nothing, 'twas only a pestering fly. Try again."

Her shoulders ached and her knees were protesting before Hester achieved the steady stream of milk.

"There, now thee have the way of it."

Hester rocked back on her heels and looked up at her young friend, handing her the piggin. "And thee must do this with how many cows twice a day?"

"I have two brothers, a sister, and now Joseph and Verity to help, so 'tisn't as much of a chore as thee would think." She set the goat's babe down, and it latched on Pumpkin for a drink. "Thee needn't worry about stripping her clean. This one will take care of that for thee. Thee can milk only as much as thee need for the babe."

Hester untied Pumpkin and patted her on the shoulder, the hair rough beneath her fingers.

She faced Hannah Jr. "I know not how to thank thee."

The younger woman ducked her head, and then looked up again. "Being my friend is thanks enough."

"That is easily accomplished." She linked her arm with Hannah Jr.'s, and they returned to the cottage. "And since we are friends, thee must also allow me to do things for thee."

Without hesitation, Hannah Jr. asked, "Would thee teach me to make baskets?"

"Baskets?"

"Not that I wish to take any of thy trade away," Hannah Jr. hastened to add. "'Tis just something I think I would enjoy, and if at some point I needed another way to earn an income..." She shrugged.

"I would be delighted to teach thee. However"—Hester stifled a yawn—"could we start the lessons after the babe learns to sleep during the night?"

Hannah Jr. chuckled. "I believe we should." Then she grew serious. "What will thee name her? She cannot remain 'the babe' forever."

Hester had struggled with that throughout her nearly sleepless night. What right had she to name a child that wasn't hers? On the other hand, the babe had clearly been left for her. That meant whoever had left her intended Hester to raise her as her own. Didn't it?

A mewling came from the basket on the table as they entered the kitchen. No doubt the babe was hungry again.

Hannah Jr. lifted and cooed to her. "I will change her while thee get things ready to feed her." With an efficiency Hester hoped she could mimic someday, Hannah Jr. got the job done. Hester had wrapped and swaddled many newborns—once—before handing them over to their mothers. Hannah Jr. had been changing and caring for her siblings for nearly twenty years. She would make a better mother than Hester could, and she'd have the support of her family around her.

Could Hester truly raise this baby on her own? Or should she consider sending the infant home with her younger and much more able friend?

The thought tore at her heart.

Chapter 11

S UNDAY MORNING DAWNED CLEAR and warm, the first Sunday in May. The first Sunday Hester would take the babe to meeting. She'd missed last week, but nobody had questioned her. Most would assume she'd been called away on her midwife duties. While the Friends were as strict as the Puritans about weekly attendance, they understood that some things were no respecter of the calendar, including illness and birth.

The babe fed and dry, Hester slipped the gown she'd stitched of soft cotton over her, then wrapped her in a blanket she'd also sewn in the fashion of the Friends. She placed her in the basket in which she'd arrived. She'd lined it with a piece of toweling to cushion the child, and tucked clean clouts at the foot. It wasn't a long walk to the meetinghouse, but it would seem longer carrying the basket. Perhaps she could fashion one with a carrying strap. She snorted softly to herself. When would she find the time? Her sleep-deprived days were now full.

Normally, a new mother would have a three- or four-week lying-in period following a birth. Family, friends, and neighbors would take care of the house, the meals, the laundry, and any younger children while the mother rested and recuperated from the birth. Hester had no such support system at hand. Even if she did, only a couple of people knew about the babe—though that was about to change.

"We shall just have to make do on our own, shall we not?" She smoothed the blanket over the sleeping infant. It had been only twelve days since she'd found the basket on her back porch, but already Hester was bonded to the little girl. For all the upheaval it had thrown her into—the lack of sleep, the constant need to launder clouts, not to mention learning to deal with a goat, and the ever-present fear that someone would discover the child's mark—when the babe was in her arms, Hester could no longer imagine handing her over to someone else to raise.

Or handing her back to whomever had left her on the porch.

She lifted the basket and exited the cottage, strolling past the goat shelter, out the back gate, and down the path, a shorter walk to the meetinghouse than going by the main street. And more private. Her footfalls were silent on the damp ground. New leaves unfurled on the branches overhead, and birds chirped. The forest smelled clean from the rainstorm of the past evening. Spring was Hester's favorite time of year. All the new growth, new birth, returning migratory birds, and flowers. Already the forest floor was dappled with white and pale pink trilliums.

The meetinghouse was a hive of activity when she arrived. Men visited in groups around the line of wagons. Women gathered nearer the building. Older boys stood in a loose knot near the forest edge. Older girls on the brink of womanhood were watching the younger ones playing in the open lot, wearing off their excess energy before entering to worship. It was a sight she'd beheld more times than she could count.

But this time, it was different. This time, she had a child of her own.

"Hester." Hannah Jr. appeared at her side. "'Tis good to see thee and the babe."

"I could not keep her a secret forever." But Hester's insides tightened, bracing for whatever greeting their arrival would bring.

Hannah Jr. leaned closer as if inspecting the basket's contents and whispered, "Only the part that need be kept secret. I will do all I can to help thee in that."

Having someone on her side brought a lump to Hester's throat. She nodded, then fell in step beside Hannah Jr. and approached the women near the building's front entrance.

"What have thee in the basket?" asked Phoebe Stokes as if she'd no idea.

Hester moved the blanket away from the babe's face to the *oohs* and *aahs* of those gathered. "A foundling. She was left on my porch."

That brought a flurry of comments, many indignant that anyone would abandon a child.

"I know not who left her, nor anything of their circumstances." Hester spoke loudly enough to be heard over the babble. "Whoever it was might have lacked the means to care for her and wished her to have a better life. That would be a sacrificial act of love, would it not?"

The murmurings died down, but the babe had roused from the noise. With Hannah Jr. to steady the basket, Hester lifted the child out. More *oohs* and *aahs* followed, for she truly was beautiful.

"Have thee named her?" Isobel O'Sullivan asked.

"Nay." Hester settled the infant at her shoulder.

"Thee should," Isobel said. "After all, she was left for thee. A gift, as it were."

"I know not what I would name her." The other women had probably picked baby names from the time of their marriages, in preparation for the children to follow. Hester had missed out on that, and now at her age of two and thirty, she didn't feel quite adequate to the task.

"A gift." Phoebe smiled and looked around at the other women. "A name that means 'gift' would be fitting, and I know of one."

"What is it?" "Do tell us." "Which name?" Several women spoke over each other.

"Theodora." Phoebe looked around the group gathered there. "'Twas my grandmother's name, and it means 'gift.'"

More murmurings arose, murmurs of agreement. When not one woman spoke out against the name, Hester said it aloud, "Theodora." The babe opened her eyes, blinked, and then settled back to sleep against Hester's shoulder. "I believe she likes it."

A flurry of questions followed about how she was feeding the babe and did she need anything, but the men approached, signaling the start of their worship time before she could answer them all.

Hester took a seat on the women's side nearest the door in case the babe—Theodora—awoke and was hungry. Nursing mothers could go to the back of the room behind a screen kept there and attend to their babes, but Hester would need to return to the cottage and the milk she'd stripped from the goat that morning.

In the silent prayer time, she thanked God for the acceptance from her community of Friends. She also prayed for Theodora's safety, as she had every day. While the women who'd gathered around and helped choose the name were supportive, they didn't know about the mark.

If they did, word could spread and reach the wrong ears. That could change everything.

"Thee knew about the foundling"—Tamson leaned so close that her breath fanned Hannah Jr.'s cheek—"and never said a word?"

"'Twasn't for me to share," she whispered back. "Now hush."

One of the older men stood and spoke about a passage from the Bible that had meant something special to him that week. He was followed by several others, and then Phoebe rose. She shared how she'd lost a healthy young goat while its runty twin had survived. She couldn't make sense of it until someone arrived in need of a milk goat with just a scrawny kid at its side. She spoke a bit longer on God providing for needs in ways people couldn't always understand, while quite a few of the women looked beyond Hannah Jr. toward Hester, nodding in agreement.

Not long after Phoebe sat down, little Theodora began to fuss.

Hannah Jr. whispered to her mother, "I shall help Hester this afternoon, if thee can spare me."

"Please do." Mother motioned for her to go. "Tamson and Verity are all the help I need."

Hannah Jr. stood and purposefully did not look at the back row on the men's side of the meetinghouse, where Isaac sat with the other young men, including Caleb Jr. Even so, she could almost feel his eyes on her as she slipped out the door.

She caught up with Hester at the bottom of the steps and took the empty basket from her. They walked out together, Theodora's fussing turning into a squall against Hester's shoulder.

"She was doing so well." Hester jostled the babe.

"'Tis too long to expect such a wee one to remain quiet." How to help without stepping on Hester's toes? Hannah Jr. knew little of her older friend's background, but it seemed the woman who had delivered so many babes had little practical experience with them. She must not have had younger siblings.

"Of course, I cannot nurse her, which is what she needs." Was that a note of defeat in Hester's voice? Or just weariness?

"What if thee brought a small pot of the goat's milk, one with a cork to seal it, and some of the linen squares thee have stitched? Then thee could take her behind the screen and feed her as she has the need."

Hester's brown eyes met hers. "I should have thought of that."

"I suspect thee are too tired to think right now."

The sigh that followed was half groan. "I fear thee are right. I fear that I cannot take care of her properly."

"Nonsense." Hannah Jr. stopped on the forest path and faced her friend. "What do thee tell first-time mothers who are having a difficult time birthing? When they are afraid and unsure? When they doubt themselves?"

Theodora squalled again, kicking her feet. As any mother would, Hester jiggled the babe and patted her bottom to quiet her. Did she even realize how naturally she did it?

"That they will do fine, to trust in me, trust in themselves, and most of all, to trust in the Lord."

"Very wise words, words thee should take to heart where thy daughter is concerned."

"My daughter." Hester smiled at the little girl and continued to the cottage with more determination in her steps, while Theodora let the forest and its creatures know that she was hungry and very likely wet.

Hannah Jr. resisted the urge to take the squirming babe. Hester had to care for Theodora to gain her confidence. Hannah Jr. would do the other chores, but not that one. It was difficult, however. She did love to care for the little ones.

At the cottage, Hester changed Theodora.

Hannah Jr. surveyed the kitchen. "I shall fetch a supply of water and then start on supper."

"I should—"

"Thee should tend to Theodora and let me tend to thee. 'Tis thy lying-in period, after all."

"But I am not worn out from giving birth, as are the women I help."

"Thee still need rest. The demands of a newborn are no easier on thee than anyone else." Hannah Jr. faced her. "I know what I say is true. Have I not seen my mother go through this five times?"

"How can I ever thank thee enough?" Hester assembled the pot of milk and her linen cloth to feed the babe.

Hannah Jr. picked up the bucket and kettle, and headed for the door, saying over her shoulder, "By allowing me to help."

She had to pass by the Puritan church on the way to the well. It was circled with buggies, wagons, and saddled horses tied to the hitching rails. At least she needn't worry about running into Benjamin again.

The last meeting with him still plagued her thoughts, especially at night. His parting words, spoken so softly she wasn't sure if he'd meant for her to hear. *I cannot.*

Watching Hester with little Theodora had brought an ache to Hannah Jr.'s chest. It was one thing to contemplate spending her life as the spinster sister to her brood of siblings when she was by herself. It was something else while being with another woman and child. The ache she'd fought down was the longing for a child of her own.

There. She'd admitted it to herself. She wanted a family of her own.

At the well, she filled Hester's bucket and kettle. On her return trip, the weight of them kept her focused on her task rather than the church when she passed it—or who was inside.

When she stepped inside, Hester had finished feeding Theodora and was rocking her to sleep, her eyelids looking as heavy as the babe's.

"Why do thee not lie down with Theodora? Both of thee need sleep." Hannah Jr. set the bucket down and hung the kettle in the fireplace, kneeling to poke the embers back to life.

"I know thee are right." Hester stood. "Yet I feel guilty for leaving thee to do all of this."

"'Tis what we women do, is it not, helping each other in times of need? I am happy to have a quiet house to putter in for a change, rather than the boisterous one I live in." She made a shooing gesture. "Get thee off to sleep."

With Hester and the babe settled in the bedroom and water heating in the kettle, Hannah Jr. plucked an apron off its peg and tied it on. She took the wooden washtub from where it hung on the far wall and set it near the hearth. She drained the water from the bucket of soiled clouts onto the garden and dumped them into the washtub. After adding a little warm water from the kettle, she grated a bar of lye soap into it and let it soften while the rest of the water came to a boil. Those things accomplished, she pulled a handful of potatoes out of a bin and scrubbed them to make a simple soup for supper.

These were things she'd done for her mother hundreds of times.

Would she ever do them for a family of her own?

She let herself imagine tending a quiet house while awaiting Benjamin's return from working in his fields or orchard. Spending her days cleaning, cooking, mending, raising a garden, visiting her mother and sisters on occasion, and anticipating the first babe on the way sounded lovely. Fulfilling. Purposeful.

Impossible.

What would their Sundays be like? Would she be off to meeting while he attended church, their Sundays spent separated? Hannah Jr. couldn't picture not sharing her faith with her husband. It would be like a living barrier between them. Women weren't allowed to speak in the Puritan church. She'd heard it said that a Puritan woman was dependent upon her husband for her salvation, which was pure nonsense. The Bible was clear that the one and only way to salvation was through Jesus Christ—the bridegroom of the church. The Lord's only begotten Son.

Even their language was different. Would he prefer her to say *you* and *your* rather than the Friends' more plain *thee* and *thy*? Would he insist that she call him Mr. Buffington in public as was the custom of Puritan wives, who referred to their own husbands in such a formal manner?

The kettle boiled over, splashing and sputtering into the fire below.

Thinking of that young man caused her nothing but trouble. Chiding herself for her daydreams, she grabbed a towel and moved the kettle from over the fire. She poured enough boiling water into the washtub's softened soap to get a nice hot lather and got to work.

By the time Hester and Theodora awoke from their naps, Hannah Jr. had the clouts washed and hung to dry, the potato soup made except for adding a bit of goat's milk, and the kitchen tidied.

"Something smells heavenly," Hester said as she came into the room with Theodora at her shoulder.

"I hope thee do not mind." Hannah Jr. wiped her hands on the apron. "I found the potatoes and poked through thy herbs to season the soup."

"Not at all." Theodora squawked and kicked as Hester put her down to change her. "I so appreciate thy help."

"While thee attend to that, shall I milk and feed Pumpkin?" Hannah Jr. pressed a hand to her forehead. "I should have thought of the goat when I fetched water. Well, I can take her bucket and fill it after I milk her."

"I doubt there will be a need." Hester looked up from changing Theodora. "A young man from the village has brought her water each morning since she's been here. The bucket is always full, although I have only caught a glimpse of him twice. I confess I do not know who he is nor why he does it, but it has made my days easier."

What young man except for her brothers had known about Pumpkin? A tingle ran up Hannah Jr.'s spine. Surely not. Had she mentioned the goat to Benjamin? She tried to remember. Even if she had, why would he bring the water each morning?

The answer was plain. To please her.

I cannot.

Chapter 12

H ESTER HAD RIGGED A long woven stole into a sling with which to carry Theodora. She'd seen a woman with such a contraption when she'd visited Boston years ago. The woman's English had been very broken, and Hester wasn't sure what country she'd immigrated from, but the sling had caught her eye. It had taken her most of an hour that morning to figure out how to fold, tie, and secure it. It might not be exactly like the one she'd seen, but it worked. Theodora was safe and snug against her, and Hester's hands were free to do other things, like shopping.

A trio of women when she arrived at the mercantile, each giving the clerk behind it her order in turn. Hester's list was short, just soft cotton fabric to sew into more clouts. Even though Hannah Jr. had stayed and done another washtub full of laundry after her butter and cheese deliveries the previous day, doing another washtub full of laundry as well as making supper and caring for Pumpkin, the babe was going through more clouts than Hester could keep up with.

Had she been an expectant mother, she'd have stitched a large pile of them before the child's birth. But all she had was the handful that had been included in Theodora's basket, clouts no doubt lovingly stitched by the babe's true mother in anticipation of her birth. How that poor woman must grieve the loss of her child. Whatever her circumstances, even if she'd done it for Theodora's safety, she must be suffering from her loss.

The Puritan woman in front of Hester turned and smiled at her. "You are the midwife, are you not?"

"I am." Hester struggled to put a name to the vaguely familiar face.

"I am Sarah Buffington, the brewer's wife." She had dark brown hair and eyes, her face tapering into a gentle point at the chin. "We have not properly met. My youngest was born just few weeks before you took up the position of midwife."

"'Tis a pleasure to meet thee."

"I did not realize you had a babe of your own." Sarah peeked at sleeping Theodora's face, all that was visible in the sling. "Does this have anything to do with our Benjamin bringing you a bucket of water each day?"

So, that was who had been filling the bucket. "'Tis for my goat," Hester said. "He fills Pumpkin's bucket."

"I see." But the wrinkles on her brow said she didn't understand, which was something they had in common.

"Theodora is a foundling." Hester couldn't keep the babe's existence a secret, so she might as well explain. "I needed a goat for the milk."

"Oh, my." Sarah's brows rose. "Have you no inkling of who the parents might be?"

"None." Hester wasn't about to admit to knowing they were Puritans. That was a piece of information no one else needed to know.

"Well, 'twould seem they wanted someone who would give her the best of care. Who better than a midwife to take in a child?" Then her smile slipped. "But you have no husband, do you?"

"I do not, but one of the young women of our community comes in two days a week to help. Thee probably know her from her dairy business, Hannah Buffum, Jr."

The woman's brows shot up. "We purchase her products." Sarah fiddled with the list in her hand and glanced around the room. "A most competent young woman with gentle manners. Of course, her cheeses are said to be the finest in the county."

"They are. And she is very kind."

The clerk asked for Sarah's order. She appeared relieved to turn back to her task, leaving Hester wondering about their brief conversation. Why had Sarah reacted nervously to her mentioning Hannah Jr.'s name?

Two middle-aged Puritan women burst into the mercantile before Hester could ponder that, one shutting the door behind them and pressing her hand to her ample chest. The other glanced around the room, breath coming in unsteady gasps.

"What has happened?" asked the young man clerking behind the counter. "Is something amiss?"

"'Tis Reverend George Burroughs." The breathless woman stepped to the counter in front of those gathered. "He has been arrested in his home in Maine, hauled back, and jailed in Salem Town. Someone has pointed the finger of accusation at him!"

The young clerk asked, "Who is he?"

The heftier woman waved a dismissive hand. "You did not live here then, but he was the village reverend for two years about ten years back. A good man he is."

"Good man?" One of the waiting women stepped forward. Goodie Putnam, but Hester couldn't remember her first name. "Did he not leave us while owing money to my cousin and half the rest of the town?"

The hefty woman answered, "Which he did return to repay, you must remember."

Goodie Putnam woman huffed, crossing her arms.

"How could he be involved with what has been happening here when he has lived in Maine these past many years?" the breathless one asked.

"It matters not where one lives if one had sold his soul to the devil," declared the Putnam woman. She scanned the crowd, and several took a cautious step back under her glare. "See that the rest of you mind your manners in this regard. The magistrates in Salem Town know what they are doing. Leave them to do their job." Her glare settled on the two women who had burst in with the news. "Tell no tales that paint the guilty as innocents." Then she swiped her bundled purchases off the counter, turned around, and leveled a glare at Hester, eyes narrowing to slits.

A cold chill broke over Hester's skin, and she clutched Theodora tighter to her bosom.

Nose lifted as she gazed around the store a final time, Goodie Putnam gave a dismissive snort and stomped out, slamming the door behind her.

Theodora startled at the noise and fussed.

"Nasty woman," Sarah whispered near Hester's ear, then spoke more loudly to the clerk. "Please see to the midwife's needs before mine." She stepped out of the way.

"Thank thee." Hester told the clerk what she needed, and he quoted her the price. While he cut the fabric, she dug the coins from her pocket and swayed from foot to foot to calm Theodora.

Voices buzzed around her about the disturbing news—and about Goodie Putnam. Words like "calculated" and "vindictive" and "retribution."

The skin on the back of Hester's neck crawled.

When the clerk finally handed her the bundled fabric, she pushed the coins across the counter and then made her escape. She hurried back to the cottage, shutting the door behind her and leaning against it.

Was it just the village, or was the whole world going mad?

"May we go with thee to Hester's next week?" Tamson pulled a clump of ramps, the damp soil clinging to the tasty wild leeks, and dropped it into her basket.

"I would love to help care for Theodora," Verity added.

Hannah Jr. stood and stretched her back. "Hester needs her rest and sleeps most of the time I am there. Two chatty girls would not be helpful. But perhaps the following week, thee can come and plant Hester's garden for her. 'Twill be about time then."

That earned her a twin pair of groans. Gardening was not the favorite pastime of either girl.

"Perhaps thee can take Theodora out in her basket while thee work in the garden and Hester sleeps."

That brought back their smiles. It should be safe enough. Hannah Jr. would just make sure that she alone changed the babe's soiled clouts.

Hester had been stitching infant gowns when Hannah Jr. had made her deliveries earlier in the week. The long gowns would more than cover the marks on the babe's torso.

Verity tugged on a stubborn ramp, then held it up and wrinkled her nose. "I have never eaten these before. What do they taste like?"

"Thee have never had ramps?" Tamson's voice rose. "They are my favorite every spring."

"They taste like leeks, but sweeter." Hannah Jr. tucked two more into her basket. "Tonight, I shall boil them, and we can make dumplings."

"Oh, aye!" Tamson squealed. "'Tis my favorite way to eat them."

"The boys like them that way too. We shall need quite a few." Hannah Jr. gestured for them to continue picking. "Be sure to leave some growing so they can produce another crop next year."

Tamson huffed. "We need not thy reminder." The girl was growing up, but she still wasn't the best at attending to details.

They'd picked for another half hour when something snapped nearby. Hannah Jr. froze where she squatted by the ramps.

The girls looked at her with rounded eyes.

A deer would have been more careful than to step on a branch, but a bear? Then a flash of red caught her eye, and she straightened.

"Are thee trying to scare us, Caleb Jr.?"

"'Twould seem we did." Their grinning brother, wearing his red knit cap, stepped from behind the leafy brambles. He was followed by Mark O'Sullivan. "Ah, ramps." Caleb Jr. licked his lips. Both boys held muskets, and each had a brace of rabbits. Mark also had a fine big turkey.

"Hannah Jr. says we can cook them with dumplings tonight." Tamson held up her basket. "So we are picking as many as we can."

Their brother rubbed his stomach. "'Twill go well with the rabbits."

"No turkey for us?" Hannah Jr. cocked her head at him.

"Caleb Jr. missed his." Mark's smirk was the tease of one good friend to another.

"Next time." Caleb Jr. shifted his feet. "Mark brings disturbing news from the village."

Mark nodded, his face a younger image of his father. "The old Puritan reverend from the village was accused of witchcraft, arrested, and jailed in Salem Town. But the thing is, the man has lived up in

Maine for years. Is anyone safe if they can drag back a man so long departed from the village?"

A chill crept over Hannah Jr. despite the warm sunshine filtering through the trees. The babbling of the nearby creek, chirping of birds, and swish of the pine branches swaying in the breeze all faded into the background.

The Puritans had turned against one of their reverends. How could anyone be safe?

The red splotch across Theodora's tummy came to mind. The child had no chance against a people who would point fingers at one they considered a holy man. And then another face flashed by her mind's eye.

Benjamin.

Was he safe in the village? Thomas had sent both Robert and Joseph away. If the brewer feared for them, was his own family also in danger?

"'Tis another Puritan." Caleb Jr. touched her arm. "We Friends have not been accused of anything."

"A blessing, for sure." She could think of nothing else to say. Then she shook her head, gathering her thoughts. "Tamson, Verity, I believe we have plenty of ramps for our supper. Let us return home." She looked at her brother. "Father will wish to know of this."

"Will thee tell him?" Caleb Jr. jiggled his brace of rabbits. "I will try to add a turkey before I return."

Mark snorted and rolled his eyes. "Perhaps I shall shoot another and share with thee." The boys walked into the woods.

Hannah Jr. and the girls started toward the farm.

"Thee turned very pale when Caleb Jr. shared the news," Tamson said. "'Twill be all right. We are avoiding the village already, except while thee help Hester." She stopped. "Are thee in danger?"

Verity slipped her hand into Hannah Jr.'s free hand. "Please say thee are safe."

"I believe so, but perhaps 'twould be best for me to continue helping Hester by myself."

Neither girl objected.

They continued to the farm in silence. Was she safe walking into the village each week? Was Hester safe to live there? Certainly Theodora wasn't should anyone discover her mark.

And Benjamin? Was he safe?

Sarah hadn't sent him or his brother to purchase any butter or cheese this past week. Hannah Jr. had been on edge throughout the day Monday, finally relieved that neither had appeared. Now, however, she wished she'd seen Benjamin, just to reassure herself that he was well.

Theodora had slept better, awakening only once during the night for a dry clout and a full belly. The extra sleep had Hester feeling more like herself. She yawned and walked onto her back porch, raising a hand to shade her eyes from the bright morning light. It gleamed with the promise of a good day, even after yesterday's disturbing news about the Puritans' former reverend.

Her front gate creaked, intruding on her morning. What if someone needed her services? She glanced back through the open door to where Theodora was tucked into her basket, one fist raised in the air. Hester had known it would happen at some point. Her responsibilities as the village midwife couldn't be ignored.

Then the long-legged young man came around the edge of the cottage with a bucket in each hand. He startled when he noticed her.

Relief flowed over Hester. Not that she didn't wish to resume her duties as midwife, just that she wasn't quite ready yet. She let her hand drop to her side and walked to the edge of the porch. "Thank thee for thy help with the goat's water."

He stopped. "'Tis no hardship."

"I do not think we have met. I am Hester Fuller, the midwife."

"I know." His face colored. "I mean, I am Benjamin Buffington, the brewer's son." He gave her a short bow without spilling from either bucket. "One of them, at least."

He didn't resemble Sarah at all, so he must favor his father. "How did thee know I had such a need?"

"Oh." He looked around as if searching for the answer somewhere in her garden. "I came across Hannah Buffum, Jr., carrying water to you about a fortnight ago."

"She has been generous with her time to help me on Tuesday afternoons."

"She mentioned the goat and your need for water and..." He lifted the buckets a bit and let them drop again. "As I say, 'tis no hardship to bring you water in the mornings."

"'Tis a kindness to me and to Pumpkin and Seed."

A lopsided grin deepened the dimple in his chin. "Are those their names?"

"Aye, they came to me already named."

"It fits them. They are a fine pair of goats."

Theodora let out a squeal, and Hester returned to the open door. "Thank thee, again."

He ducked his head in a bashful sort of nod before continuing to the goat shelter.

Hester gathered Theodora into her arms. The babe was happy and squealed again, reassuring Hester that she recognized her now. It made her heart swell to the point of overflowing. She walked to the window as Benjamin poured water into Pumpkin's bucket. What had Hannah Jr. said to him? And why? Not that she distrusted the young woman—she didn't.

But what had Hannah Jr. to do with the brewer's son?

Chapter 13

A S IF POUNDING ON her door weren't enough to awaken both her and her nearest neighbors, the shout of "Midwife! Midwife!" surely did it. The noise also awakened Theodora, who fussed as Hester scooped her up and headed for the door.

"Midwife! Mid—"

She opened the door, and the frantic young man cut off the word. His eyes were wild, darting around but probably not seeing anything. His hair was in total disarray, his coat hung unevenly, and his hat askew. "Thank the Lord you are home." The words came out in a rush. "You must come at once, my goodwife is in terrible pain with the coming child."

"Her first?" It wasn't a guess. Hester had seen enough first-time fathers to recognize them.

"Aye. I shall help you to the cart." He reached for her arm.

She stepped back. "I will need to dress, and then thee must drive me to the Buffums' farm before I can continue on with thee."

"There is no time." He raked his fingers through his hair, making more of a mess of it. "My goodwife needs you now."

"Has she anyone with her?"

"Aye, her mother and a sister, but they are not midwives."

"First babes take their time to arrive, and I cannot care for thy goodwife and my daughter at the same time. We must drop her off with the Buffums first. Where do thee live?"

"North of town off the main road, before the turn to Boxford."

"Good." Hester pointed to the top step of her front porch. "Sit there while I dress, change the babe, and gather what I need. I shall make haste."

She didn't wait to see if he obeyed, just shut the door and hurried to her room. Theodora was wet but not cranky, so she only needed changing, not feeding. Hester put clean clouts and nursing cloths into Theodora's basket, then snatched the corked pot with goat's milk and added that. She hung the handle and that of her other things over her arm on the way out the door.

"There you are." The young man leaped to his feet and started for the two-wheeled cart behind the dark horse tied to the hitching rail in front of her cottage.

It was predawn, the eastern sky a palette of brilliant colors, the air cool with a hint of dampness on the breeze. Hester put her midwife basket and bag on the floor of the cart. It sat much lower than a wagon, making it easier for her to settle herself on the bench seat with Theodora's basket on her lap.

The young man had untied the horse and leaped onto the seat beside her. "Where is this farm we must go to?"

Hester gave him the directions, and he slapped the reins on the poor horse's rump. The startled beast jumped forward, nearly cracking Hester's neck as she held onto the seat with one hand and Theodora's basket with the other. She spent the rest of the ride in silent prayer for their safety.

The sun was breaking above the horizon when the cart careened down the lane to the Buffums' farm. Hannah Jr. was on her way from the barn to the house as the young man stopped his horse.

Hester climbed out of the cart, thankful for the firm ground under her feet, and met her friend. "I do hope thee were sincere with thy offer." Theodora chose that moment to let out a long wail. The poor babe had probably been too shaken up to cry on the ride.

"Thee are needed elsewhere, 'twould seem." Hannah Jr. set down the bucket she'd been carrying and took Theodora. "I am more than happy to care for this one while thee help another be born. Rest easy." She raised her blue eyes to Hester's. "All will be well."

"I cannot thank thee enough for—"

"We must make haste," the young man called from the cart.

"I can handle this one." Hannah Jr. lifted her chin in his direction, lowering her voice. "If thee can handle that one."

"That remains to be seen. 'Tis his goodwife's first babe, so I may be a long time."

"Worry not. I will take good care of Theodora."

"Of that, I have no doubt." Hester hurried back to the impatient young father-to-be, yet her heart was heavy at leaving Theodora behind. Not because of worry, but because...because she was truly becoming a mother.

Hannah Jr. entered the kitchen while Theodora worked herself into a full-throated cry.

"Who is this?" Mother set her dishcloth down and approached.

"'Tis Theodora. Hester has been called to a birthing."

"Theodora!" Tamson crowded close to see the babe.

"Would thee bring in the bucket of milk I left outside?" she asked her sister. "I could not carry both that and the babe's basket."

"Aye, but do not feed Theodora until I return. I wish to learn how." Tamson ran out the door.

"Mother," Hannah Jr. lowered her voice. "Thee must know something, but only thee."

"What is it?"

"The reason Theodora is a foundling is because of a mark on her body. 'Tis large and red. Hester said she has seen the like before, although not as large, and they are harmless—normally."

Mother glanced around the kitchen, but they were still alone. "So the mother feared it might mean the child was tainted by what is going on? How tragic."

"Hester suspects that to be the case, or that the mother feared what would happen to the child if someone in her household found out."

"'Tis good thee told me. Not that we believe such nonsense, but 'tis best to keep it to ourselves."

"If only thee and I change her clouts, none other will see it."

Tamson banged through the door into the back room off the kitchen.

At Hannah Jr.'s raised brow, Mother nodded. Tamson had a heart of gold but a tongue that seldom stilled.

Her sister set the milk bucket on the work table. "Can I help feed her?"

"Fetch Verity first," Hannah Jr. said. "I am sure she will also wish to help."

By the time the men came in from finishing the barn chores, Mother had breakfast ready. Theodora was fed, content, and well entertained with both of the little boys bringing her a favorite toy and Verity keeping an eye on them all. Tamson and Hannah Jr. finished setting the table while the older boys washed up.

After the silent prayer, Hannah Jr. asked Father, "May I remain home from meeting today with Theodora? 'Tis awkward to feed her even with the table close. I know not how I would manage at the meetinghouse."

Mother looked down the table at Father. "I believe 'twould be best."

"If thy mother thinks so, then I agree."

"I believe I can fashion a better way to feed her," Tamson said, "than dipping and re-dipping the nursing cloths."

"I am sure Hester would be delighted." If anyone could, it was probably her sister. Although Tamson kicked against the goads often enough, her feisty personality allowed her to look at things in unconventional ways. "Theodora will not be able to sip from a cup for a few months yet."

Tamson smiled. "Let me think on it."

They finished their meal, and the rest of the family left the kitchen to change into their best clothing. The Friends had no fancy clothing, but they kept their newest pieces for Sunday meeting—not as a matter of pride, but as a way of showing of respect for the Lord and a proper manner of offering their worship.

Theodora had drifted off to sleep in her basket, leaving Hannah Jr. free to tidy the kitchen. While she was happy to fulfill her promise to her friend by watching the child, she was disappointed that she wouldn't see Benjamin again this Sunday. Would he wait outside the brewery to watch their wagon pass? Did he even know that she hadn't been riding with her family these past few Sundays? That she walked home with Hester to help her after meetings?

Most importantly, was he staying safe from all the witch accusations and ramifications in the village?

"Goodie Hanson." Hester faced the laboring woman's nervous and excitable mother. "Thy daughter will need a restorative broth after the babe arrives. 'Twould benefit her greatly if thee would pick a bowlful of tender dandelion shoots, no longer than thy first finger, and simmer them with chicken or beef bones, whichever thee have. Add a good bit of salt and a pinch of sugar, and if thee find any rosemary, a pinch of that as well. Would thee do that?"

"You think I should leave my daughter?"

Hester did—emphatically. The woman was no help at all. Quite the opposite. Her jerky pacing, hand-wringing, and fearful conjectures were wearing on Hester's nerves. The first-time mother needed to be calmed and reassured, but her mother's behavior was the exact opposite. "Indeed, 'twill be a great help. Thy daughter will benefit from it."

"Well, if you think so." Before she left, she threw her arms around her daughter one last time, tears in her eyes. "I will not be far away, my love."

"'Tis all right, Momma." Goodie Tweed gave her mother a wan smile. "The midwife knows best."

"Indeed, she does." The sister escorted their mother from the room, closed the door, and collapsed into a chair with a groan. "How I wish my midwife had banished her from the birth of my first. 'Tis why I never informed her of the expectant dates of the next two." She giggled.

"Momma means well." Goodie Tweed grimaced against another pain.

Which was probably true, but some women lacked the temperament—and common sense—to be in the birthing room. The dandelion greens were a good source of nutrition, but mostly, they were time consuming to pick and wash and had to be tended closely to prevent them overcooking into an inedible green slime. They should keep Goodie Hanson busy until the babe arrived, Lord willing.

Goodie Tweed's sister, on the other hand, was an asset. She walked around the room arm in arm with her sister, keeping her talking, even laughing, and shared the local gossip from around the county. She was smart enough, however, to avoid any mention of Salem Village and the witch trials.

Then the mother-to-be groaned long and deep, both hands going to her extended middle, her breath coming in a series of short gasps.

"Time to check thee again." Hester helped lower the pregnant woman to the bed.

There had been little for Hester to do until the babe's head crowned. Now it was time to get to work. She'd already assembled the birthing stool, so she guided the young woman to it. It was an option she offered to all the women who called her. Although some preferred to lie abed, in Hester's experience, the birthing stool eased delivery. "Thy time is at hand." From the sunbeam's angle through the west windows, it was well into the afternoon.

With her sister's support on one side, Goodie Tweed lowered herself into position. She'd no more than taken the seat when another pain hit. She bit her lip, turning it white where her teeth marked it.

"'Tis a fine thing to cry out if thee need to," Hester said.

"Nay, I cannot do that." Determination filled the young woman's voice. "I will not upset my husband more than he already is."

"Nor Momma." Her sister took her hand. "Squeeze as much as you want, 'twill not harm me and 'twill help."

Less than an hour later, a wee girl child slipped onto the receiving blanket in Hester's hands, red and wrinkled and without blemish. Amid the exclamations of mother and aunt, Hester lifted the child for their inspection before cleaning her. How many such babes had she held in that way?

Never had one touched her heart as this one did.

Because never before had she had a child of her own. Never before had she truly understood what it meant to be a mother.

As she washed the infant and swaddled it, it was with hands much more accustomed to the task. When she handed the babe over to the exhausted and exhilarated mother, it was without even a twinge of sorrow for her own motherless state. Theodora had not only made her a mother, but a better midwife.

With babe and mother cleaned and tucked into bed, the long-suffering father and Goodie Hanson were called in.

Hester repacked her basket and returned the birthing stool into its canvas bag, anxious to return to her daughter.

Back on the cart, the new father was like a different person. Gone was the silent driver urging the horse to greater speed. Instead, the gentle man holding the reins kept up a steady stream of conversation. Hester had to hide her grin as he told her for the third time how beautiful his daughter was, as if Hester hadn't been there to see it all.

Hannah Jr. stepped outside when the cart pulled up to the farmhouse and waved him off, insisting that they would see Hester the rest of the way home.

"Thee may as well stay for supper," her friend said. "Theodora is content, and 'twill save thee needing to prepare something when thee return home."

Hester's stomach grumbled in agreement. "That sounds wonderful." She'd eaten only a slice of bread and a piece of cheese that day, and it was nearly suppertime.

"Thee must see what Tamson has devised for feeding Theodora. She is quite clever, my sister." Hannah Jr. held the door open. "I trust the birthing went well?"

"It did." Hester climbed the steps. "A beautiful little girl."

Hannah Jr. froze, her attention on something behind Hester.

Hester turned as the cart that had brought her passed a wagon on the farm's lane. She didn't recognize the man driving it, but his clothing suggested he was a Puritan. Why would he come to the Buffum farm on a Sunday evening? Neither Puritans nor Friends conducted any business on the Lord's day.

"Father?" Hannah Jr. called into the house. "A Puritan man is coming up the lane."

Caleb Buffum joined them on the small porch. "'Tis Alexander Osborne. It cannot be anything good."

"Is not his goodwife one of those accused and housed in Salem Town jail?" Hester asked.

"Indeed." He moved to the side away from the door. "Thee should wait inside and allow me to deal with this."

Hester followed Hannah Jr. into the back room, where Hannah waited just beyond the open door. The three women exchanged tense glances.

The wagon stopped outside, horses blowing, bits jingling as they shook their heads.

"Caleb Buffum, 'tis sorry I am to disturb you on the Lord's day, but I am in need of a coffin."

Chapter 14

S ARAH OSBORNE WAS DEAD.

Hannah Jr. poured the freshly separated cream into a bucket, then wiped her brow with the back of her trembling hand.

The first victim of the witch trials had died of a fever in the Salem Village jail.

Mother and Father had tried to prepare her, and Hannah Jr. had thought she'd understood the direness of the situation, but now someone was dead.

Widow Scudder had died at that cave where she'd held Verity, but that had been accidental. This was different. This was a shock.

She wasn't the only one who felt that way. The previous night's supper had been a nearly silent affair. Everyone had been subdued, even little Theodora, who had slept through it.

Father always stocked a couple of coffins in the corner of the carpentry shop. He'd given one to Alexander. He couldn't sell it on the Lord's day, but she was pretty sure he would not have charged the man anyway. Father was generous with people, and even more so when they were grieving.

He would need to make another to replace it, but would one be enough? How many people would die before the witch trials were over? Everyone knew of the hangings some years ago in Boston... but knowing it had happened there and facing it happening here...

Hannah Jr. shuddered. She'd never seen a gallows, but she could picture one all too clearly from what she'd heard.

Keeping busy would help hold the dark thoughts at bay. At least, she hoped it would. She carried the buckets to the springhouse and set them in the trough Father had built to channel the cold spring water. The fresh water would cool the milk and cream and keep them from turning sour until she was ready to churn butter or make cheese.

As she exited the springhouse, a familiar wagon turned into the lane, a heavy wagon pulled by a matched team with bells tied to the harnesses.

The brewer's wagon.

With all the upset of last evening, she hadn't given a thought to Sarah Buffington sending one of her sons to fetch butter and cheese on this Monday. She strode toward the door to the dairy, hoping it was Benjamin and not bothering to chide herself over it. She wanted to see him, to speak with him, to know he was safe. Or at least as safe as any of them could be.

A shout from the barn said the boys had seen the wagon too. Joseph, who had been in the hay loft window, came sliding down the pulley rope all the way to the ground. Thankfully, the younger boys weren't out yet and hadn't witnessed that. She'd speak to Joseph later about setting a better, less dangerous, example.

Her heart lurched as the wagon drew closer and Benjamin's eyes found hers.

He was safe. He was here. And once her siblings had been shooed back to their chores, she would speak to him. With a slight tip of her chin in that direction, she turned and entered to the dairy to wait.

How could a day go from such heights only to plunge into such lows? A new birth, a new life, the start of a family, all of which had touched Hester's heart in a deeper way than ever before, and then the senseless death of Sarah Osborne.

What did it matter if Sarah had married her indentured servant? Or if she had been trying to regain control of her deceased husband's farm, which had been willed to their sons instead of her? Or if the same farm had a decades-old boundary dispute with the Putnam family? Were any of those adequate reasons to jail an ill woman in a cold, damp cell?

Of course not.

Hester changed Theodora's clout, while the babe blinked up at her. Such innocence. Pure innocence that could be torn apart should the wrong person learn of the mark on her belly.

An overwhelming flood of protectiveness infused Hester from the soles of her feet to the hairs on her head. Whatever it took—short of defying God's law—she would do it to keep Theodora safe.

She tucked the babe in her basket and carried it and her milk piggin to the goat shelter. Pumpkin's water bucket was full already. The young man usually came early. She almost never heard him, but appreciated his acts of kindness. She stuffed an armful of hay into the feeder, then slid onto the small stool and milked the goat. The little goat, Seed, watched over Theodora's basket, her face cocked and her too-long ears swiveling.

"'Tis just a babe the same age as thee." Hester could milk the goat without looking now, which freed her to keep an eye on the two youngsters—human and goat.

Seed, filling out from a scrawny runt to a miniature and darker image of her mother, was nursing more, but Pumpkin's udder had expanded to accommodate the need to produce more milk to feed both babes.

If Seed had been a human, born runty and surviving while the healthy twin died, would she have been accused of witchcraft? And what then? Put to death for the crime of survival?

Pumpkin stamped a back hoof.

"Forgive me." Hester dropped her hands from the goat's udder. "I did not mean to squeeze so hard." She had enough milk for Theodora for the day, and perhaps enough to make pancakes for her supper. She stood and scratched the goat's back. "I will keep my thoughts more pleasant when I milk thee. 'Tis not thy fault that people can be so... so insensible and cruel."

She carried Theodora's basket and the piggin back to the cottage. She'd planned to spend the day planting her garden, but she had no interest in being outside. The day was pleasant enough, but she felt safer in the house, away from prying eyes and the threat of pointing fingers. For the first time, she battled fear at living within the village, surrounded by Puritans.

Not that all Puritans were bad, in the same way not all Friends were saints. She need only look at her goat's full bucket to see unwarranted kindness. Others in the village treated her with respect. She couldn't claim any as true friends, but many, like Jane Biddle, were amiable acquaintances.

Theodora yawned, her eyelids weighty. While the babe drifted off to sleep, Hester started a kettle boiling and pulled down the washtub. Instead of gardening, she'd launder Theodora's things. After all, she couldn't assume that Hannah Jr. would arrive on the morrow after her deliveries. Nor could she blame the young woman if she chose to stay away.

Hester couldn't remain shut up in her cottage forever, and no one knew how long the witch trials would last. She'd have to make a decision, to stay or find another place to live. A place where Theodora would be safe from suspicion—if, indeed, such a place existed.

For the first time in a very long time, Hester wished she had a husband to lean on, even if it wasn't Timothy.

The wait for Benjamin to enter the dairy seemed an eternity. Did Hannah Jr.'s siblings have no chores to be about? Did they have so much time to waste?

She shook off her unkind thoughts. She was being peevish.

And why seest thou the mote, that is in thy brother's eye, and perceivest not the beam that is in thine own eye?

Never had a verse from the scriptures applied more to her. She took a deep breath, then plunged into her own work, which she'd been neglecting as much as her siblings were neglecting theirs. The loyal customers among the Friends gave her a list each week of what they wanted delivered the following week. Hannah Jr. was busy pouring thick sour cream into an earthenware pot when the door finally opened.

Benjamin was backlit in the doorway, his face shadowed but no less handsome for it. He swept the tricorn hat from his head, sunlight glinting off his dark curls as it would from a raven's wing.

Setting down the bucket of sour cream, her hands trembling slightly but no longer out of fear or uncertainty over what had happened to Sarah Osborne. She wiped them on her apron and faced him. "Good morning, Benjamin."

He stepped fully into the room, leaving the door open as propriety dictated he should. "I have missed seeing you."

"'Tis good to see that thee are safe and well." She wished she could say more, but it wouldn't be appropriate. Nothing had changed between them. He was still a Puritan and she a Friend.

"Your family's wagon passed again yesterday, but you were not in it." He took another step closer.

Her heart beat like a trotting horse against her stays. "I remained at home."

"Were you feeling poorly?" Concern filled his voice.

"Nay. I was watching Hester's babe while she delivered another for one of the Puritans near Boxford."

Wrinkles creased his brow. "One of the Puritans. Is that how you see me as well?"

"'Tis what thee are, as I am one of the Friends."

He took one more step closer, and the roomy dairy seemed to shrink. "'Tis not all that I am. Nor is being a Friend all that you are."

"Perhaps not, but 'tis enough to keep us apart." She retreated a step, the workbench pressing against her lower back. "I am someone thy mother orders her dairy products from. That is all I can be, no matter what thee may say."

He held his ground this time. "Thee are generous and kind. I know 'twas thee who devised the plan to get food to the orphans. As I know 'twas thee who befriended the one who lives with thy family now, Joseph's little friend."

"Verity is her name. 'Twas the proper thing to do, caring for the widows and orphans."

"Aye, but *you* did it when others did not."

"The initial idea was mine, but 'twas the efforts of many who made it happen, including thy mother. Yet in the end, 'twasn't enough. The orphans had to be removed from the widow's care for their well-being."

A slow, warm, and dangerously intriguing smile stretched his lips—lips she ought not be noticing. "You are as modest as you are beautiful."

"Have thee the order from thy mother?" Hannah Jr. thrust out her hand to take whatever paper he'd brought, desperate to stop the direction their conversation had taken.

Instead, he took her hand in his. "Not written down this morning because she lacked the time. She bid me to request two rolls of butter, two pounds of soft white cheese, and a wheel of whatever hard cheese you have available." He didn't release her hand.

And she didn't pull it away. "Did she send a pot for the soft cheese?"

He raised his free palm to his forehead. "Of course she did. I left it in the wagon."

Hannah Jr. eased her hand free of his, missing the warmth of his fingers as soon as hers slid away. "While thee fetch it, I shall wrap the rest of her order."

He left the dairy, and she hurried to do what she'd said, choosing her very best hard cheese and two of the largest rolls of butter to wrap in heavy paper. When he returned and gave her the pot, she filled it to the brim, then quoted him the price.

Taking her hand in his again, he laid the coins in her palm and folded her fingers over them. Keeping hold of her hand, his eyes met hers, the moment drawing out, creating uncomfortable yet at the same time delightful sensations in her middle. "I am not going to give up."

"I am glad thee are safe." She stepped back, and he let her hand go. "I was worried for thee, especially at the news of Sarah Osborne's death."

He straightened and blinked. "Sarah Osborne? Did they hang her?"

"Nay, she died of a fever. Thee had not heard?"

The shake of his head sent his curls dancing. "I left early to—" His eyes flashed to hers and away.

"To take a bucket of water to Hester's goats?"

He shrugged, still looking out the window. "You are not the only one who can do a kind deed."

"But every day? 'Tis a commitment, I would say."

He turned back to her. "'Tis little enough to help an unmarried woman who has taken in a foundling. Is she not the same as a widow with no one to support her and the child?" His voice took on a defensive tone.

She had to squash the urge to slip her hand back into his. "Thee are right, of course, and I appreciate that thee are helping her and Theodora. As am I. 'Tis why thee do not see me on the wagon after meeting. I walk to the cottage with Hester and help her in the afternoon."

"Working on a Sunday?"

"Not working, helping."

His smile returned, as slow and enticing as before. "I suppose there is a difference in the middle of that somewhere."

Her cheeks heated at the combination of his smile and his teasing. "I suppose there is. But now I must get back to my real work, and thee must deliver these"—she gestured to his mother's order on the workbench—"to thy mother."

"Since I cannot see you on Sunday, I shall look forward to next Monday when I bring Mother's order."

So much for avoiding him when he came to the farm, as she'd promised Mother she would do.

Hannah Jr. ushered him out the door and whispered to his retreating back, "As will I."

Chapter 15

HANNAH JR. RUSHED THROUGH her deliveries the next day, eager to see Hester. Once they'd learned of Sarah Osborne's death on Sunday evening, it hadn't seemed the right time to show her Tamson's idea for feeding Theodora. She'd packed what she needed and now hurried along the forest path to the cottage, the afternoon sunshine filtering through the tree leaves overhead.

Hester was planting her garden when Hannah Jr. arrived, little Theodora on a blanket shaded by a large bush. The goats were loose in the fenced yard. Pumpkin nibbled at the leafy shrubs and weeds while Seed frolicked along, bouncing in the way young goats and lambs did.

The gate squeaked when Hannah Jr. opened it.

"Hello." Hester straightened and dusted off her hands. "I was not sure thee would come today."

"Nothing could keep me away. Theodora is already growing and changing. I do not wish to miss a full week."

Hester looked around and lowered her voice. "But with Sarah Osborne's death, I am hardly comfortable in my own garden. I do not expect thee to—"

"Worry not." Hannah Jr. interrupted. "I do nothing because of thy expectations but out of my own wishes to be here and to lend thee a hand as I am able."

Hester's smile was genuine, but troubled. "Thee are a godsend, I must say."

"Today, I wish to show thee the way Tamson devised to feed Theodora. We only tried it once, but she seemed happy with it, and the feeding was less, well... messy."

"Less messy would be wonderful." Hester motioned to the house. "Take Theodora into the house while I shoo the goats back into their shelter, lest Pumpkin start browsing in my herbs again."

Hannah Jr. lifted the infant and snuggled her close, enjoying the fresh scent of the babe mixed with the earthy smell of grass that clung to her blanket. "Come along, wee one. Let us do as thy mother said."

The babe tried to stuff her fist into her mouth keeping her owl-eyed stare on Hannah Jr.'s face. Was she starting to recognize her? That brought a flurry of emotions that Hannah Jr. didn't take the time to sort through as she entered the cottage. What good would it do her? She had no future that included a babe of her own, not as long as her heart was connected to a certain curly-haired Puritan with a dimple in his chin.

Hester entered the cottage and closed the door. It was such a nice afternoon, warm for the middle of May. The cottage had several windows, but most women kept their doors open to allow in the cool breeze as well as the sunshine. Hester moved to a basin on the workbench and washed the garden dirt from her hands. She turned her head to look at Hannah Jr. "So what do I need for this new way of feeding Theodora?" She wiped her clean hands on a piece of toweling.

"I brought reeds with me." Hannah Jr. held one up. "It works with the nursing clothes."

Right on cue, Theodora began to fuss, and Hannah Jr. sat at the table with her.

Hester chuckled. "Thee have impeccable timing, 'twould seem." She handed Hannah Jr. the corked pot of goat's milk and a nursing cloth.

Hannah Jr. uncorked the jug and dipped in the reed, the same kind her little brothers used to blow bubbles in the creek, and the older boys used to breathe through when they swam. When Hester sat beside her, she dipped the nursing cloth into the milk and offered it to the babe. Theodora sucked on it, quickly removing the milk. Hannah Jr. held her finger over one end of the reed and then drew it out and touched the other end to the top of the nursing cloth. When she let her finger come slighting away from the reed's other end, milk dribbled onto the cloth, and Theodora sucked it off.

"Amazing." Hester leaned closer. "Such a simple concept, and yet never would I have dreamed of it."

"Nor I. Tamson is the clever one."

"Indeed, she must be." Hester held out her arms. "Let me try."

Hannah Jr. handed the babe over, who fussed at having her feeding interrupted. Hester had her in place and was delivering the milk-filled reed to the cloth before the infant's fuss could turn into a full-throated protest.

"'Tis amazing." Hester laughed. "I said that already, did I not? But such a simple tool, yet 'twill make her feedings so much easier and, as thee said, less messy. Why, I shall be able to manage this even at meeting." She raised shining eyes to Hannah Jr. "Able to feed my daughter with ease, if not in the same way as the other mothers."

"Not every mother can successfully nurse her babe."

"Indeed." Hester's attention went back to keeping the milk supplied to Theodora. "I have had to help a couple learn to use the nursing clothes. But never"—she lifted the reed and dipped it into the pot again—"would I have thought to do this."

"And now thee can help other mothers when 'tis necessary." All because of her clever sister. Pride washed through Hannah Jr. at the thought. "We have plenty of these reeds. They grow near where the spring feeds into our pond." She lifted a half dozen out of her basket that she'd brought with her. "Each should last for a few days with washing in between feedings. I can bring more next week."

Hester studied the reed in her hand. "I believe they also grow near where I harvest the flat reeds for baskets in the fall."

Theodora fussed when her nursing cloth was dry of milk.

"Patience, sweet girl." Hester resumed feeding until the babe was satisfied, then lifted her to her shoulder and patted her back. "Thee must tell Tamson how wonderfully it worked. I will thank her myself at meeting on Sunday."

"She will be pleased."

After a satisfied burp from Theodora, Hester changed the girl and moved to her rocking chair.

"I shall fetch water, but then what can I do to assist thee today?" Hannah Jr. had already noticed that the laundry bucket was almost empty, and a pot of something savory was stewing over the hearth.

"I could show thee some of the simple steps in making baskets while this one naps, if thee like."

"Oh, but I thought to help thee today, not have thee help me."

"And thee have." Hester nodded to the pot and reed on the table.

"Very well." Hannah Jr. picked up the water bucket and the large kettle and left the cottage. A glance at the sun said it was already mid-afternoon, but she could stay and learn with Hester for a couple of hours, at least. The village street was not busy, but neither was it empty as it had been in past weeks. People were trying to get back to normal with the witch trials moved to Salem Town.

She did her best to ignore her treacherous heartbeat, which grew more rapid as she neared the brewery. Surely, Benjamin would be busy working for his father and not watching for her. She'd told him about helping Hester Sundays, but not Tuesdays. Therefore, it was silly of her to anticipate seeing him. Yet she couldn't help herself and glanced toward the brewery.

Right into the eyes of Isaac Kerley.

He stepped off the brewery's porch and headed toward her. There was no escaping him this time, no brother to intervene, and hurrying on would be rude since he knew she'd seen him, so she stopped and waited.

"Hannah Jr." He took the heavy kettle from her hand. "Allow me to assist thee."

"'Tisn't necessary, I—"

"I know thee are capable of carrying water," he said, "but I wish to help. As these are empty, I assume thee are headed for the well."

Hannah Jr. glanced up at him, but she caught movement in the brewery's square front window.

Benjamin. Probably. At that distance, perhaps Thomas Jr. She couldn't be sure but was flustered all the same.

"Shall we?" Isaac motioned for her to continue, unaware of the turmoil inside of her.

Maybe it was a good thing for Benjamin to see her with a young man of the Friends. Perhaps it would cause him to rethink his assertion that he would not give up. If she were to encourage Isaac—for a little while—it might put Benjamin off. And that was what she wanted.

Well, not *wanted*, but it was for the best. For both of them.

"I know thee must have a well on thy farm." Isaac brought her attention back to him. "I assume thee are doing a good turn for someone in the village."

"For Hester Fuller, aye."

"The midwife? She lives in the village?"

Hannah Jr. shot him a glance. "Thee did not know?"

His cheeks pinked as he shrugged. "'Tisn't as if I have had any dealings with her." Then he met her eyes. "Not yet."

Oh, no. The thought of encouraging him left her in a rush. He was shopping for a wife, and it was never going to be her. It was best if she made that plain to him now. But how? She couldn't exactly blurt out that she wasn't interested in Isaac. Tamson could have done so, but not her.

Although she'd made things plain enough with Benjamin, what had that accomplished? Nothing, as far as he was concerned.

They reached the well, and he hauled up the water bucket and filled both vessels, then lifted them and nodded to her. "Show me the way."

"Thee need not carry them both, I can take one."

He stepped back and shook his head. "'Tis my pleasure to help thee."

She started toward the cottage. "'Tis actually Hester thee are helping."

"'Tis thee I have an interest in helping, Hannah Jr." He leaned toward her while still walking, kettle in the hand closest to her, bucket in the other. "As I think thee know."

He couldn't have handed her a better opening to say what she needed to say, but her mouth went dry. Or maybe it went dry because of who stood outside the brewery as they passed, leaning against the building, arms crossed and one foot raised, heel resting against the wall behind him. There was no mistaking him for Thomas Jr. this time. Gone was his usual smile and easy manner. Benjamin looked... angry.

And heaven help her, it lifted her spirits. Maybe it even gave her the courage she needed, because several steps past the brewery, she stopped and faced Isaac.

"Thee are correct, Isaac. I do know of thy interest, but I do not return it." She took the kettle and bucket from his hands while he was too dumbfounded to stop her. "'Tis nothing against thee, please understand, but my interest lies elsewhere. To not tell thee plainly would be dishonest. Now, I shall be on my way." She turned and left him standing there.

She resisted the temptation to glance back at Benjamin. Because turning Isaac away didn't change things between Benjamin and her. Not one bit. All the same, her heart was lighter as she returned to the cottage.

It was obvious since Hannah Jr.'s return that something had happened while she had fetched the water. Hester let her hands drop to the top of the table. There was no sense in trying to teach someone basket making when that someone's attention was far away from the willow twigs and woodbine vines on the table between them.

"Will thee tell me what has upset thee?" she asked.

Hannah Jr. startled, then blushed and picked up the basket bottom she'd started. "'Tis nothing of concern."

Hester reached across the table and put her hand over the young woman's. "Thee can tell me. I promise to keep thy confidence. After all"—she cut a glance at Theodora, who was sleeping in her basket—"thee are keeping mine."

Dampness gathered in Hannah Jr.'s eyes, but she blinked it away. "'Tis a mess of my own making and one I need to think my way out of, lest it hurt my family."

That may have been the last thing Hester expected to hear. "I cannot imagine thee doing anything that would dishonor thy family."

"Nor can I, and yet"—she pressed a hand to her breast—"my heart is torn."

"A matter of the heart?" Hadn't she told Hester that none of the young men among the Friends had caught her interest? Oh. Oh, dear. "With someone outside of the Friends?" Hannah Jr. cringed, and Hester's heart hurt for her young friend. She softened her voice and asked, "May I know in whom thee are interested?"

There followed a pause while the younger woman collected herself, or perhaps worked up the courage to voice what she'd held in secret for too long.

"'Tis the brewer's son, Benjamin. The one who brings water for the goats."

"Ah." That also explained Sarah Buffington's reaction in the mercantile. The mother must know of her son's interest in Hannah Jr. "So his kindness is a way to keep thy attention, not a way to assist a midwife he knows not."

"'Tis what I accused him of, but he said 'twas not for me alone to do a kindness for others." She shrugged. "He seemed hurt that I had accused him of having improper motives."

"Whatever his motives, he makes mornings easier for me." Hester squeezed Hannah Jr.'s hand. "But I will ask him to stop if 'twill bring thee peace."

"Nay, please do not. 'Tis good for thee and Theodora." The younger woman's shoulders rounded. "I have told him, several times, that there is no future for the two of us."

A flare of admiration filled Hester. Would she have been so direct had Timothy not been a Friend? She doubted it. She'd been so young and so in love. "What has been his response?"

Troubled blue eyes met Hester's. "He says that he will not give up."

The pain in her friend's voice touched something deep within her. She wished she could urge Hannah Jr. to follow her heart. Yet as the older woman, it was her job to mentor the younger in the ways of the Friends, in their shared belief in the Lord and shared desire to follow only Him. The heart wasn't the best rudder in a storm. What was it the Bible said? *The heart is deceitful and wicked above all else, who can know it?* How best could she help steer her friend clear of the pitfalls, disappointment, and further heartbreak that surely must lie ahead?

Chapter 16

IT'D BEEN THREE DAYS since Hannah Jr. had shared her burden with Hester. Three days of mulling over the midwife's words. Filled with the heartbreak of losing Timothy, Hester had poured herself into helping others. She'd found fulfillment in becoming a midwife and all the duties that entailed, from attending pregnant women who were ill, delivering babies, attending to newborns and mothers who had problems after birth, and even helping grief-stricken women who suffered a miscarriage, a still birth, or the loss of a young babe. Being a blessing to others had eased Hester's grief.

Hannah Jr.'s grief was different, but not entirely. Benjamin wasn't dead, of course, but no less lost to her. She already kept busy in the dairy as well as in the house and garden, helping Mother. Tuesday and Sunday afternoons she spent with Hester. Was there more she could do?

Who else could possibly need her help?

Father's advice on most everything came to her loud and clear in the quiet dairy. *Have thee prayed about it, daughter?* She had not. Why? Perhaps because she didn't wish to hear the answer. It was hard enough knowing the right thing to do without having it confirmed. Or was it? Was she just being willful? Probably. She grabbed the broom and swept the wood plank floor, then kneeled, and bowed her head.

Lord, I have been wrestling with this for too long without bringing it to Thee. Mother knows, Caleb Jr. suspects, Tamson thinks she knows, and now Hester. Yet I have neglected to come to Thee. Thee are aware of my thoughts, wayward as they are, and my desires, which are equally wayward. Lord, I cannot seem to stop these feelings on my own. I need Thee to settle my heart and keep me true to Thee alone. If that be through remaining a spinster and helping others, please show me who to help and when and where. Amen.

She waited there on her knees for some time, a habit she'd learned from Father. Waiting for the nudge, as he called it, in her spirit which would direct her. But it didn't come. Often it didn't. Father said that happened to him as well, and that those times were when the Lord wished for him to figure things out on his own, as when Father made her brothers figure things out without his help. People often learned best that way.

Hannah Jr. would have preferred a nudge after laying bare her heart, but it wasn't to be.

"Hannah Jr.?" Tamson's voice reached her, and she climbed to her feet and dusted off her petticoat.

"In the dairy." She'd left the door open to catch the cooling breeze.

Her sister popped inside, Verity just behind her. "Mother says we must finish planting the potatoes this morning, and the carrots as well. Verity has never planted carrots. Can thee finish the potatoes while I help her with them?"

When she'd prayed for someone to help, she hadn't planned on it being her sister, but who was she to question the outcome of a prayer? "Gather the seed potatoes, the carrot seeds, and the hoes. I must check the wrappings on the hard cheese, and then I shall join thee."

The girls scampered away, chattering like chipmunks, Button barking and running alongside.

When Hannah Jr. joined them in the garden, the sun was overhead without a cloud, warming the dirt under her bare feet. She took the hoe Verity offered her, thankful that Father had been able to replace the iron head. A wooden hoe would have made the work that much harder. She moved to the long row of potato hills they'd started the day before. It took a lot of potatoes to feed a family their size throughout the winter months. She'd need to plant two more rows beside the one already there. The work was mindless. Heap up a hill of dirt, dig a hole in its middle, drop in a seed potato, cover it up, tamp down the rich soil, and then make another hill next to that one. At least the breeze was cool enough to keep things pleasant.

The family's wagon was rolling up the lane by the time Hannah Jr. had finished the second row. It was pulled by Dandy and Scout, since Dolly was still nursing her foal. Father drove, Caleb Jr. beside him. The back of the wagon was piled with milled boards. One of the Friends had a sawmill along the creek on the very northern edge of their community. Father took his logs there to be cut. What was he making that required so many boards? He hadn't mentioned getting a new carpentry order since finishing the doctor's furniture. He'd been too busy in the fields getting their wheat, rye, oats, and peas planted. He'd wait to plant the corn for another week or so. Springtime was for planting—not carpentry work.

"Hannah Jr.!" Caleb Jr. shouted and waved for her to join them.

She set down the hoe to mark her spot and left the sack of seed potatoes beside it. "If I cannot return, thee will need to plant the last row." She ignored Tamson's moan of protest.

Father grabbed one end of a stack of boards while Caleb Jr. grabbed the other. "Hold the door for us, will thee?" He nodded to the outside door to the carpentry shop. The same breeze that had cooled her in the garden pushed against the door as she opened and held it steady while they carried in stack after stack, lining one wall of the shop almost to waist height.

"Thank thee, daughter." Father removed his hat and wiped his brow. "'Twas very helpful."

"May the boys and I go fishing now?" Caleb Jr. brushed the sawdust off his hands and onto the seat of his breeches. "Mark said the bass were biting in the shallows."

"See thee come home with a nice catch of bass, and thy mother will forgive me for excusing thee from chores."

"The girls will wish to tag along," Hannah Jr. said. "Tell them the carrots will not plant themselves, but they may join thee after. I shall finish planting the potatoes." Caleb Jr. sprinted off, and she turned to Father. "Did thee get a large order for the carpentry shop?"

His brow wrinkled, and he shook his head. "Nay, 'tis just that with the death of Sarah Osborne, it seemed prudent to have more wood on hand." He went into the shop.

She followed and closed the door behind her. "To make more coffins?"

"Indeed." He sank onto a stool and glared at the wood, as if he were angry with it instead of the people who had started the whole witch business. "I cannot think she will be the only one to die."

"What can we do?" Hannah Jr. hadn't planned to ask that, but the question slipped out all the same.

"Do?" Father shook his head. "We will sow and tend and reap the harvest. Thee will run the dairy. Thy mother will keep all else in line, I have no fear."

"But is there nothing we can do to help those who are..." She struggled for the right word.

Father's brown eyes were full of understanding. "Victims of the madness, what the doctor calls hysteria? I know not what we can do to help them. Or if, in trying to help them, we would put our own family in danger."

Danger. That word sent a prickle across her flesh. But hadn't she prayed about finding a way to help others? Was God answering her prayer even now? She rubbed her upper arms. What could it mean?

For the past fortnight, Hester had enjoyed a gentle rhythm to her days. Rise with Theodora and tend to her, milk Pumpkin, spend an hour in the cool of the morning working in her garden while the goats grazed, then keep busy with Theodora and her housework. She made baskets, took trips to the mercantile if necessary, and visited with Hannah Jr. when she came.

Hester loved the routine. Loved being part of a family, even with just the two of them. Having someone else to love and care for, someone who needed her, fulfilled her in ways she'd never have understood without Theodora.

It was the end of May, and there were no babies due within the Friends' community for several weeks yet. She knew of no expectant mothers among the Puritans, although she rarely knew of them ahead of time. If she had, she might have an idea who Theodora's mother was. She pushed that thought away, as she did every time it crept up on her.

Her life was full, the weather lovely, and her daughter progressing beautifully. Hester could almost forget the cloud of uncertainty that still cloaked the village, although not as heavy and ominous since the proceedings had moved to Salem Town. Was this simply the quiet before the storm? Even the thought of that made her cringe. That and the memory of Goodie Putnam's glare.

She tucked Theodora into her sling and headed out the door to the mercantile for a brick of flax to spin into thread for her baskets. Halfway to the store, she met Jane Biddle coming toward her. The woman's red-rimmed eyes didn't meet hers.

"Jane? Is anything amiss?" Hester touched the other woman's arm to stop her from passing. "Is thy new babe doing poorly?"

"Richard? Nay, he is fine." She dabbed her eyes with a handkerchief, then lowered her voice. "'Tis my aunt, Sarah Cloyce."

"I am so sorry. Thee said she had been accused."

Jane latched on to Hester's arm. "'Tis worse, I fear. They have arrested her and ordered her moved to Boston jail. Boston." The last word was almost a wail.

As well it should be. Boston, where the so-called witches had been hung during the last outbreak of accusations.

"She has not been convicted of anything, has she?"

"Nay. 'Tis not just my aunt, but also Goodie Nurse, Goodie Corey, John and Goodie Proctor, and the child, Dorcas Good. A child? Can you imagine?"

A stab of fear shot through Hester, and she hugged Theodora's sling tighter.

Jane dabbed her eyes again. "I hold out hope, now that Governor Phips is returned from England, good man that he is. Surely, he will see things set to rights." She turned pleading eyes on Hester. "Will he not?"

"Let us hope so and pray that he listens to the Lord's direction."

"Pray, of course, as we all have been. But just now down the street, several women were saying that additional shackles have been ordered for the jails. The money had to be borrowed to cover it. There appears not to be an end in sight." She sniffed and shook her head.

"But where are my manners? 'Tis good to see you out and about with the foundling." Jane peered at Theodora in her sling.

Hester's heart seized for a moment, but her quick glance assured her that the babe's gown covered her mark.

"She is a beautiful girl." Jane looked up at her. "Will you keep her? Or find a family for her?"

"As she was given to me, I have decided to keep her. Her name is Theodora, which means gift."

"How lovely." Jane smoothed the back of her finger across Theodora's cheek. "I wish all were as pure and innocent as this one and my Richard. Only they are safe from the madness that surrounds us." That brought on another rush of tears that she dabbed away. "Forgive me." She sniffed again. "I must hurry home. 'Twas good to see you again, Midwife."

"I shall pray for thy aunt." Hester stepped aside and let the other woman pass, then walked on, steps heavier than before. What must it be like for the families of the accused? Jane had lost her mother years before, so her aunt Sarah had been a source of encouragement to Jane during that false alarm. She'd been loving and helpful. How could a woman like that be accused of such a horrible thing?

Hester gazed into the face of her daughter. What would happen if Theodora were ripped away from her? The heartbreak of losing Timothy dimmed compared to what threatened to overcome her with that thought. She'd witnessed the miracle of motherhood more times than most, the instant bonding of mother and child that couldn't be explained with mortal words. The full magnitude of it had to be experienced.

And now Hester had experienced it.

The past fortnight, with its illusion of normality, had lulled her into a false sense of security. Walking along the street, nodding politely to those she passed, she felt again the lurking sense of evil that hung over the village. Evil that would accuse a gentle woman like Sarah Cloyce of being a witch. Evil that had caused Sarah Osborne to die in the dank cellar of the jail in Salem Town. Evil that would fall upon Theodora should anyone see her mark.

Hester had to fight the urge to turn and flee. Above all things, she must not bring attention to herself or her daughter.

Entering the mercantile, she gave her order to the clerk and waited while he weighed the brick of flax. There were no other customers, perhaps because it was midday and many would be home for their meal. She pushed the coins across the counter and took her packaged flax as Theodora began to fuss.

Pushing past the door and stepping into the bright sunshine, she almost ran into Benjamin Buffington.

"Pardon me." He was steadying her when Hester took a hasty step back against the building's wall. "I was not watching where I was going."

"No harm done. 'Twas entirely my fault."

Theodora cried, no doubt hungry more than frightened, her face puckered and red.

He shifted his feet awkwardly. "I could carry your package home for you, if you like."

"There is no need, but thank thee for the kind offer."

"Then I wish you a good day, Midwife."

She dipped her head in acknowledgment and walked past him, forcing her steps to be casual and unhurried.

How kind it had been of Hannah Jr.'s admirer to offer his help, especially after she'd practically run him down, charging out the door the way she had without a look to the left or right.

Seeing him up close, she could understand Hannah Jr.'s attraction. That curly hair and the dimple on his chin would have had her looking at him twice if she were fifteen years younger. But good looks and fine manners didn't change the core of the problem.

He was still a Puritan and Hannah Jr. a Friend.

Hannah Jr. had a secret love she couldn't acknowledge, while Hester had a daughter whose mark she must keep secret. The Friends weren't big on keeping secrets, but sometimes, there was no other choice.

Especially when evil lurked all around them.

Chapter 17

"**Y**OU HAVE BEEN AVOIDING me."

Hannah Jr. jumped, slopping some of the heavy cream onto the workbench. She set the bucket down and gulped in a deep breath before turning. "Benjamin."

"I did not mean to frighten you."

"Then why did thee sneak up on me?" she snapped. And why hadn't she heard the arrival of his wagon? She had been avoiding him for the past three weeks. Quite successfully. The bells on his wagon always gave away his arrival. But not today.

"To prevent you from sending your sister to take my order again." He shrugged. "It worked."

"How did thee arrive?"

The grin that creased his face and put a sparkle in his eyes was far too appealing. "On horseback."

"I did not know thee had a riding horse." But then again, how should she? For all her silly emotions concerning him, they did not know each other that well.

"Nor did I until last Friday." He frowned and brushed at a smear of dirt along the side of his buff breeches. "Blaze and I are still learning to get along."

"He threw thee? Are thee hurt?"

"Blaze is a she, and I am not hurt, unless you count my pride. That, I fear, took a bruising." He looked out the open door. "Where is everyone?"

"Salem Town. Father took everyone except me, Verity, and the little boys. She is minding them in the house." Verity had no wish to go into Salem Town again, considering what had happened the last time. But she would have come to the dairy to take Benjamin's order, saving Hannah Jr. from seeing him.

Hannah Jr. had told herself all morning that it wasn't because it was Monday and Benjamin might come that she had decided to remain home. After all, she'd only seen him from the upper window of the house for the past three weeks while Tamson filled his mother's order, and twice while passing the brewery to fetch water for Hester. They hadn't spoken. She'd hoped not to speak with him again.

Except if that were true, why was her heart so lightened by his appearance?

"I would speak with you, since we are alone, about the man I saw you with in the village, the one who walked you to the well."

"Isaac Kerley."

"I suppose him to be one of your Friends."

"He is."

"And yet"—the grin tugged at his lips again—"you took back the bucket and kettle and left him standing in the street with his mouth hanging open."

"Did I?" She turned, grabbed a rag, and mopped up the spill.

He came behind her, and while her heart sped, it wasn't from fear. He reached around her and stopped her hand, took the rag away and set it aside, then turned her by the shoulders to face him. "It gave me hope."

With more effort than it should've taken, she stepped to the side and moved away from him. "Please, do not let it."

"Do not have hope when I see you turn another man away? And more the fool him that he left." Benjamin moved and stood in front of her, but didn't touch her this time. "I would not have."

"But thee should. Thee should take thy mother's order and go."

He caught her hand then and gave it a gentle tug. "Come and meet Blaze."

Was he serious? She glanced up at him. She had enough brothers to know that look, the challenge in his eyes. He was daring her. If she refused, would he call her a coward? The urge to stamp her foot was strong, but she was far too old and poised for that. At least, she thought she was. "Fine." She walked past him, out of the dairy, and stopped to stare at the pale horse tied to the hitching rail.

"She is white."

"Aye, I know." Humor filled his voice. "I did not name her. She came with the moniker."

"A fully white horse named Blaze." Hannah Jr. shook her head. "I thought her named for a white mark on her face."

"Come. She likes my mother's sweet biscuits." He pulled one from his inner coat pocket and broke it in half, handing it to Hannah Jr. "Go ahead. Make friends with her."

Hannah Jr. held the biscuit piece out, and the horse's velvety lips slicked it off her palm. "She has a kind eye." She stroked the animal's long face and cut a glance toward Benjamin. "Whatever did thee do to her for her to toss thee in the road?"

He straightened his waistcoat and eyed the horse. "I rode her in a direction she preferred not to go." With a shrug, he gave the horse the other half biscuit. "The former owner warned me that she is barn sour, having not been ridden much in the past two years. She does not like leaving the comfort of her barnyard."

Hannah Jr. stroked the white face again. "Perhaps she just needs a little persuading."

"Ah, then I am in luck." He hiked a brow at her. "If I can win over the heart of this girl"—he patted the white shoulder—"it could be good practice for winning yours."

"Hello!" Verity called as she, Benji, and Jonathan hurried toward them. Rags and Button raced ahead, tails wagging. So the dogs had been in the house too. That was why they hadn't raised an alarm at Benjamin's arrival.

"Give me thy mother's order, and I shall fill it while thee introduce everyone to Blaze."

He handed her the slip of paper with an air of reluctance, then turned his attention and smile to the younger children.

Hannah Jr. filled the order, peeking out the open door when laughter and giggles got the best of her curiosity. Benjamin was leading the mare around the large yard with all three children on her back, the two boys sharing the saddle and Verity holding on behind. The laughter and giggles must have been from the story he appeared to be telling, waving his arms to emphasize something or other.

He'd make a good father someday.

And a good husband to some Puritan woman.

"You can bring the babe, Midwife, 'twill be fine." The man on her doorstep twisted the hat in his hands. "But my Martha, this being our first child together, and her feeling so poorly this morning..." He shrugged. "If you would but come and comfort her?"

Hester patted Theodora's back as the babe rested against her shoulder. Already changed and fed, she would be good for at least an hour. Since the Puritan couple didn't live far outside the village, that should be enough.

"Give me a moment to pack my daughter's things." She left the door open while he waited on the porch. Just in case, she tucked the corked pot of goat's milk, a nursing cloth, and a reed in among her midwife supplies.

Moments later, she was seated on the cart next to James Rupert, who clicked to the chestnut horse.

"I had heard you took in a foundling." He nodded toward Theodora. "That must not be easy for you, a woman alone." There was no condemnation in his voice. She'd known him for six years, having delivered his first wife's three children. Her death had been a shock when Hester had learned of it. The healthy young woman had delivered her babes without fuss and seemed the type who would overcome anything. Anything but a cut on her leg that had gone bad. She'd died of infection.

"'Tis an adjustment, but one well worth it."

"I know when my wife died"—he ducked his head, then looked up and forward—"I was at a loss what to do with the young ones by myself."

No one could fault him for marrying again right away, with children who'd been just five, three, and barely a year old. There had been gossip around the village about him choosing a girl nearly ten years his junior. The women Hester had overheard gossiping had sons around his new wife's age and had probably been casting eyes at the girl for a future daughter-in-law.

They pulled up to a modest farmhouse, whitewashed, with a deep porch and a line of laundered sheets hanging under it, flapping in the breeze. The young woman, Martha, stood at the top of the steps. "Good morning, Midwife, thank you for coming." Two young boys were sitting on the top rail of the porch, while a little girl clung to the woman's petticoat.

"Good morning." Hester got off the cart, then lifted out Theodora's basket and her basket of supplies.

"I shall tie the horse by the barn, and return you when you are ready." James drove off.

"Fetch one of Midwife's baskets, Silas."

The older boy scrambled down, and Hester handed him her supplies. He looked in the other basket. "She gots a babe."

"She *has* a babe." The young woman corrected him but smiled at Hester. "I am Martha Rupert."

"Hester Fuller."

"Come in, and welcome." Martha moved aside and shooed the children out of the way. "Silas, take your brother and sister outside to play under the maple tree. Midwife and I will be here in the kitchen."

The boy did as she said without a fuss.

"They have accepted thee well, 'twould seem." It never hurt to start a conversation with a compliment.

"We have had our moments, but we have worked them out. For the most part." She gestured to a chair near the hearth. "Have a seat. Would you like tea?"

"No, thank thee." Hester sat and put Theodora's basket at her feet, in which the babe was sound asleep, lips twitching with a dream. Hester looked up as Martha sat in the chair across from her. "What can I do for thee?"

The young woman smoothed her hands over the gentle mound of her middle. "I told James there was no need to fetch you."

"And yet he did, so tell me what is troubling *him.*"

Her cheeks flushed, and she picked at a loose thread on her apron. "'Tis only that I have had a couple of times recently when things make me cry and"—she raised troubled eyes to Hester—"I cannot seem to stop it or even tell him why."

"Because thee know not?"

"Exactly. I wish I did, but I..." She pressed the back of one hand to her mouth, turning her face to the side.

Hester sat back in her chair. "'Tis all very common, what thee are describing. Many women go through such a phase when they are still two or three months from delivering."

"They do?" She faced Hester again. "Truly, you are not just saying that to comfort me?"

Hester chuckled. "I can assure thee, I am not. I have heard the same complaint from countless women."

"James says his first wife never felt this way." The words came out tumbled with vulnerability. What must it be like to try and fill another woman's place?

Hester's heart went out to her. Martha couldn't be more than ten and seven, yet she'd stepped into the role of not just wife, but mother to three children, and that not even a full year ago.

"Some women, I suspect, are just better at hiding these things from their husbands." Hester had held the hands of more than one crying woman who couldn't let her feelings out around her husband, whether from fear of his reaction or the wish to spare him the emotional upheaval.

"I wish he had not bothered you with this." Martha clasped her hands in her lap, fingers laced tightly enough that her knuckles whitened. "I do not expect the babe until the end of July."

"Thy husband's concern is a good thing. It shows how much he cares for thee."

One side of her lips tugged into a half-smile. "I hope he does."

"I have had many men fetch me for their wives, and have seen all kinds of responses. Thee can trust me in this, the man who came to my cottage cares very much for the woman carrying his child."

There was nothing wrong with Martha that a good woman-to-woman talk wouldn't clear up. The next half hour was spent with Hester reaffirming the young wife that she was loved and cared for by the man outside waiting to take Hester back to the village.

Theodora was still asleep when Hester gathered her basket and headed for the door. Martha followed with the other basket. "'Twould seem my husband was right. I did need thee to come."

"Hesitate not a moment to call me out again if thee have a need, even if 'tis just to talk. Thee might wish to talk about what will happen when things get closer."

"'Twould be good to know more. My mother died when I was ten, and my father never remarried. He did his best," Martha hastened to add, "but there are things he could not tell me."

"Send thy husband again, or thee are welcome to come to my cottage in the village." She glanced at the man stepping in to the cart to drive it to them. "I am sure he could watch the little ones for a while."

"Aye. He is a good father. A good man." She glanced toward the tree where the children were watching, the little girl holding onto her eldest brother's hand.

Martha had lost her mother at an early age. It made sense that her heart went out to the three motherless children she'd taken on as her own. While they were a bit separated by age, Hester had the feeling that James and Martha were a good match. Their children were very lucky to have them.

"Midwife, I put a load of firewood in the cart for you," James said as he pulled the horse to a stop.

"There was no need—"

"I insist. 'Tis the least I could do."

Hester stepped into the cart and settled her baskets. Theodora awoke, so Hester lifted her out and brought her to her shoulder, then nodded to James.

The horse started forward, and Hester waved to Martha.

James cleared his throat. "Was everything all right?"

"Thy wife is fine." Hester smiled at his rushed sigh and relieved smile. "Every woman goes through this a little differently, and Martha has not a mother to turn to for advice. Fetch me anytime she needs to speak with me, or I have invited her to come to my cottage, too. Whichever pleases her best."

"I know not how to thank you."

"The firewood is more than enough." Hester had half a mind to thank him for bringing her out to their farm for a peaceful morning without worry of what was happening in the village outside of her walls. A morning of doing what she was meant to do—helping others bring their children into the world. No worry about witches, or pointing fingers, or saying the wrong thing to the wrong person. No need to fret over someone discovering Theodora's mark.

"'Tis glad I am that you would come. Only a few weeks ago, friends of ours had a babe. A wee girl." He let out a long breath. "It did not survive. The husband had to bury it in the night, fearful that seeing the dead infant would be too distressful on his goodwife. The poor woman took it hard. At least he buried it in the basket she had purchased for the babe and wrapped it in a blanket of many colors that she had woven herself. That gave her some comfort." He clicked to the horse when it slowed its pace. "The poor man blames himself for not fetching a midwife, but the babe came so quickly, he had not the time."

Hester's tongue stuck to the roof of her mouth. A purchased basket. A woven blanket of many colors. All joy in the day leached out of her.

James was speaking of Theodora's parents, but he didn't know the truth. Did anyone, other than Hester and the husband who *hadn't* buried his child? How could one keep such a secret so close to the village?

What would happen when the truth came out?

Chapter 18

Hannah Jr. held the end of the long board still while Father cut the length needed for another coffin. The fields were all planted, the lambs and calves born, and the sheep sheared. There was finally time for something other than spring farm chores. Although the boys were busy hoeing the cornfield, Father could take the time to replace the coffin given to Alexander Osborne three and a half weeks past.

The dogs' barking broke above the rasp of the saw. Father stopped, mopped his brow, and went to the window. "'Tis David."

Outside of meetings, they hadn't seen the O'Sullivans much. "Is he alone?"

"Aye." Father glanced at her. "If thee wish, thee can do something else while we talk."

"May I stay?" She wasn't sure what made her ask that, to leave and enjoy a refreshing breeze somewhere under a tree.

"Very well. 'Tis no big guess that he brings news." He left the shop to greet his friend.

They entered together a few minutes later, David stopping when he caught sight of her. "Good afternoon, Hannah Jr."

"The same to thee." She gestured to a stool. "Will thee have a seat?"

He cut a glance at Father. "Is thy industrious daughter taking over thy carpentry shop now?"

Father chuckled. "Nay, but if she put her mind to it, she could probably do the job as well as any of the boys. Have a seat."

David sat on the stool and slumped forward, hands clasped between his knees. "'Tis not good news I bring to thee."

"I feared as much." Father took the other stool.

Hannah Jr. sat on a low crate and wrapped her arms around her bent knees, half wishing she'd left before doing so would have been rude.

"The governor set up the Court of Oyer and Terminer in Salem Town two days ago, on Monday," David said.

Father rubbed the side of his nose. "Law terminology is beyond my learning."

"I had to ask as well," David said. "It means to hear and determine."

"Then why could they not just call it that?" Father asked.

"Because they need those fancy French words"—David winked at Hannah Jr.—"to make them feel like they know more than the rest of us."

"Undoubtedly." Father waved dismissively. "But that is not what thee came to say."

"Nay." All levity left David's face and voice. "'Tis that on the first day they indicted both John Willard and Rebecca Nurse for witchcraft."

Father's quick intake of breath sounded loud in the shop. "So they must stand trial?"

"'Tis my understanding." David wagged his head. "I fear it will not go well for either of them."

A rock settled in the pit of Hannah Jr.'s stomach. Rebecca Nurse had been a customer of hers for several years. The woman was elderly, hard of hearing, and had struggled with her health off and on for the past months. Hannah Jr. couldn't think of anyone less likely to be a witch than that kind old woman.

"On what evidence did they indict them?" Father asked.

David snorted. "On those girls' say-so, the ones they say have been afflicted. Not a one of them accused either Rebecca or John of physically touching or speaking to them either."

"How can they have harmed the girls if they did not touch or speak to them?" Hannah Jr. usually remained silent when adults were speaking, a habit held over from her childhood, but what David had just said made no sense.

David turned to her. "The girls claim that the specter of the accused person visited them and did harmful things to them, then demanded they sign the devil's book."

"Specters?" Father straightened on his stool. "What nonsense is that?"

David held up a finger. "I had to ask that as well. They say 'tis when the person's spirit leaves their body and goes roaming about the countryside."

"Never have I heard anything so daft." Father shook his head. "And the judges of the court, they believed the girls?"

"'Twould appear so." David shifted on his stool. "Will this change thy mind on leaving here?"

"I must speak with Hannah, of course. 'Tis not a decision to be lightly made, but I have no desire to leave."

"Indeed. I shall be speaking with Isobel tonight. And if we decide to leave, I will let thee know. Perhaps we can travel together." He shrugged. "Safety in numbers."

"Do thee have an idea of where to go?" Father asked.

"I do." David nodded to Hannah Jr. "But it must stay between the three of us for now."

Hannah Jr. stood. "I should leave the two of thee to make plans."

"Nay." Father raised a hand to stop her. "Sit and listen. 'Twould be good for someone else in our family to know of these plans."

A sense of something heavy covered her with those words. She was an adult, of course, but she wasn't used to Father treating her like... like an equal. He'd always treated her as someone he could count on, yes, but not an equal. She should have been proud of his trust and faith in her, but instead, niggling in the back of her mind was her infatuation with Benjamin—a young man Father would never approve of.

"Of course." David leaned forward until Hannah Jr. worried he might tip the stool. "Thomas Danforth is allowing any under suspicion to take refuge in his forests. 'Tisn't well known, thee understand, but word had reached my ear, so it will have reached others."

"I have heard the name," Father said, "but I know not where the land is."

David pointed. "'Tis southwest of Boston, close enough to move even a large family in three or four days. Far enough to be out of sight and, Lord willing, out of harm's way. 'Tis said he owns over fifteen thousand acres of untamed land."

The large canvas sacks she and Mother had sewn and stored the past winter, when fear of being accused had first appeared, might yet be put to use. They had a place of refuge to flee to and friends to travel with. Dolly's filly was old enough to travel with them, but what would happen to the cows, sheep, and chickens?

She didn't wish to leave their home or her life here near Salem Village.

She put a tight clamp on any thoughts of Benjamin. But what would become of Hester and Theodora if Hannah Jr. went into hiding?

Hannah Jr. was filled with the conviction that she ought to stay here, even if the rest of her family left.

Tuesday arrived, and Hester was eager for Hannah Jr.'s visit. They'd barely spoken at meeting. When the older women had flocked around Theodora to coo and smile at her, Hannah Jr. had stepped back and moved off to be with her siblings. Hester'd had the distinct impression that something was on the young woman's mind, but Hannah Jr. hadn't said anything that afternoon. Perhaps her young friend would open up on this visit. Hester hadn't felt right about pressing the matter, especially since she was holding back a secret of her own.

Should Hester share what she'd learned about Theodora's parents? Hannah Jr. already knew that Theodora was a Puritan child, and that her mother must live close by to have purchased one of Hester's baskets. What good would it do to share that the mother thought her child was dead? That the father had lied about burying the child? Hester didn't know the mother's name. She hadn't asked James Rupert because she didn't want to know it. The father had seen the babe's mark and made a decision—one he would have to live with.

And so would Hester.

She tugged on a particularly stubborn tuft of grass growing among her potato plants. It gave way, almost dumping her on her rear end. She glared at Pumpkin, who grazed on the other side of the fenced back yard. "Why could thee not eat the grass and weeds out of my garden and let the other plants alone?" She'd had to chase the beast away from her pea vines that morning when she'd turned her back for just a moment.

Pumpkin lifted her head, bottom jaw swinging as she chewed, and then went back to grazing, completely unimpressed with Hester's outburst.

Theodora napped in her basket beneath a shady bush, her little foot resting on the basket's rim. She was outgrowing it already. Not already. The babe was six weeks old. How could so much time have passed so quickly?

"Good day, Hester." The back gate squeaked as Hannah Jr. came through it.

"Good day." Hester rose and shook the clinging dirt from her petticoat and apron. "Thee caught me wool-gathering."

"Deep thoughts, then?"

Hester sighed. "Deep enough. It dawned on me that Theodora is six weeks old already. The time has gone by so fast."

Hannah Jr. smiled. "'Tis like that with the little ones. Thee turn around, and they are halfway grown, helping thee in the garden."

Hester planted her hands on her hips and glared at Pumpkin. "If only 'twas that easy with a goat."

"Oh, my." Hannah Jr. laughed. "What has happened this time?"

"I will tell thee over a cup of tea." She shooed her friend toward the cottage. "Go on in while I put the goats away."

Hannah Jr. took Theodora inside and set the order of butter and cheese on the table, then watched Theodora sleep until Hester arrived.

"Oh, that goat." Hester recounted the antics of the animal while making tea. "Did thee happen to bring any fresh cream today?"

With a smile, Hannah Jr. lifted a crock. "I had a feeling thee might need some."

"What would I do without thee?" Hester smiled, but Hannah Jr. sobered. "Is something amiss?"

"Have thee not heard the news of Bridget Bishop?"

"I have not." Hester poured the tea and sat across from Hannah Jr. "I do not believe I know her."

"Nor I. She is from Salem Town." Hannah Jr. picked up her cup but didn't sip from it. "They found her guilty of witchcraft yesterday. She is to hang this very afternoon."

Hester gasped. "Where did thee hear this?"

"David sent Matthew to our farm this morning at first light. He told my father and then rode on to spread the word."

"Why would they do this?" Hester didn't want to believe that anyone was going to be hanged for witchcraft, even though it had happened in other counties before. This was Salem Village. Her home.

"David may be something of a gossip"—Hannah Jr. shrugged—"but he is reliable. He came by the farm last week and told Father of this new court the governor established. He called it the Court of Oyer and Terminer. It means—"

"To hear and determine." Hester glanced up at her friend's raised brows. "Father insisted I learn a little French as some of the medical journals he kept were in that language."

"I fear this may be only the beginning," Hannah Jr. said.

Hester wanted to argue with her but how could she, when she agreed? Would Sarah Cloyce face the same fate, working out Jane Biddle's worst fears?

"What will thee do if...?" Hannah Jr. looked down at her hands, still clenching the untouched cup of tea. "What will thee do if others move on?"

Move on? Did Hannah Jr. mean that some of the Friends were considering leaving the area? Of course she did. Why wouldn't they? She leaned against the edge of the table. "Will thy family go?"

Hannah Jr. met her eyes. "Father and Mother have yet to make that decision, but preparations have been made."

"Of course." Hester scanned the room. Would she have to pack up and leave everything behind?

Theodora awoke, cranky from being wet and hungry, no doubt.

The sound flooded Hester with an odd sense of peace under the circumstances. She wouldn't leave everything behind. If she lost every belonging in the cottage, even Father's medical books and Mother's tatted doilies, it wouldn't matter as long as she had Theodora. Nothing was more important than that.

Where she would go, how she would travel, how would she support herself and her daughter? All of that she could work out in time while trusting the Lord to see her through.

Hannah Jr. had lain awake well into the night for the past several nights, considering all she'd learned, and then pondered even more on her delivery route this morning after Matthew's news had arrived. Through it all, she'd only strengthened her resolve to remain rather than flee to some unknown wilderness to the south, regardless of what Mother and Father decided was best for the rest of her family.

After all, for the livestock, the garden, even the fields, would still need tending, as much as one person could. And how could she leave Hester and Theodora alone? Hester had become like an older sister, Theodora, a treasured niece.

"If thy parents decide to leave, do they have a place in mind?" Hester asked.

"They do." Hannah Jr. put her elbows on the table and leaned forward. "But I have no desire to go with them."

Her friend cocked her head and seemed to peer into Hannah Jr.'s soul. "Would thy decision be influenced by a certain young man in the village?"

"Not by him only." Hannah Jr. wouldn't lie to her friend. "I would worry myself sick if I left thee and Theodora here alone to face whatever may come."

"'Care not then for the morrow, for the morrow shall care for itself: the day hath enough with his own grief.'" Hester shifted Theodora from her shoulder to the crook of her arm, the babe's eyelids drifting shut. "Those words supported me through the grief of losing Timothy. They are wise words. I shall take each day as it comes, and trust in the Lord to see me through." She lifted her face to Hannah Jr. "Thee should do that same. Worry not for me or Benjamin or even thyself, but trust in the Lord."

"I know what thee are saying is right and true, but 'tisn't easy, not with everything happening around us."

"Life is not easy, nor does it get easier as thee travel its paths." Hester rose and put the sleeping babe in her basket, then returned to the table. "I wish it could be otherwise. I have my own fears and have to turn them over to the Lord daily. 'Tis what thee should do as well."

Hannah Jr. hung her head, closing her eyes and listening with her heart as well as her ears. "I know thee are right." She lifted her face with a sigh. "Thee would counsel me to leave with my family, then?"

"Not necessarily. I would counsel thee to listen to the Lord and what He puts on thy heart."

"I have been trying to do that for weeks." Frustration leaked into Hannah Jr's voice despite her best efforts to remain calm. "In regard to my fears for the village and my family and thee, and in regard to my feelings for Benjamin." She pressed a fist to her lips as the last word came out more sob than not.

"Oh, my dear." Hester took her other hand and squeezed it. "I know not what the future holds, and neither do thee, but I will keep thee in prayer to the One who does."

Hannah Jr. held onto her friend's hand as if it were a rope thrown to a drowning person. That was how she felt, like a drowning person, drowning in the fear and uncertainty and unhappiness surrounding her.

When would it stop? *Please, Lord, see us all safely through.*

Chapter 19

MURKY DARKNESS PAINTED THE clouds overhead, dawn's first color-ful strands still well below the horizon. The wagon, driven by an impatient husband, pulled into the Buffums' farm lane, and Hester pointed to the light shining from the window in the back room off the kitchen. "Someone is awake. Stop by that door."

A dog barked from the barn, the black-and-white collie.

Someone opened the back door as they approached, and the other dog, the red-and-white one, shot out and added to the barking.

The human silhouetted by the light of the doorway was familiar, so Hester called out. "'Tis Hester. I need thee to care for Theodora while I attend a birthing."

"Of course." Hannah Jr. stepped off the porch and met the wagon as it rolled to a stop. "Hand her to me." She reached up and took Theodora's basket.

"I packed extra goat's milk." Hester handed down a second basket with the babe's necessary items, since Theodora barely fit in the basket by herself. "The goodwife is a ways out of the village. I may be a while."

"Take all the time thee need," Hannah Jr. said. "Theodora is in good hands. We shall be doting on her *here*." Hannah Jr.'s stress on the last word reassured Hester that the family was not leaving this day, at least.

Hester let out a breath of relief and lowered her voice. "Thee are still in my prayers."

What would Hester do with Theodora without Hannah Jr.'s support during birthings? If the child had not a mark on her body, she could come along. But Hester dared not let one of the new mother's family or a friend tend to Theodora—especially not if they were Puritans.

"Are you ready, Midwife?" The husband who had banged on her door was impatient to be off. He had cows to milk and a farm to run. He'd been very vocal about that on her porch, if silent since then. This one wasn't anxious or worried for his goodwife—only for his own work. But as it was to be his seventh child, perhaps she shouldn't judge him harshly. They were relatively new to the area, and he knew better than she did how easily his wife delivered her babes.

"Indeed." She glanced back down at Hannah Jr. "Thank thee."

Hannah Jr. waved.

The wagon lurched forward and turned in a tight circle. They were back on the road in no time and heading east at a fast clip, which made Hester a little nervous considering the darkness around them. The horses moved out without a fuss. She'd heard their eyesight in the dark was much better than a human's. That, and the silent prayer she sent up, should see them safely arrived.

Donald Hoffman, as he'd introduced himself, said nothing, so Hester felt no need to speak either. A silvery flash lit the clouds, but the delayed thunder was barely audible above the wagon's noises, so the storm was a long way off. Still, the air was heavy, and the scent of rain carried on the breeze.

Approaching storms often heralded a birth. Hester wasn't sure why it happened that way, but she'd driven to many a birthing in the rain or arrived moments before the first drops. Father had once said it had to do with pressure, or so he'd learned from an old sailor who'd been a doctor in his youth.

The farm finally came into view, and her heart sank. Even through the pre-dawn gloom, the house was obviously run down, devoid of whitewash, various items lying scattered around the yard. The barns beyond with their sagging rooflines were no better. A single window on the main floor had a candle shining from it.

Donald stopped the horses, who blew out their breaths and shook their manes. "Go on in the house," he said as she climbed down unaided with things in hand. "The only bedroom downstairs."

As soon as both of her feet were on the ground, he slapped the reins on the broad rumps of the team. "Get up there."

Hester mounted the steps to the porch, grabbing the railing when one sagged alarmingly beneath her. She almost missed the black dog lying beside the door, until it raised its head and growled.

"Easy dog." Every farm had at least one dog, and most of them were harmless enough, but as another shaft of lightning split the sky and the deep rumble of thunder followed, the eeriness of the place made Hester nervous. That was never a good thing. Dogs could detect nervousness and become more territorial.

The door creaked open, and a child of no more than ten stood in the dark entryway. "You the midwife?"

"I am."

"Come in. Ma is needing you."

With another quick glance at the dog, Hester stepped past it, letting out a breath when teeth didn't sink into her leg. The room beyond was dark, but a gentle light came from down a hallway.

"This way." On closer inspection, the child was a girl wearing only a shift.

"Could we not light a candle?" It seemed silly to have to wander through a strange house in the dark.

"Pa says one candle is enough."

Of course he did. He must be as stingy with candles as he was with words. But Hester couldn't allow her ire at the husband to affect how she did her job. "I see. Well, then lead the way."

She followed the little girl into a bedroom lit with exactly one candle, the one in the window. That wouldn't do. Hester needed more light to work by, no matter what Donald Hoffman said.

The woman on the bed may have been anywhere from thirty to fifty. Her hair was braided back and slick with sweat. Her face, in the feeble glow, was grayish and deeply lined. She was the only person in the room.

"Midwife?" The voice was thin and weary, and sent a shaft of alarm through Hester.

"'Tis I. And thy name is?"

"Pearl Hoffman." She struggled to rise.

Hester rushed to her side. "Be easy. Let me help thee."

"Thee? Be you a Quaker?" There was accusation in her tone now.

"We call ourselves the Society of Friends, but others refer to us as Quakers."

Pearl scooted away from her across the bed. "I cannot have a Quaker attend to me."

Hester glanced around the room. "'Twould appear there is no one else. Have thee no family? No friends to assist?"

"Nay. But I cannot have a Quaker."

This was a situation Hester hadn't faced before. She was well known in the area as a Quaker and a midwife. Had no one thought to tell the woman's husband that? Would he even have cared if he'd known?

Pearl groaned and curled around her bulging middle.

There wasn't time to find anyone else. Hester turned to the young girl, but she was gone.

"Pearl, may I call thee Pearl?" Some Puritans were very touchy about names, so Hester always asked.

"Call me nothing. Just go away." The woman groaned again, arms around unborn babe as if to protect it from Hester.

"There is no one else to assist thee. Even thy daughter, who is far too young, has left the room, and thy babe is ready to be born. "

"She is watching over the little ones for me." The woman shot her a glare, a flush of color flooding into her face. "As I asked of her. She is a dutiful daughter." It was good she had enough spark to defend her little girl.

"Then allow me to watch over thee and the new babe, lest thee be all alone."

"How can I trust you? A Quaker?" Another groan grated through her clenched teeth after that question.

"I have a very good reputation in Salem Village with both the Puritans and the Friends. I have delivered half the children now living in and around the village." Hester put her basket on a small table along the wall, then took the candle from the windowsill and put it on the trunk at the end of the bed. "Will thee allow me to see how far along the babe is?"

"'Tis starting to crown, I can feel it."

Hester didn't push the issue. Her husband had said this was babe number seven, so the woman would know. "I brought with me a birthing chair, if thee wish to use it. Or we can deliver the babe on the bed."

"A birthing chair?"

"Aye. I have found it helps many women deliver more comfortably."

"Nay. 'Tisn't natural."

Arguing the naturalness of birthing positions wouldn't win the woman's trust. "Then we shall not use it. Would thee like to take a turn about the room?" Walking often helped, if only to distract the woman from the pain.

"I would like that."

Hester steadied her while she stood, and they walked around the bed and back again twice, until Pearl doubled over, hands grasping the bed's headboard. Hester supported her until the pain abated.

"'Twould seem the babe is ready indeed," Hester said.

"Aye." Pearl's breath heaved out with the word. "That it does. I had not expected the babe this soon, but 'tis a fact I am more than large enough."

Hester helped her back onto the bed, then surveyed the dingy room. "I require more light. Where may I find more candles?"

"Husband does not like us wasting candles."

Hester pushed down her irritation at the man. "'Tisn't a waste if we need it to safely deliver his child, is it?"

Pearl groaned again, eyes shut. When she opened them she said, "There is one in the parlor and one in the kitchen."

"I shall fetch them both."

"He will not be happy with you if you bring them in here."

"Then he will just have to be unhappy with me. I cannot deliver a babe in the dark." Hester left the room. The sky should have been lighter by then, but the storm's clouds had thickened. When another stab of lightning lit the parlor, she located the candle.

Upstairs, a child cried. Someone shushed it, perhaps the one who'd opened the door for her.

The candle in the kitchen was easy to locate on the mantel above the hearth. Hester hurried back to the bedroom and lit them both from the taper there. Once the room was aglow, she laced her fingers in front of her and faced Pearl. "Thee should allow me to see how the babe progresses now."

Another powerful contraction passed before the woman nodded. What else could she do with her child on the way?

The babe was fully crowned, and as it wasn't the first, would likely be born in a matter of minutes. Hester readied the receiving blanket and clean clothes. She poured water from the pitcher on the stand into the basin and sniffed it. It smelled clean. Another woman to help with boiling fresh water was a luxury she didn't have, so it would have to do.

"Midwife!" Pearl's call was just short of a shout.

Hester rushed to the bedside and assisted her into a delivery pose. She took Pearl's hands and placed them on the bed's headboard where she could grip. "Hold on, squeeze as tight as thee must, but relax everything below thy hands and let thy body do its work."

"I know." Pearl panted a few quick breaths. "I have done this before."

The next few minutes passed with Hester encouraging the woman when and how to push as she guided the babe into the world. The babe was smallish, but he tightened his little body in the receiving blanket and then let the whole world know how unhappy he was with his new location.

Pearl stretched to try and see. "Boy or girl?"

"'Tis a fine boy thee have."

"Husband will be happy. He said we had too many girls already."

Hester shot a glance at the doorway, relieved that the little girl in the shift wasn't there to hear that comment. While men typically wished for sons to work alongside them, some went too far and denigrated the daughters born to them with such careless words. It never failed to raise Hester's dander.

"I see no reason he should not be happy with this one. Let me clean him up, and then I shall hand him to thee." The babe howled again at the tepid water, but she bathed every inch after tying off the cord. His dark hair curled tightly against his head, and even after Hester washed it, the curl remained. "He shall be a handsome one, he will."

"Midwife? Something feels amiss."

Hester swaddled the babe and laid it on the bed, and turned to the wide-eyed Pearl. "This is likely just the—" But it wasn't the normal afterbirth. Two tiny feet were protruding. "'Tis another babe." Hester's heart dropped—a backwards presentation. She took hold of the feet and encouraged Pearl to push. The twin slipped into Hester's hands, little more than half the size of the boy crying where he lay.

"I need to hand thee the first one while I work on this one." Hester did, then picked up the other—a girl.

Pearl put the first twin to her breast to quiet it. "Why has it not cried? What is wrong?"

"She is a tiny thing." Hester rubbed the babe with a dry cloth, willing it to take a first breath. She turned the wee girl over, belly to her palm, and patted her back. She was so small...

A squeak, not unlike a mouse, and then a hesitant breath.

Hester raised her eyes to Pearl's. "She breathed." Then she bent over the babe again, rubbing and patting, stimulating the babe to respond. Finally, a thin cry issued forth. Hester breathed a cautious sigh of relief. But the babe was so small. Could she survive beyond her birth?

She moved to the basin and washed the infant. When she got to the babe's hands, she bit her lip to keep from crying out. One of them, the right, was fine, but the left hand was deformed, twisted and thin with fingers that didn't sit on it properly.

A deformed babe born during the witch trials.

"What is it, Midwife?" Either Hester hadn't covered her reaction as well as she'd thought, or Pearl's motherly instincts were heightened. Or both.

Hester swaddled the little girl and carried her to the bed. "She lives, but she is so very small." She met Pearl's eyes and read the fear in them. There was no easy way to tell the mother what needed to be said. "There is more." She peeled back enough of the swaddling to expose the left hand. "Her hand..." There was no need to say any more.

Pearl's eyes filled with tears, but she laid the now sleeping boy on the bed beside her and reached for the girl.

Hester handed her over.

"Once we finish here, Midwife, 'twill be fine. Me and the twins—both of them—we will do just fine." She raised her eyes to Hester. "No need to bother my husband with too many details. I shall deal with all that in due time." Her gaze intense enough to scorch Hester, she added. "No one needs to know any details. No one."

Was this woman the modern-day Jochebed Hester had envisioned at the start of all the witch madness? Would Pearl be able to hide the babe's deformity from her husband—and others—until the witch accusations passed?

"I agree. Thee have my word, before the God of heaven, that I will not tell a soul of thy daughter's deformity." With all her heart, Hester prayed the woman would succeed in keeping the child's secret.

Just as Hester kept Theodora's.

Chapter 20

H ESTER STAYED WITH THE Hoffmans until after supper, which she
prepared with varying degrees of assistance from the six other
children, ranging in age from the ten-year-old girl who had opened
the door to a girl almost two years old, and including another set of
girl twins who were eight years old. Hester's heart went out to Pearl.
How the woman coped with it all was beyond her.

Her initial uncharitable impression of the run-down farmhouse left
her feeling guilty.

Donald Hoffman stomped his feet on the porch before entering. He
was layered in dirt and mud, having worked in the field for the entire
day, even through the brief downpour that morning. Sweat soaked
through his clothing and created a dark ring around the base of his
straw hat. He hung the hat on a peg, exposing dark curls that glistened
with sweat. He scanned the room, the children seated at the table
eating a simple supper of soup and biscuits, then back to Hester.

"Did she have a boy?"

Hester had to rein in her knee-jerk desire to tell him what she
thought of that question, but as with her first thought of the house,
she needed to look at the larger picture. The man had been up since
before dawn to fetch her, and hadn't come in from the fields until now.

He had six—now eight—young mouths to feed as well as himself and Pearl. He was as overworked as his wife.

"Aye, she did. And a wee girl too."

"Twins again, eh?" He shook his head. "The last midwife told us how rare that is."

"'Tis rare, I assure thee, but it can run in families." Father had told her that, not that she'd seen it herself. This was the third set of twins she'd delivered. The other times, she'd half expected there to be two because of the size of the mother and their early delivery dates. If she'd known Pearl beforehand, she might have suspected it in this case as well, or maybe not, since the girl twin was so tiny.

"Are you ready to leave?" He gestured toward the door.

"Why do thee not sit and eat something first?" In the daylight, and underneath the dirt, the man was little more than skin and bones. "And see thy wife and babes. My daughter is in good hands until thee return me." He'd have to return her. It'd been all of five miles from the Buffums' farm, too far for her to walk this late in the day.

He headed down the hall toward the bedroom.

With the help of the two oldest children, both girls, they encouraged the little ones to finish their suppers, then cleared the table and washed the dishes. Hester was starting to grow concerned when Donald reappeared in the kitchen.

"My apologies, Midwife." For a moment, he looked like a chagrinned youth. "I fell asleep on the chair."

"Thee must have needed the rest." Hester ladled a bowl full of soup and put it on the table along with three biscuits she'd held back from the children. "Eat first, and then thee can drive me back to the farm where we left Theodora. They will see me the rest of the way home."

She'd never seen anyone wolf down a meal in such a short amount of time. Hester went to the bedroom to say goodbye to Pearl, but she was sleeping with a babe on each side of her. Hester tiptoed out, her basket and bag in hand, and followed Donald to the wagon.

In the waning daylight, she had a better view of the farm. It was run-down, but the fields were worked, the garden was planted, chickens and geese roamed the yard, and a lone cow stood by the fence next to the largest barn. One cow? To feed all those children?

Hester's heart was touched by this Puritan family who struggled to survive and did the best they could under the circumstances. It wasn't her place to judge them, and the Lord had driven that point home. People like the Hoffmans didn't have time to worry about things like witch trials and accusations. They were too busy worrying about their day-to-day needs.

Maybe that wasn't such a bad way to live.

The morning after Hester had picked up Theodora, after delivering a set of Puritan twins, Hannah Jr. was once again helping Father in the carpentry shop. Since the word of Bridget Bishop's hanging, he'd decided to make more coffins. A grim job, but a necessary one.

"I have been thinking, Father."

He didn't look up from marking the next board laid across his trestle supports. "What about?"

"How will the people of the village know that thee have these coffins made?"

That brought his head up. "Who else would make them?"

"Thee are the most sought-after carpenter in the area, but will some assume thee will not make a coffin for a person who was hanged as a witch?"

"Oh." He set down his piece of marking charcoal. "I see. Will they think me unwilling to sell a coffin for an accused witch's remains? Alexander Osborne had no qualms about asking."

"Aye, but Sarah had not been tried and convicted, only accused."

Father rubbed his jaw. "I had not thought of that." He slanted her a glance. "Have thee landed upon an idea?"

Her cheeks heated at the teasing in his voice, but she nodded. "Much as we did with the orphans, could we not work with the Puritans to get the word out discreetly?"

"I suppose 'twould be easy enough. The doctor for sure, and Thomas Buffington. They proved themselves more than trustworthy in helping us fetch Verity home."

"Thee could speak with the Buffington son who picks up Sarah's order, if one comes this Monday." Hannah Jr. ignored the flash of anticipation that the prospect of seeing Benjamin always brought. "I know not how best to approach the doctor without going into the village."

"Do thee think Hester might approach him for us? 'Twould not seem odd for the midwife to speak with the doctor, I should think."

"I shall ask her on Sunday after meeting."

Father leaned against the board he'd been marking. "Do thee understand why I feel led to do this?"

"Thee are the carpenter. 'Tis what thee do."

"Aye, that, but 'tis even more. Every family should be able to bury their dead with dignity, even if their Puritan church will not allow them to be buried in their churchyard."

Because of their Puritan code of hierarchy, which Hannah Jr. would never understand.

He waved a hand in the direction of the hill where his parents were buried. "Every family should have a place to lay their family members, a place to visit. A place of respect for who they were and remembrance for those left behind. To withhold that, 'tis cruel."

How much would such a place mean to Jane Biddle if, the Lord forbid, her aunt were convicted and hanged for witchcraft?

Father picked up and pointed his charcoal stick at her. "Thee and I have it within our means to help, to be of service to the families who will soon grieve the loss of their loved ones." He pressed his hand against his chest. "I feel it here, that God has called me to do this."

"If thee feel His calling..." Hannah Jr. took a moment to search out the right words, praying silently that she wasn't about to utter them out of any selfishness on her part. "If thee are, indeed, called for this purpose, then how can thee consider moving away?"

Father stepped back and dropped onto one of the stools. "Thee are a wise young woman, my daughter." He shook his head. "How had I not seen that for myself?"

"Perhaps because thee have so much weighing on thy shoulders already."

He rubbed the back of his neck and rotated his head, working out the kinks formed from bending over the wood, no doubt. "A wise young woman, indeed. After we are finished here, I shall speak with thy mother concerning what thee have said."

Hannah Jr.'s cheeks heated again, but this time from his obvious pride in her. It hurt to think that, if she weren't careful, she might do something that would tear that pride away.

Please, Lord, let it be Thomas Jr. who arrives with Sarah's order on Monday.

After supper, the entire O'Sullivan family arrived at the farm. The younger Buffum children paired up with David and Isobel's crew, the older ones running off to the pond, while the youngest played under the shady maple trees. It was hot for the middle of June, so Hannah Jr. prepared cups of cider from the keg Caleb Jr. carried up from the cool cellar. She arranged them on the table with slices of cheese and dried apple rings.

"Hannah Jr.?" Mother called to her. "Come and join us outside where 'tis cooler. Everyone can help themselves from what thee have set out."

To keep the flies away, Hannah Jr. draped a cheesecloth over the food and another over the cups, then she followed the rest of the adults to a shady spot where they could keep an eye on the youngest children while enjoying the evening breeze.

In addition to herself and Caleb Jr., Matthew, Mark, and Mary—the other young adults—all stayed to listen.

Mother spread a pair of old quilts on the ground for the women to sit on while the men sat on the grass.

"Matthew and Mark went to the land Thomas Danforth owns," David said. "Boys, tell us what thee saw."

Only a year apart, the two couldn't look more different, with Matthew favoring his mother and Mark the spitting image of a young David. They shared the duty of retelling their adventures, describing a forest with minimal openings for grazing livestock, a stream teeming with fish and frogs, and the many types of trees from maples and pines to hickory, walnut, and even some butternut, one of Hannah Jr.'s favorites. They'd seen deer and bear, squirrels and rabbit, grouse and turkeys. They'd even crossed the tracks of a moose and calf. The land was rocky in places, and they'd found one shallow unoccupied cave. In short, it had food, water, and shelter. At least enough to keep them through the summer and into the fall.

Winter, however, would be difficult unless they built permanent structures. Since they didn't own the land, they couldn't do that.

The young men had also come across others living in different parts of the forest in separate encampments. The people who had already taken refuge there lived in family groups and avoided the others. Matthew said the place fairly stank of suspicion and fear, nobody knowing who they could trust and who they couldn't. Mark said it was enough to make the hair stand up on the back of his neck.

What had sounded like paradise at first transformed into something dark and disturbing. Hannah Jr. didn't think she was the only one to feel it. Mother shifted uncomfortably as the boys described the people, and Isobel and Mary exchanged worried frowns.

"What say thee?" Father looked at David. "Thee have had longer to think on their report than I."

"'Twould seem we would be trading uncertainty here at home for uncertainty in a faraway place." David leaned back, his arms stiff, hands against the ground, and crossed his ankles. "Between the two, I believe I would prefer to keep my family under my own roof."

"I agree," said Isobel. "I told David the same last evening."

Father turned to Mother next. "And thee?"

"The boys painted a beautiful picture, until it came to the people there." Mother shook her head. "If moving there means living in fear somewhere else, I see no point in it. We can do that here at home."

"Then it looks as if we have reached the final decision," Father said. "We stay on and see this through."

"Unless and until"—Mother looked around the circle—"the houses start burning."

Isobel said, "Agreed," with Father and David nodding.

"Too bad." Mark shrugged. "There were some very large fish in that river down there. I would not have minded a chance to bring a few ashore."

Matthew shoved his brother over onto the grass. "He is right. 'Tis a beautiful land down there. Maybe someday, when things get back to normal, we can make another trip for fishing and hunting."

When things get back to normal.

Hannah Jr. held on to those words. It was mid-June. The rumors of witches had started around the middle of January. Could it only have been five months? It seemed much more. How much longer would it continue? How many more people would be accused? Convicted?

Hanged?

Which families would it touch? Hers? The O'Sullivans? Benjamin's? Hester and Theodora?

So many questions with no answers, but one thing was finally settled. They were staying home. The relief that had flooded Hannah Jr. with Father's decision would have weakened her knees had she not been seated. She didn't want to think too hard about why, afraid that not all of her motivations were as pure as they should be.

Chapter 21

S UNDAY MEETING WENT LONGER than usual. Hannah Jr. did her best not to fidget on the hard bench. The words shared by those who stood were all inspirational. It wasn't that. It was her excitement to share with Hester her family's decision to stay. Hester had arrived just as the meeting started, so they'd had no chance to speak.

Elias Barwick finally stood and called for a last silent prayer.

"About time," Tamson whispered.

Hannah Jr. elbowed her sister and caught her eye, then tipped her chin toward Verity, whose head was bowed, hands clasped in her lap.

Tamson flushed and ducked her head.

How would Mother keep Tamson in line? At twelve years old, her sister was almost to the threshold of womanhood, and she needed a steady hand. Left to her own devices, the girl might... Might what? Fall for a Puritan young man?

Hannah Jr. bowed her head. *Lord, please watch over Tamson and guard her heart. Do not let her have wayward thoughts about anyone Thee would not approve of—* She snapped her eyes open and glanced around. Everyone else was still in silent prayer. Nobody realized that she'd just been shocked to the roots of her hair.

Did the Lord not approve of Benjamin and the other Puritans? Did He only approve of those among the Friends? Were the Friends the only true followers of Him?

The thought made her stomach twist. Surely not. Did Jesus not go to the Samaritans? Did he not eat with tax collectors and sinners? Did He not forgive the robber on the cross and promise him a place in heaven? Benjamin and his family were, at this very moment, worshipping the Lord in their church down the road.

When the prayer ended, Hester came to Hannah Jr. "I must hurry back to the cottage. I did not bring enough supplies for Theodora for such a"—she glanced around and lowered her voice—"lengthy meeting."

"I shall join thee." Hannah Jr. signaled to Mother, waited for her nod, and then followed Hester out to the door. "'Twas rather a long meeting."

"Not that I mind, in general, but Theodora is wet again, and will soon be crying for her milk." There was pride in her friend's voice that plucked the thread of jealousy Hannah Jr. had worked so hard to bury. Once they were on the path and it was just the two of them, Hester stopped and faced her.

"Thee should know, 'twas Thomas Jr. who has been filling Pumpkin's bucket these past couple of days."

"Thomas Jr.?" Hannah Jr.'s heart dropped. "Is Benjamin ill?"

"Nay. I did not mean to alarm thee." Hester jiggled Theodora who was beginning to fuss in earnest. "'Twould seem Benjamin was sent on an errand out of town. He asked his brother to keep filling the bucket for me every morning." Theodora's cry split the air around them. "We should make haste."

Flustered, Hannah Jr. hurried after her friend. Reaching the cottage first, she opened the door and held it while Hester entered and set about changing her daughter.

Surely, Thomas would not have sent Benjamin off on a dangerous errand, but travel during these times had a feeling of unease about it. Hannah Jr. couldn't help worrying as she set out a cold meal of cheese and ham Hester had set aside, along with the dried apple rings and hickory nut scones she'd brought from the farm. "Verity baked the scones yesterday. She seems to enjoy baking."

"She will miss that if thee leave." Hester held Theodora, now dry, and worked the reed to apply milk to the nursing cloth.

"That is my news." Hannah Jr. flashed her friend a grin. "We are not leaving. The decision to stay was made last Thursday."

"Oh, I am so glad." Hester shook her head. "That might be selfishness on my part, but I am."

"As am I."

Hester dabbed a dribble of milk from Theodora's chin. "What settled the decision?"

"Matthew and Mark O'Sullivan went to the place where people are taking refuge." Hannah Jr. explained the situation, the fear and suspicion even there so far from the village and Salem Town. "I think Father's heart was not in leaving anyway. He seems driven to want to help those in need here."

"In what way?"

"He is making coffins."

Hester paused Theodora's feeding and met Hannah Jr.'s eyes. "I am sorry to say, that may be the most comforting thing he can do if things do not change course—and soon." Theodora squeaked, and Hester began feeding her again.

"I told Father I would speak to thee today, to see if thee are able and willing to help."

Hester chuckled. "I cannot see myself with a saw in my hand."

Hannah Jr. joined her in a moment of mirth, then sobered. "We wondered if thee could speak with the doctor and let him know that Father will have coffins made and ready for... for in case they are necessary. I thought 'twould not seem too out of step for thee—as the midwife—to approach the doctor."

"Nor would it be against the decree of the Friends for the rest of thee to avoid the village." Hester glanced up at her. "Speaking of helping people, I had a thought to ask thy father for a favor."

"What do thee need? I am sure he will help if he can."

"'Tisn't for me." A crease marred Hester's brow. "'Tis for the Hoffman family, the one I helped deliver twins for last Wednesday while thee watched Theodora."

"What could Father do for them?"

"They have eight children now, but just one cow, one that looks well past its prime. I know not how Donald feeds the lot of them with so little."

With her cheese sales limited to the Friends and Sarah Buffington, they had more than enough milk for the family and the dairy. Father had three young cows that had freshened in the past fortnight besides Buttercup with her new heifer. The run of late-night calvings had all gone smoothly.

"I shall ask Father about loaning out one of our cows."

"If he agrees, it might be best for me to accompany him to approach Donald Hoffman." Hester made a wry face. "I found the man to be less than personable."

"And yet, thee wish to help him?"

"The Lord convicted me that I was too quick to judge my fellow humans that night."

Theodora spit out the nursing cloth and turned her face away.

Hester set the reed aside and moved her daughter to her shoulder. "She has learned how to let me know when she is full."

"Clever girl." Hannah Jr. touched Theodora's downy head. "'Twill not be long before she takes pap from a cup."

"Do not rush her, please." Hester pointed to a shelf. "There is a pot of plum preserves I have been saving over there. 'Twill go nicely with the scones."

Hannah Jr. set it on the table and sat across from Hester. After a silent prayer except for Theodora's burp, she spread the preserves on one scone and put it on a plate next to a wedge of cheese, a slice of ham, and several apple rings. She pushed it across the table to Hester and filled a second plate for herself.

"About speaking with the doctor, only do so if thee are comfortable making the call. I would not see suspicion cast onto thee."

"Worry not. 'Twould be fine for me to approach him on any number of topics without raising an eyebrow. Several village women will have their babes in summer yet or early fall, as most everyone knows. Should any notice my errand, they would assume my mission applies to my trade."

"'Tis just that we have heard that the doctor's niece is one of the accusers, and if thee should run into her..." Hannah Jr. shrugged.

"'Twould appear their niece has moved in with the Putnams. I overheard my neighbors speaking of that the other day." Hester held up a hand. "I did not mean to eavesdrop, but those two women will speak over the fence just opposite my garden, and I cannot always ignore my work to avoid them."

"I feel better knowing thee will avoid the doctor's niece."

"As do I."

Hannah Jr. picked up an apple ring and twisted it into a figure eight and back again.

"What else is on thy mind?" Hester asked.

Letting the apple ring fall to the plate, Hannah Jr. gazed out the window toward the brewery even though it wasn't in her line of sight. "Benjamin. Did Thomas Jr. mention where he had gone?"

"Nay, and I did not think it my place to ask."

"Nor was it." She had to force herself not to fidget with something else while she chose her next words. "Do thee think the Lord disapproves of the Puritans?"

"What?" Hester's brow wrinkled.

"'Tis just that, as I was praying at meeting, I knew the Lord would not approve of my attachment to Benjamin. It occurred to me that maybe the Lord did not approve of Benjamin at all, or any other Puritans."

"I do not believe that." Hester rose. "Let me put this one down, and we can have a long talk. Just the thing for a quiet Sunday."

Hannah Jr. took heart from Hester's initial response and tried to tame the butterflies in her middle while she waited for her friend to settle Theodora.

The next morning, after rehearsing what she should say several times and reassuring herself that Theodora was properly covered in her sling, Hester hesitated on the doctor's porch. "Shall we see what the man has to say?" When her daughter blinked up at her, Hester drew in a deep breath and knocked.

A woman with gray hair covered with a loose linen cap opened the door. Her face was neither warm and welcoming nor harsh and disapproving, being a somewhat confusing combination of all. "Can I help you?" Her voice was crisp, but not unkind, as her eyes settled on Theodora. "Is your child ill?"

"Nay. She is in good health." Not a wrinkle moved on the woman's face, but Hester continued on. "My name is Hester Fuller, I am the village midwife. I wonder if the doctor might have a moment to speak with me."

The woman pulled the door open wider. "Come in. I shall see if he is busy." She left Hester standing just inside the door and disappeared through a doorway off the kitchen.

The house was larger than the cottage, the kitchen tidy and sparsely furnished. But of course, they'd had Caleb build all their furniture. A crock on the table held a spray of wildflowers, the blooms' scent mingling with the lingering tang of fried bacon.

"Hello?" The doctor came into the room. He looked much the same as when they'd first met, his wispy gray hair uncovered, his waistcoat wrinkled, and a pair of round spectacles gracing the bridge of his nose with kindly blue eyes peering from behind them. "How can I assist you?"

"Thee may not remember our meeting at the mercantile. I am the village midwife, Hester Fuller." She pushed the edge of the sling out of the way so the doctor could see into it. "This is my daughter, Theodora."

"Of course I remember. My goodwife said you wished to speak with me but assured me that your child is not ill. I am glad to hear that. Please"—he gestured to a chair by the table—"have a seat."

"Thank thee." She settled herself and made sure Theodora was comfortable. "I am here are the behest of Caleb Buffum."

"Caleb?" His scraggly eyebrows hiked. "Is one of his family ill?"

"Nay. 'Tis nothing of that sort." She tried to remember the words she'd rehearsed. Why was she so nervous? He was the village doctor, a man dedicated to helping people. Nobody to be fearful of.

He sat back in his chair, laced his fingers together, and rested them on his lean belly. "What is my friend Caleb up to, then?"

His friend? The words she'd rehearsed came back in a flood. "Caleb has been making coffins." She paused when the creases on his face pulled into sorrowful lines.

He gestured for her to continue.

"After Alexander Osborne came looking for a coffin for Sarah, Caleb started building more. He wishes to help those who lose loved ones during this difficult time. Due to the circumstances, he cannot approach the church elders, and he thought perhaps thee might be willing to direct those grieving and in need his way, should a coffin be required." The last words left her in a rush, and she waited while the doctor rubbed a spot on his chest, apparently deep in thought.

"I hate that it has come to this." Sorrow filled his voice. "But I fear Caleb is right. Coffins will be needed." Then he blinked and glanced at her. "Would you like a cup of tea?"

"Thank thee, but I have delivered the message, and I should be on my way." She rose.

The doctor stood and walked her to the door. "I have heard many compliments of your skills as the midwife, but should you ever need me, please do not hesitate to come or send someone for me." Before he opened the door, he brushed Theodora's cheek with a gnarled finger. "An adorable child. I believe I heard that she was a foundling, did I not?"

"She was." Hester offered what she hoped was a natural smile, while inside she fought the urge to hide Theodora and scuttle away. The babe's mark was covered with both her gown and the sling. She was safe. "I prefer to think of her as a gift."

"I would have to agree. 'Tis a fine thing you have done to take her in." He opened the door. "When you see Caleb, tell him that I will"—he raised a finger—"discreetly inform the grief-stricken where to turn for help."

"He will be pleased, I am sure." With a parting nod, Hester walked toward the cottage, relief lightening her steps.

While she'd been to the mercantile with Theodora, she'd not actually sought anyone out before—any Puritan—while holding her daughter. It felt like she'd taken a first step to being just another mother in the village and not an imposter. There was no reason to believe any Puritan would ever see Theodora's mark. No reason to feel as if she needed to keep her daughter hidden away. By helping Caleb, Hester had helped herself gain another layer of confidence. The only thing marring her morning now was the underlying reason for her visit to the doctor.

The coffins.

Chapter 22

H ANNAH JR. SNAPPED HER head up at the thud of hooves outside the open door to the dairy. A moment later, Benjamin appeared in the doorway, and she slapped a hand to her heart. "Thee frightened me."

He slicked the tricorn hat from his curls and held it in front of him. "I did not mean to." He pointed the hat toward the main entrance to the barn. "'Twould seem no one else is around."

"Father and the boys went to help a neighbor gather his sheep that were scattered by a bear."

"I hope they find them all."

"Indeed." Hannah Jr. smoothed her apron. "What can I do for thee?"

He dug a scrap of paper from his pocket and handed it over. "Mother's list." He took a step closer, letting his hat hang to one side.

The flutter overpowered her common sense. More than anything, she wished he'd put his arms around her, hold her as she'd seen Father hold Mother on the rare occasions when they thought no one was looking. Instead, she stepped back. "Where did thee go last week?"

"An errand for my father. Nothing of importance."

Yet she had the feeling he wasn't being entirely truthful, and she'd never felt that way about Benjamin before. Frustrating, even exasperating, and always intriguing, but never evasive. She cocked her head, folded her arms, and waited, a trick that often produced results with her brothers.

He lowered his head and shuffled his feet, but when he looked at her again, the truth was in his eyes. "Father sent me with a load of supplies, carefully hidden under kegs of cider and ale, to a place where people have taken refuge. I should say no more about it. Father was adamant that I not tell anyone."

"I should not have pried."

"'Tis no matter. I trust you will not say ought of this to anyone else."

"I will not." On impulse, she took his hand and squeezed it. He'd been in danger after all. "'Twas a brave thing to do, under the circumstances."

"Nay." He shrugged. "If anyone had stopped me, I had a load of kegs to deliver with its bill of sale. None would suspect that the bottom barrels contained salt pork, corn meal, and beans."

"Would thy father consider helping in another way?" It was the perfect opportunity to ask.

"I am sure he would."

"Father and I are building coffins." She glanced down, and he squeezed her hand. She should pull hers away, but the comfort of his grip warmed a place in her heart. "He asked me to tell thee of that, thinking perhaps thy father could discreetly get word to the grieving families that the coffins are here in the carpentry shop. Father cares not if anyone can pay. He only wishes to do what he can to help."

"He is a generous man, as is my father." His grip tightened. "Two such men will someday come to the conclusion that you and I are right for each other. Mark my words."

Hannah Jr. pulled her fingers free. "Thee cannot know that."

"But I can have faith." This time, he cocked his head at her. "Would it be so bad if you had a little faith too?"

She stiffened. "I have faith in the Lord and wish to do only as He would have me do."

The slow grin that left Benjamin's lips parted sent her flutter into a gallop.

"Then I shall pray all the harder for the Lord to put it into the hearts of two kind and faithful men that their son and daughter were meant to be together."

Despite her best efforts, hope blossomed at his words as she turned away and filled his mother's order.

Hannah Jr. followed Father to the carpentry shop after the midday meal. It was the first time she'd had to speak to him alone. "I spoke to Benjamin Buffington this morning and asked him to let his father know about the coffins."

"What did he say?" Father spread the precut coffin boards on his workbench.

"He said his father will gladly help."

Father took down the small saw he used to cut dovetail joints. "As I was sure he would."

"Yesterday, Hester requested I ask thee for another type of help."

"Oh." He looked up from where he bent over the workbench. "What kind of help?"

"'Tis for the family she assisted the day Theodora spent with us. 'Twould seem they have eight children and only one cow. Hester thought the cow looked quite old."

"They are a Puritan family, I believe she said. Does she wish thee to sell thy dairy products to them?"

"Nay." Hannah Jr. drew her fingertip though the sawdust coating the workbench. "She hoped thee would lend them a cow."

Father straightened. "Lend them a cow?"

"'Tisn't unheard of."

"Between neighbors, Friends we know and trust." His brows drew together. "What do we know of this family?"

"Hester said Donald Hoffman is a prickly sort, but hard working, with more daughters than sons and none of them above ten years old." She offered him a smile. "And with fewer customers, we have more than we need here, especially with the young cows now milking."

"Hannah Jr.?" Mother's voice reached them. "Join me in the garden?"

"Go." Father nodded toward the door. "I can work here on my own this afternoon. I will think on loaning out a cow."

Hannah Jr. stepped outside into the bright sunshine. Tamson and Verity watched the little boys under the shade tree while shelling the early peas they'd picked that morning. The older boys hoed weeds in the cornfield, a never-ending chore lest the weeds steal the moisture so needed for the corn. Mother was almost to the garden when Hannah Jr. caught up with her.

After handing Hannah Jr. one of the hoes she carried, Mother got right to the point. "I saw Benjamin ride to the dairy this morning. Thee were with him for a long time."

Hannah Jr. sank her hoe deep in the warm earth and uprooted a patch of encroaching grass. "He brought his mother's order, but Father had asked me to speak to Benjamin concerning the coffins. He thinks Thomas will help spread the word that Father has them here and ready for... for whenever a family needs one."

"What did Benjamin think?"

"He agreed." She met mother's searching look. "He said his father and mine are both kind, generous, and faithful men."

"That is true." Mother tucked a loose strand of hair under her linen cap, over which was pinned a flat straw hat with a wide brim to keep the sun off her face. "We owe Thomas a debt for his help in rescuing Verity and securing her place with us."

Hannah Jr. straightened and faced her. "Do thee believe Puritans can be favored by the Lord?"

"Oh, my. Where did that question come from?"

"'Tis something Hester and I spoke about yesterday. She believes—and I want to believe it too—that the Lord's favor falls on all who believe in Him, and not just on the Friends."

"Of course it does." Mother whacked at another patch of grass with her hoe. "I know not why thee would think otherwise. The Light of Christ is a gift to any who shall receive it. Surely thee know that."

Hannah Jr. planted her hoe in the dirt and leaned against it. "Then why the disputes between Puritans and Friends?"

"It did not start with the Friends, I can assure thee of that. Oh." Mother stopped her hoe and looked at Hannah Jr. "This has to do with Benjamin."

"I have told him, more than once"—Hannah Jr. kept steady eye contact—"that there can be nothing between us."

"And does he listen?"

Her eye contact slipped. "Not as he ought."

Mother swiped a clod of dirt and grass roots from her hoe with her bare toes. "I know not what to tell thee today. Our world has turned upside down. When this is all over, Lord willing, we should discuss this with thy father."

"Father?" Hannah Jr. took a step back.

"He has been asking questions. Questions I have put off answering." She fluttered a hand in the air. "Which has not been difficult, with everything else going on. But until the situation with the village and Salem Town has been resolved, we will hold our peace."

Hannah Jr. nodded, her throat too tight to answer.

What if Benjamin was correct? Dare she let the hope his words had sprouted that morning take root like the grass creeping into the garden? Or would it, like the grass, creep in and crowd out the good things already in her life?

It would take patience and courage to find out. Hannah Jr. had always had plenty of the former, but maybe not enough of the latter.

Supper was over, and the steamy hot kitchen held little appeal after Hannah Jr. wiped the last plate dry. Tamson and Verity had taken the little boys to the pond to cool off, Caleb Jr. had taken Robert and Joseph fishing and probably swimming in the river, and Father had driven Mother to visit Arthur Stokes. The old man's rheumatism had caused him to miss Sunday meeting, so Mother had made him a tonic and raspberry pie. No doubt he'd get more pleasure from the pie.

Hannah Jr. swiped the table clean. That done, she needed to get out of the heat. She removed her apron and hung it on a peg, then stepped outside. The air was thick with humidity, barely stirred by a languid breeze. From the look of the gathering clouds, they would have a summer storm later.

She strolled to the barn, stopping at the horse corral and watching Dolly and her filly, whom the family called Honey. Tamson and Verity had begged to use that name. The three-month-old horse was growing fast and getting more independent, stretching her short neck, front legs splayed apart so she could crop the grass on the other side of the paddock from Dolly. Father would start hitching Dolly again soon, tethering Honey to her side and letting the youngster learn the role of a work horse even before she was weaned.

Honey jerked her head up, nostrils flared, ears perked toward the road, and let loose a long, high-pitched whinny. Then she kicked her heels higher than her withers and raced across the paddock to Dolly.

Father and Mother wouldn't return this soon—unless something was wrong. At the too-familiar dread that seemed to plague her daily, Hannah Jr. whirled to watch the lane. The single horse and cart were unfamiliar to her, as was the man hunched over on the seat, reins dangling from hands hung between his knees, face hidden by a broad-brimmed hat he wore. The type of hat many of the Puritans favored.

Hannah Jr. cast a glance toward the pond. The girls were splashing in the shallow end while the young boys hunted frogs along the shore nearby, well away from whatever bad news was approaching.

When the cart pulled to a stop, the man lifted his head. He was young, not much older than she, but his expression was drawn, dark circles shadowing his eyes. "The brewer said I should come here." He wiped a hand down his face, looked off into the distance, and then back at Hannah Jr. "For a coffin."

She couldn't stop the hand that flew to her collar. "I am so sorry—" She let the word drag out because she didn't have a name.

"Roger Toothaker, Jr., at your service." He inclined his head. "There is no need to be sorry. My father was estranged from our family for many years. I only happened to hear that he had been accused of witchcraft while visiting cousins in the village."

"He was hanged?" Hannah Jr. shouldn't have blurted that out, but she hadn't heard of any man being hanged or even sentenced to hang.

"Nay. He died in prison of what the jailor said were natural causes." He shrugged. "I have no doubt 'twas true. The last time I saw him, he was not in a good way, from lack of proper food and care."

"How sad."

"As I said, 'twas his own doing, staying away from our family as he did. When I got to the jail in Salem Town this morning, he was dead. To tell the truth, I thought to leave him there for the town to deal with, but when my cousin and I went to the brewery, the brewer said I could get a coffin here." He shook his head. "Even after all these years, our mother would find comfort in burying him nearby."

"Where do thee live?"

"Billerica. I am a doctor there."

Which explained why he understood his father's condition.

Hannah Jr. gestured to the carpentry's door. "The coffins are in here." She opened the door and held it while he climbed down and secured the horse to the hitching rail.

He glanced around the shop, then walked to where five coffins stood upright, tilted against the wall. He chose the one of middle length. "Father was not a tall man, and painfully thin. This one will do." He raised his eyes to her. "How much do I owe you?"

"'Tisn't necessary. Father is making them for the unfortunate people who have been—"

He stopped her with a raised hand as he dug coins from his waist-coat pocket with the other. "I can afford to pay." He dropped several coins on the workbench, then pulled the coffin away from the wall.

Hannah Jr. hurried to take one end and helped him load it on the cart. "Again, I am sorry for thy loss, even if thee were not close."

He touched the brim of his hat. "Thank you." He untied the horse, mounted the cart, and drove off.

How terribly sad. She couldn't imagine a father who had turned his back on his family. She was blessed to have her parents, steady and reliable and committed to their faith and each other. That made it even harder to think about Benjamin and a chance for the two of them.

She would never do anything to disappoint the parents who loved her, provided for her, and had raised her in the community of Friends. When the witch trials were over, if Father wouldn't approve of Benjamin, she would find a way to live a fulfilling life as a single woman.

With a broken heart.

Chapter 23

T HE RATTLE OF A cart out front brought Hester to the window. Instead of a frantic husband fetching the midwife, Hannah Jr. stepped out of the one-horse cart and walked to the door.

Hester pulled it open.

"Thee are arriving in style today."

Hannah Jr. entered. "I thought to save thee a long walk."

"Oh?"

"Father will speak with thee about loaning the cow. Can thee spare the time this afternoon? And stay for supper with us, of course."

When had Hester last had a day out other than delivering a babe? She grinned, feeling a little like a child outside the window of the chocolatiers. "Give me a moment to ready Theodora."

Between the two of them, Theodora was fed, changed, and in her sling. When her basket was packed with the necessities, Hester and Hannah Jr. were in the cart in short order, the steady clop of the horse's hooves taking them out of the village.

"Caleb is agreeable to loaning the cow?" Hester asked.

"He would like to meet the farmer and see the farm for himself, to be sure the animal would have proper shelter and enough area for grazing."

"Of course, 'tis prudent of him." But would he see only the shabby house, the sagging barn roofs, and the unkempt garden that had formed her first opinion of the place? Maybe not, as they would arrive in the daylight, for sure.

At the farm, Caleb ran a hand across his chin. "Hoffman, thee said. I have heard that name not long ago. A farmer with a large family of young children."

"Eight all together, including the twins I assisted Pearl to deliver last week. I should make a visit to see how she is getting on, so if thee will drive me out there, thee could see the place and meet Donald. 'Twould work out well for both of us."

"I can keep Theodora here," Hannah Jr. said.

"Nay," Caleb said. "Let thy mother and the girls do that. I think it best if thee come with us. Thee know the cows better than I and which one might be best to loan him, should we find the situation agreeable."

"I must say, I did not think things would progress quite so swiftly," Hester said.

"Father lets no grass grow beneath his feet." Hannah Jr. chuckled, then sobered. "And in these times, helping others is a way to show the Light of Christ, is it not? I shall pack a basket of cheese and butter for the family."

"I suspect Donald will not look favorably on charity," Hester said, "but if thee were to present it as a gift to the mother, he should not argue it. After all, 'tis common enough for women to help the mothers of newborns."

With Theodora more than adequately entertained by the younger Buffums and supervised by Hannah, Hester slid onto the cart seat beside Hannah Jr., who took the middle of the bench next to her father. It was a tight squeeze, three across, but as soon as the horse started forward at a fast clip, the breeze cooled Hester and brought the refreshing scent of pines and cedars that lined one side of the lane.

Hester had paid close attention when Donald had returned her to the Buffums', and it was a good thing. The farm lane off the main road was almost hidden by a pair of bowed cedars. "There it is." She pointed the way for Caleb.

"I have passed by this many times and never knew there was a farm down that track. I thought it abandoned."

"I suspect it was for some time." Hester leaned forward and spoke across Hannah Jr. "The buildings are not in good shape. I know not how long the Hoffmans have lived here, but I think not very long."

The lane turned, and the house and outbuildings came into view. They looked as sad in the daylight as they had on the stormy night when she'd first arrived. This afternoon, however, several of the children were sitting on the porch, the large black dog with them. As the cart approached, Donald stepped out of the barn, a musket held across his chest. He barked some command, and the children scrambled into the house.

"'Tisn't the best sign," Caleb muttered.

Hester waved, hoping to head off any unpleasantries. "'Tis I, the midwife, come to see how Pearl and the babes fares."

Donald let his arms drop as he walked to the house, the musket hanging to one side. "Aye. Come on up then."

Caleb stopped the horse by a hitching rail that had seen better days. "I am Caleb Buffum. Thee brought Hester and her babe to my farm last week."

"The dairyman?"

"More of a carpenter and farmer." Caleb nodded toward Hannah Jr. "'Tis my daughter, Hannah Jr., who runs the dairy."

The man grunted. "A girl?"

"A young woman, and a very capable one." Hester climbed off the cart and straightened her petticoats. "As thee will know from the basket she has brought for Pearl."

"We have no need of charity." The man's dark brows pulled into a scowl.

"Perhaps 'tisn't a custom where thee are from." Hannah Jr.'s tone was the perfect mixture of kindness and respect. "In these parts, we bring gifts when a new babe arrives. Or in thy case, two of them."

"May I see Pearl now?" Hester took the basket Hannah Jr. had packed from the back of the cart.

"Aye, Midwife." He gestured toward the door with the muzzle of his rifle. "Go on in."

The man's scowl was enough to make Hannah Jr. wish they hadn't come, and the musket didn't help either. Father, however, stepped out of the cart and tied Dandy to the decaying hitching rail before addressing the man again.

"Thee have barns and pastures, yet but one cow to be seen." He pointed to the light brown animal who looked more bones than flesh—the picture of a cow in her declining years.

"She is enough." Donald Hoffman shifted his feet, the musket across his chest again.

That didn't stop Father. "'Twould seem slim offerings with so many mouths to feed, judging by how full the porch was on our arrival."

"'Tis none of your business." The voice was gruff. Final.

Hannah Jr. remained on the cart. Perhaps the whole visit had been a bad idea.

"Not yet, but it could be." Father crossed his arms and planted his feet. "We have a problem on our farm of too many cows at the moment." He pointed to the outbuildings, all of which, as Hester had said, looked to have been abandoned for years. "Thee have space and adequate grazing, while we are in danger of pouring milk out on the ground."

"How can you have too many cows?" Distrust radiated from the man like the summer sun off a flat rock.

"Thee must have heard of the goings-on in the village and Salem Town, have thee not?"

"That witch business, aye." Another grunt. "I have no time for such."

"Nor I. But it has affected Hannah Jr.'s dairy. I cannot allow her to deliver her butter and cheeses to the goodwives of the village anymore." Father leaned toward Donald. "As a father, I am sure thee understand."

That earned Father a jerky nod, as if the man were unfamiliar with such a motion.

"So thee see the problem. If I could loan out a pair of young cows, with their calves at their sides, until the village settles down, 'twould save us having to waste time milking cows only to empty the buckets on the ground."

Donald shot a glance at the barns and the pasture beyond, then back to Father. "Why me?"

Father relaxed and leaned against the hitching rail. "Hester thought thee would be a good person to approach. I can see she was right about the work thee have put into the place in such a short time." He pointed to the fields planted with corn, rye, wheat, and beans. "'Tis a lot of work for one man."

"My sons are not yet old enough to be much help." The scowl was gone. A thoughtful gleam in his eye, Donald's voice remained less than friendly. "Milking two cows, even with calves to help, would add work to my day."

Hannah Jr. sat straighter on the cart seat. As much as she didn't want to, she felt the nudge Father often talked about prompting her. "Hester said thy eldest daughter is ten years old. 'Tis the same age I began milking cows. I would be happy to show her how to do it."

Donald leaned the musket against the upright post of the hitching rail. "For how long would I keep them? I cannot put up enough hay by myself to see too many animals through the winter."

"With the Lord's help," Father said, "only until the snow flies." The two men worked out the details of bringing the cows over, and Hannah Jr. agreed to come with them and help the eldest daughter learn to milk, even though she was not comfortable with Donald Hoffman, his gruff voice, or his unfriendly manner.

But after that nudge she'd felt as surely as if the Lord had put a hand to her heart, she knew it was the right thing to do. She'd prayed for a way to be helpful, useful to others, and He'd provided.

Never had she thought it would be to a disagreeable Puritan farmer.

Hester walked past the dog and tapped on the door. It was opened by the same girl as before, only this time she was fully dressed with a linen cap covering her hair.

"May I come in and see thy mother?"

"Aye." She opened the door wider and turned to say over her shoulder, "'Tis the midwife, Momma."

Pearl appeared, wiping her hands on a piece of toweling. "Welcome." There was hesitancy in her tone, perhaps even fearfulness.

Hester smiled in what she hoped was a reassuring manner. "Hello, Pearl. I thought to come and see how thee and the babes were doing. I like to assure myself that all is well after a birthing."

"All are fine here."

"I am happy to hear it." Hester handed her the basket. "This is from Hannah Jr., who owns a dairy about five miles from here. She asked me to bring it in to thee."

Pearl took the basket and moved the cloth covering aside, her eyes widening as they met Hester's again. "We cannot accept this."

"Of course thee can, gifts to the mother of a newborn is a custom here."

It was obvious that she wanted to accept.

"Thy husband did not object to me bringing it into the house."

The stiff line of Pearl's shoulders eased. "I know not what to say, 'tis such a bounty."

"One thee will enjoy. No one makes a hard cheese like Hannah Jr." Hester glanced around the room at the children watching in silence. "May I see the babes?"

"Of course." Pearl set the basket on the workbench, then whispered something to the eldest girl before leading Hester to the same bedroom where she'd delivered the twins.

They were snuggled together in a single cradle, the boy curled almost protectively toward his wee sister.

"They both have good color and round tummies." Hester pressed her forefinger against the boy's hand, and he curled his fingers around it. Then she did the same with the girl. Neither awoke, but Hester was satisfied. She nudged her finger against the girl's deformed hand. Although those fingers didn't open or grasp, the hand moved away from her touch, so it had feeling.

"How has thy family reacted to her hand?" Hester asked in a low voice, lest any curious children be lurking in the hallway.

"Husband saw it just yesterday. It did not seem of great concern to him. Had it been the boy..." She let her sentence trail off.

Hester could finish the thought. Donald wasn't concerned about a crippled girl, but a boy who couldn't work would have disappointed him. As callous as it sounded on the surface, the man needed strong and able sons to help him work the farm.

"The girls think her the sweetest of babes, and in truth, she is a happy one. She rarely cries or fusses. The boy, on the other hand, wants what he wants when he wants it and lets the whole house know." Pearl's voice was filled with pride in her children.

The boy would likely take after his father, then. Hester turned her attention to Pearl. "And thee? Have thee enough milk for both?"

Pearl nodded, but the knot on her brow said there was more.

"Thee can tell me. There are things to do which can help bring in more milk."

"'Tis just that I worry. They do not require much now, but when they do, will I be able to feed them well enough? I am not as young as I was with the first set of twins."

"Eating dairy products is the best, like the cheese we brought. Thee must make sure thee eat some and not feed it all to the children. Thee should drink at least a small cup of milk every day."

"Our cow did not breed in the fall." Pearl shrugged. "Husband says she is too old. She gives maybe half a gallon of milk a day. I save it for the children. I know not what we shall do when she dries up altogether."

What a load of worry the poor woman carried. "Caleb Buffum, the man who drove me here, and his daughter are speaking with thy husband now. Caleb has too many cows and hopes to arrange with thy husband to keep some here for a while."

Pearl pressed a hand to her mouth, eyes brimming, but no tears fell. When she pulled her hand away, her voice was barely a whisper. "'Tis an answer to my prayers."

Hester folded her hands at her waist. "The Lord uses people to do that, I believe."

"I owe you an apology, Midwife, for the way I spoke to you when you arrived that night."

"Worry not. 'Tisn't the first time a woman in the throes of delivery has said things she regretted after."

"I was not prepared for you to be a Quaker, and I had always been told Quakers were heretics and worse." Pearl covered her mouth again, taking a moment to either collect her thoughts or control her emotions, Hester wasn't sure which. "You were so comforting and kind that night, not only with the babes, but with my other children and even my husband. I am ashamed."

Hester gripped Pearl's arm. "Thee need not be. 'Tis all forgotten. I knew thee to be a good woman when thee did not flinch at thy daughter's deformity."

"And I knew you to be a good woman when you did not either."

Hester nodded, her own throat tight with unshed tears. It wasn't often that a Puritan called her "a good woman," and it touched her. Deeply. It also gave her hope. Hope that someday the gap between the Friends and Puritans might be bridged once and for all. Maybe not in her lifetime, or even Theodora's, but someday.

Chapter 24

T HE SECOND HALF OF June passed without a birth, without any new witch accusations of the villagers, and without a drop of rain. Hester walked along the rows in her garden, ladling out water to the parched plants while it was still early morning, before the sun could steal the moisture away. She sent a silent prayer of thanks for the Buffington brothers who made sure Pumpkin's bucket was filled every morning, as well filling the bucket she kept at the back door and used to water the garden. She still needed to load Theodora into her sling and carry water for her household needs, but having the other two buckets filled eased her workload.

Hester paused and wiped the back of her wrist across her sweaty brow. She shot a glance at Theodora in the shade on her blanket and gasped. Lying on her tummy, the little girl held her head up and gazed around. She was growing up far too fast. Hester had marked April twenty-second for Theodora's birthday, the day she'd arrived on the porch. Today being the first day of July, that made her ten weeks old.

Ten weeks of motherhood, and Hester couldn't imagine not having Theodora in her life.

Pumpkin's head snapped up, ears perked toward the gate at the forest path, and she let out a garbled *baa*, her mouth full of the weeds she'd been browsing.

A leafy bush just beyond the gate swayed, but there wasn't a whiff of breeze. How odd. Hester dropped the ladle into the bucket and went to Theodora, scooping her off the blanket.

It was far too early for Hannah Jr.'s Tuesday visit, unless she'd started well before dawn to escape walking in the heat of the day. Except, Hannah Jr. didn't emerge from the forest.

Nobody did.

Pumpkin dropped her head and returned to browsing, but the hairs on the nape of Hester's neck tingled. Several minutes passed while she scanned the area, looking for so much as a leaf out of place. Finally, reassured with Pumpkin was no longer interested, she moved Theodora's blanket to the very edge of the garden, within easy reach, and finished watering her plants.

Perhaps it had been nothing more than a stray dog or a large bird that had launched into flight from the bush. She wanted to believe that. Yet with all the accusation and talk of witchcraft, it was hard to ignore the feeling of dread that had assailed her in that moment. Was there something evil lurking out there?

Hannah Jr.'s head was still spinning with the news they'd received last night.

Father and the boys had returned after helping repair the neighbor's fence that the wandering bear had torn apart a fortnight ago. They'd brought bad news home with them. Five more of the accused women had been tried and convicted of witchcraft in Salem Town—including Rebecca Nurse and Sarah Good, both from Salem Village.

They were sentenced to hang on the nineteenth of July.

In the weeks that had passed since, Hannah Jr. had hardly been able to concentrate on assembling her orders to deliver to the Friends who remained her loyal customers. Every time Rebecca came to mind, her eyes filled with tears. That dear old woman had never said a bad word about anyone, much less acted maliciously. The injustice of it all robbed Hannah Jr. of peace.

Or maybe it was knowing that she and Father would need to finish more coffins—and soon.

A shout arose outside, happy greetings from her brothers. The voice that called out in answer caused a familiar flutter in her middle. She rushed to the open door of the dairy.

Benjamin sat on his white horse, tall and straight with his tricorn hat at a jaunty angle on his ebony curls, speaking with Robert and Joseph. Why was he here on a Tuesday? If he had business with her and the dairy, he was lucky she hadn't started her deliveries early. As it was, her baskets were almost packed and ready to go.

When he looked her way, she stepped back into the building. Even though Mother had said they'd speak with Father, that wouldn't be for some time yet. And it certainly didn't guarantee he'd be open to the idea of his daughter and a Puritan man, even the son of his Puritan friend.

She'd just tucked the last few items from her list into the second basket when the floor creaked behind her. Taking a calming breath, she turned.

"I apologize for coming a day late, but Father could not spare me yesterday. Thomas Jr. is down with a summer cold. Mother insisted I make time to come today." He drew a scrap of paper from his waistcoat pocket. "I fear her list is rather long."

"I hope I have enough on hand to fill it." She took the paper and scanned it. "We are short two cows at present, but I can fill this, as long as I can substitute plain soft white cheese for the herbed."

"I am sure that will be fine." He poked a thumb toward the cow's pasture, the corner of which was visible from the open doorway. "Did you lose two cows?"

"Nay. We loaned them out."

He cocked his head. "Is that a common practice?"

"I do not believe so." She busied herself putting Sarah's order together. "But the family had a need, and with my customer list shortened, we could afford to share them."

"'Twas your idea, was it not?" Was that admiration in his voice? "You found another way to help someone in need."

"Nay." Hannah Jr. looked up and met his brown eyes. "'Twas Hester's idea. She knew of the need and thought we could help. Father was agreeable." She gave him an impish grin. "Even though the family is Puritan."

His chuckle was deep and rich and caused the flutter to speed up to an alarming rate.

Then he sobered. "At least someone is still doing good around here. Have you heard the news?"

Hannah Jr. nodded, her teasing wiped away. "I am heartbroken for Rebecca Nurse."

"As are most in the village." He shrugged. "Father is more agitated than I have ever seen him. I think he worries lest someone were to point a finger at Mother."

"Oh, I pray not." Hannah Jr. pressed her hand over her heart. "We Friends live with the same fears, so I do understand."

"As of yet, not a single Quake—Friend has been accused. Have you not considered why?"

"Father has thought about it, even spoken with the doctor on the subject. I do not believe either found any comforting conclusion. But I pray 'twill continue." She motioned for him to hand her the sack dangling forgotten by his side. "I also pray every day for thee and thy family."

"As I pray for you and yours."

"Now." She picked up her two delivery baskets. "I must be about my deliveries. As it is, I am late today."

"I wish I could offer you a ride, but..."

"But 'twouldn't be proper." She faced him then, allowed herself a moment to enjoy just being with him, and then smiled. "I am glad thee came today. Tell Thomas Jr. I hope he gets better quickly. Summer colds are dreadful things."

"I shall tell him." A sheepish expression added a ruddy hue to Benjamin's cheeks. "He knows about us, you know. Well, about my feelings for you."

"Thee told him?" It shouldn't shock her. Did her own siblings, at least Tamson and Caleb Jr. not also know?

"We are twins. I did not need to tell him, he just... he knew."

She mentally shook herself and stepped toward the door, passing him on the way out of the dairy. "I must be on my way. Take care, Benjamin, and stay safe."

"The same to you. I know not what I would do if I should lose you."

Lose her? He did not yet have her to lose. At least, not more than her heart.

"Rebecca Nurse too?" Hester thumped onto the chair so hard that pain shot the length of her back and into her neck. If the chair hadn't been there, she'd have sprawled on the floor.

"Are thee all right?" Hannah Jr's rushed to her side.

"I think so. But Rebecca Nurse? She is a harmless old woman. I do not understand how anyone could accuse her, much less convict her. 'Tis wrong. Horribly wrong."

"They did not convict her at first." Hannah Jr. took the chair beside Hester. "Father said she was found not guilty, but when the spectators at the trial raised a loud protest, the judge demanded a reexamination of the evidence. They discovered one question she had not answered, and convicted her because of that alone."

"She was all but deaf in one ear and hard of hearing in the other." Hester dropped her face into her hands, as if hiding her face could stop the horror of what her young friend had shared. "I cannot believe it."

"I wish I could not." Hannah Jr. slumped against the back of her chair, making it creak.

Hester raised her head. "Thee must be exhausted, walking thy deliveries around in such heat. Would thee like a cup of tea?"

"Water would be better. I am parched."

"Of course." Hester rose and waited on her.

Hannah Jr. took the cup of water and drank it down. "I am supposed to be helping thee, not the other way around."

"Today, we shall help each other." Hester refilled the cup and handed it back. "Five women to hang all on the same day." A shutter ran through her. "What a ghastly spectacle that shall be."

"Father started making extra coffins this morning. He was working on them when Benjamin arrived for Sarah's order." Hannah Jr. ducked her head. "He came a day late because his brother was too ill to work in the brewery yesterday."

Hester leaned forward. "I thought thee had decided to dissuade the young man for good?"

"I had, but Mother said something to me."

"What did she say?"

Hannah Jr. raised her eyes to Hester's. "She said when all this is over, Lord willing, we will discuss the issue of Benjamin with Father."

"Oh." She took the younger woman's hands. "That does not mean he will accept the idea of thee and Benjamin, only that thy mother is willing to discuss it with him. Do not get thy hopes too high."

"I know, and yet..."

"And yet, how can thee not?" Hester squeezed her hands, then let go. "I understand. Truly, I do. I will pray for thee every night, I promise."

They spent the rest of the afternoon cleaning and cooking, then Hannah Jr. milked Pumpkin and carried water to the cottage before she left.

Once Hester was alone with Theodora, she had plenty of time to think about what was happening over in Salem Town. Sarah Good was a disagreeable woman at best, but hardly a witch. If she had been, she'd have spit her venom over the village long ago, so much did she dislike the people around her.

But gentle Rebecca Nurse?

Tears streamed down her face as she put Theodora to her shoulder and rocked her. What hope was there in this world for such an injustice to occur? What hope had any of them? Had she been right to stay in the village? The feeling as if something evil lurked just beyond her back gate that had assailed her that morning threatened to overwhelm her again. Should she pack up her things and find somewhere else to live until everything came back to rights?

Lord, I know not what to do. Give me Thy direction, and not my own.

Theodora burped and then cooed, her little hands grasping Hester's neckline and tugging.

"Thee are interrupting a prayer, my dear." She put her nose to her daughter's. "I am fairly certain the Lord will understand—this time. He is a loving heavenly Father who wants only the best for His children. Even when they misbehave." As they were in Salem Village and Salem Town. Hester would trust Him to see her through, whether she was to stay or to run, she would leave the matter in His hands. Where else was she to find peace in such a time?

Chapter 25

J ULY NINETEENTH, IN THE year of the Lord, 1692. Would anyone in the village ever forget the date? Would anyone in all of Massachusetts Colony?

Hester pushed her half-finished basket to the middle of the table. Her heart wasn't in working on it. Or doing anything else. She picked up a fan she'd made of birchbark laced to an oak stave and waved it in front of her face.

The date five women—two from Salem Village—were hanged for witchcraft in Salem Town.

Theodora awoke with a squall, no doubt hot and sweaty along with wet and hungry.

Hester tended to her, then moved to the rocking chair until the little girl burped. She was starting to take notice of the world, lifting her head from Hester's shoulder and focusing on the things nearby. The smallest things could fascinate the precious little girl, and this afternoon, it was the ties on Hester's linen cap. Pudgy fingers grasped the narrow linen strips and tugged them toward her mouth.

"Thee are no longer hungry." Hester untangled the fingers from her ties. "But if thee are going to be awake for a while, we should visit the garden and remove a few more weeds."

After letting the goats out to browse, Hester spread a blanket in the shade for Theodora, then knelt beside her herbs and worked on removing the weeds that insisted on growing there. Seed bounced over and sniffed at the babe. Hester would need to ask Phoebe about weaning the young goat. She'd no idea when it was normally done. But then Pumpkin would be all alone, and somewhere in her memory was a tidbit about goats needing to be with more of their kind. She'd ask Phoebe about that, too.

The neighbor's porch creaked, and then a shadow fell over the back of Hester's garden.

"Good afternoon." It was her gossipy neighbor, who had never approached or spoken to her in the backyard before.

Hester tried to remember the woman's name but came up empty. She stood and brushed the debris from her apron. "Good afternoon. Can I help thee?"

"Nay. 'Tis just that..." The woman looked around and then came closer until she pressed against the fence that separated their yards. "'Tis just that I have seen a man lingering around your back gate."

"A man?" That tingle was back at the nape of Hester's neck. "Do thee know him?"

"He remains in the shadows, you know." She pointed to the bush Hester had seen move a fortnight ago. "So I have not had a good look, just the outline of his wide-trimmed hat. It could have belonged to any farmer in the colony."

Hester wiped her damp palms against her sides. "Thank thee for telling me."

"I worry about you, I do. Living here all alone with just the babe." She tipped her chin toward where Theodora was entertained by watching Seed, who grazed nearby. "'Twas a generous thing you did, taking in a foundling."

Hester suppressed her annoyance at that word. "She is a blessing."

"Of course she is. 'Tisn't the child's fault that someone cast her aside, poor little mite."

"The man"—Hester needed to change the conversation before she took offense at whatever the woman might say next about her daughter—"when have thee seen him? How often?"

"Let me think. The first time was about a fortnight ago. Then again a few days after, and last evening he was there again when I poured the wash water on my garden. I called to my husband, but before he joined me on the porch, the man had moved away."

Three times. The tingling grew to a ripple that wormed its way down Hester's neck.

"A dog would be a comfort, if you had one."

"Indeed." Where would she find a dog, and how would she feed and care for one along with Theodora and herself? Already, her coins were dwindling with no births, and her baskets were collecting dust in the short hallway because she had no way to get them to Salem Town.

Seed wandered away from Theodora, and the little girl cried.

"Excuse me. I must see to her. Thank thee for telling me. I shall be on the alert from now on."

"I will tell my husband to keep his eyes open," said her neighbor.

She scooped up Theodora, then herded the goats back into their shelter before practically running into the cottage and shutting the door. What reason had anyone to watch her?

Unless they were intent on finding a reason to accuse her of witchcraft.

Hannah Jr. spread small clothes on the bushes to dry in the morning sun, but the normalcy of that chore did nothing to dispel the oppressive feeling that had nothing to do with the heat and humidity—and everything to do with what was happening in Salem Town. She laid out the last from her basket and turned to Mother.

"Is it not odd how, in the beginning, we feared what was happening in the village every day. But now, 'twould seem we almost forget about it until something like this."

"We have learned to live with the evil happening around us as long as it does not touch our family." Mother shook her head. "I am not sure that is a good thing. Nay." She sighed. "I am fairly certain 'tis a bad thing."

"Would it be better to live in fear and worry daily?"

"Better? That is perhaps not the right way to think of it." Mother smoothed the last piece of toweling over the laundry rope, then picked up her empty basket. "We should always be aware of what is happening around us. We should be watching for the opportunity to do a good turn for others, and always we should be sensitive to the direction of the Lord. If we forget about the bad things happening to other people, we could miss those things."

"Yet, if we dwell on the fear, we might be afraid to step up should we be needed, would we not?"

"Thee are asking such deep questions." Mother walked toward the house, and Hannah Jr. followed. "I suppose the hangings today have us all questioning."

"I wonder if there is more I could be doing."

Father and the boys were working in the fields. The garden had been weeded the day before and wouldn't need to be picked again until Monday. Their laundry was drying in the breeze. Hannah Jr. was even caught up on work in the dairy. Time was heavy on her hands, giving her too much opportunity to think about what was happening in Salem Town.

"Have thee been back to the Hoffmans' since taking the cows over and teaching the young girl to milk?"

"I have not. Tess learned quickly. I did not think I needed to return."

Mother stopped and turned to her. "Why do thee not pack a basket with whatever thee have extra in the dairy? Take Tamson and Verity, and go help Pearl Hoffman for the day. 'Twould take thy mind off Salem Town, and I am sure 'twould bless the woman."

"Leave thee alone to feed Father and the boys?"

Mother gave her a wry grin. "I am sure I can handle that task."

"Of course." As much as Donald Hoffman had frightened her on her first visit, when they had delivered the cows, he'd been perfectly polite. She had no reason to be reluctant. "Then I shall tell the girls and fill a basket."

Half an hour later, they were on the road with Dandy and the cart.

"Why are we going to work at someone else's farm?" Tamson asked.

"Pearl Hoffman has a house full of young children and no one to help her." Hannah Jr. put as much cheerfulness into her tone as she could. "We are going to be a blessing to her today. I know not what we will be doing, exactly. We shall ask her what needs attention the most."

"I think 'twill be nice." Verity looked up at her from her position in the middle of the seat. "I like to meet new people."

"Donald Hoffman can seem rather..." Hannah Jr. searched for the right word. "Rather reserved. Not a man given to many words, for sure."

"And his wife?" Tamson asked.

"I have not met her, only Donald and the oldest daughter, Tess."

"How old is she?" Verity asked.

"About thy age, I would guess." Hannah Jr. smiled at Verity's squeal of delight. "Hester said there are eight children in all. Two of them are newborn twins."

"Like Benjamin and Thomas Jr.?" Tamson's eyes danced with teasing mischief.

"Nay. Not like them at all. One is a boy, and the other a girl, brother and sister twins."

Verity let her chin droop to her chest.

Her hands full of the reins, Hannah Jr. nudged the girl's hunched shoulders. "What is wrong?"

"Nothing." The little girl's voice was a whisper on the wind.

"She gets that way when she thinks about her brother and sister," Tamson said. "'Twill pass soon enough."

Hannah Jr. had almost forgotten that Verity had a previous family, so smoothly had the girl fit into theirs. She gave another nudge. "'Tis good thee remember them, even if it makes thee sad for a few moments."

Verity nodded, wiped the back of her hand across her eyes, and then smiled up at Hannah Jr. "I am glad thee and Tamson are my sisters now."

Hannah Jr. nodded, her throat too tight to speak.

They reached the overgrown turn onto the farm's lane.

"It looks spooky," Tamson said.

"'Tis only because no one has trimmed the branches." Hannah Jr. turned the horse into the lane and started down it. "Donald has been too busy getting his crops in the fields and tending them to work on the lane, I would imagine. I should warn thee, the house is also in need of work. The Hoffmans have not lived here long, and with Pearl giving birth last month, well... thee will see. There is much work to be done."

Donald was in the field along the lane, and when they came into sight, he walked toward them, a scowl creasing his face. "Have you come for the cows?"

Tamson and Verity shrunk against the cart seat's backrest. Hannah Jr. didn't blame them. The man was intimidating. But she stopped

Dandy and tried to be as calm as Mother would have been. "Nay. We have come to see if Pearl needs a hand around the house. We have finished our chores for the day."

The man removed his wide-brimmed hat, wiped his forehead, and resettled it. He glanced at the house, where four of the children sat on the porch, a black dog with them. "I guess that would be all right."

"Thank thee." Although why she should thank him for allowing them to help his wife, Hannah Jr. wasn't quite sure. But she steered Dandy toward the house and let out a deep sigh.

"He is a fright," Tamson said.

Verity bobbed her head in response, glancing behind them at Donald, who had resumed working in the field.

"Nevertheless, we are here to help Pearl, not him."

The dog growled as they climbed off the cart, but a little girl in faded blue dress shushed it.

"Hello." Hannah Jr. smiled at the trio of girls and one boy, Tess not among them. "I am Hannah Jr. and these are Tamson and Verity. We have come to help thy mother today."

"I shall fetch her." The oldest one sprinted into the house.

The youngest poked a thumb in her mouth and held out a hand to Verity.

Verity took the little hand in hers and let herself be drawn down to sit beside the girl and pet the dog, its tail thwacking against the porch boards.

"Hello?" A lean woman with a babe in her arms came to the door.

"Thee must be Pearl." Hannah Jr. introduced herself and her sisters. "Mother suggested we come and offer our services to thee today. We have finished our chores at home, and there is plenty of day left to be productive."

"Oh. My." Pearl took a step back and allowed them to enter the kitchen, where Tess and another girl were washing dishes, the shorter one standing on a crate to reach the basin. "I know not what to say."

"Say that thee will allow us to work here." Hannah Jr. smiled. "Verity is particularly good with young children, while Tamson and I know our way around cleaning a house."

"'Tis so generous of you..." Her words trailed off when a babe wailed from down the hallway.

"Can I take that one while thee tend to the other?" Tamson held out her hands.

"His name is Charles." Pearl handed the infant over. "The others can introduce themselves." Another cry had her heading down the hallway.

"Momma is very busy." Tess turned, drying her hands on a scrap of toweling. "I remember you. You taught me to milk the cows." There was pride in the girl's voice. "We get buckets full of milk every day now. All we want to drink and more left over for the porridge and sometimes a hasty pudding."

"That is wonderful." Hannah Jr. looked around the kitchen. It needed a good scrubbing from top to bottom, and that's why they'd come. Within minutes, she had the younger children organized with Verity in charge of Charles and Emma, the infant and a toddler, and Tamson heading outside with Molly and George, both old enough to help set the porch and yard to rights. That left her and Tess with the eight-year-old twins, Gretta and Lena, to attack the kitchen.

One thing was for sure, by the end of the day, she'd have no energy left to worry about what was happening in Salem Town.

Chapter 26

H ANNAH Jr. HAD SEEN her little brothers both bathed and put to bed early, so they'd be ready for meeting in the morning. She had also bathed, washing away the sweat from working at the Hoffmans' all afternoon. Sleep was all she longed for when a knock came on their door. She pulled the curtain aside from the upstairs window, looking out into the inky darkness of a cloud-covered night.

A wagon pulled by two heavy horses stood outside the back door. It looked like the brewer's wagon, but she'd heard no bells, not even the jingle of the harnesses.

She pulled a wrapper off its peg on the wall and tugged it on while she hurried downstairs. Thomas's voice reached her at the doorway to the kitchen.

"The boys came to me for help, and I could not refuse them." All levity was gone as the big man shook his head, dark curls so like his sons' but showing the beginnings of gray swaying with the action. "To treat anyone that way, 'tis a disgrace."

Mother came up behind Hannah Jr., put a hand on her shoulder, and addressed Father and Thomas. "What has happened?"

"The hangings today." Father met Mother's eyes and then Hannah Jr.'s. "They cut the dead down and threw their bodies into a rocky ravine, then told everyone that they were not to be properly buried, by decree of the court, but left to rot and be eaten by wild animals."

"How could they?" Mother moved past Hannah Jr. "'Tisn't decent."

Caleb Jr. entered the kitchen, with Robert and Joseph behind him.

Tamson and Verity had been so tired from working at the Hoffmans', Hannah Jr. hoped they would sleep through the noise.

"The women were excommunicated from the church upon their convictions," Thomas said. "The church will not allow them burial in the churchyard."

"But to leave their bodies to lie on the open ground"—Mother shook her head—"'tis barbaric."

"No offense to the Puritan church, Thomas," Father said.

"None taken. I quite agree. 'Tis why I came myself to get a coffin. The Nurse grandsons are in the wagon. We shall go from here to the place where they threw the bodies and bring them out. At least, the two we know. I would retrieve them all, but I suspect the other families will do the same, edict from the church or no."

"Thee can bury them properly, even if 'tisn't in the churchyard," Mother said.

"Thee will want two coffins," Father said. "One for Rebecca and one for Sarah."

"Indeed, if you have two on hand."

Father gave the man a sad smile. "I have that many and more." Then he turned to Mother. "I will go with Thomas to retrieve the bodies and help the families bury their dead."

"I can help," Caleb Jr. said.

Mother stiffened, and Hannah Jr. could almost feel the protest that never came to her lips.

"Nay," Father said. "I may not return until the morning. I need thee here to see to the farm."

Mother took a deep breath. "Be careful. All of thee."

Someone had lit several candles in the kitchen. Hannah Jr. took one and followed the rest outside. No wonder she hadn't heard anything. The bells had been removed from the harnesses, and rags were wrapped around the chains that connected the leather straps to the doubletree and the doubletree to the wagon.

The young men in the wagon were not familiar to her, so must have been the Nurse grandsons. Francis Nurse, Rebecca's husband, sat on the seat. He was well into his seventies, too old and frail to attempt such a thing on his own.

Father led the way to the carpenter shop, the wagon following.

Mother put her arm around Hannah Jr. and urged her back into the house. "Come into the parlor with me. We shall pray for them until thy father returns home." Unspoken was the underlying danger.

If they were caught retrieving the bodies, they would be arrested by the authorities in Salem Town. What would the charges be? Disobeying the court, for one. Could they be charged with stealing the bodies? Even worse would be if they found themselves charged with... She failed to stifle a shudder as the word filled her mind.

Witchcraft.

Dozing in the chair despite her efforts to stay awake and pray, Hannah Jr. was startled at another knock on the door. Had the men returned? But Father wouldn't have knocked. Fear had her on her feet, while Mother was already crossing the hall to the kitchen. Hannah Jr. took a minute to light another candle with the stub she'd brought from the parlor.

"Hester?" Mother's single word was filled with relief.

"I am sorry to bother thee, but babes will come in the dark of night."

Hannah Jr. hurried to the door. "'Tisn't a bother." She took Theodora, who blinked a few times and then settled on her shoulder. "I shall be praying for the mother and child."

"Thank thee." Hester handed a basket to Mother and hurried back to the cart waiting for her in the yard.

Mother shut the door and pressed a hand to her chest. "I thought..." She heaved a sigh.

"As did I." Hannah Jr. rested her cheek against the babe's downy head. "I am so relieved."

"I will be, once thy father is home." She looked around the kitchen. "Should I brew us a pot of tea?"

Hannah Jr. lifted her head and nodded. "I am sorry for falling asleep when I had intended to pray until they returned. Perhaps the tea will help."

"I nodded off myself." Mother looked out the window. "Clouds are covering the stars, but it must be well past midnight."

"They likely had to wait until the lights went out in the houses around the town before they dared to move the bodies." Even saying that made Hannah Jr. shiver. It was one thing to see a dead animal—she'd seen more than her share of them—but a human body? One made in the image of God? She shivered again.

"I know." Mother set the water to heat. "'Tisn't likely they will return before dawn."

Hannah Jr. pulled a blanket from Theodora's basket and settled the sleeping child on it. She was too big to fit comfortably in the basket anymore. How she envied the infant's blissful sleep.

Her only comfort that night was that Benjamin hadn't been part of the mission to retrieve the bodies.

Guilt picked at her for thinking that way.

The cart bounced over a rut in the road, almost unseating Hester.

"I am sorry." James Rupert shot her a rather frantic look. "I cannot see the ruts in the dark, and they do not bother the horse." But he didn't slow the vehicle, his grip firm on the reins held in front of him, his jawline stark even in the darkness. This might be his fourth child, but it was Martha's first, and he was worried.

Hester estimated it to be around two in the morning, but without the moon or stars visible, that was only her best guess.

They were traveling south, and suddenly, out of the darkness loomed a large wagon pulled by a team. Other than the clomp of the horses' hooves, it made no sound.

James pulled the cart to the far side of the road to let the larger vehicle pass, shooting her a glance.

When the wagon rolled by, Thomas was driving with Frances Nurse beside him. Caleb Buffum sat on the edge of the wagon's bed. He dipped his chin at her, then shook his head slightly. Why was the wagon silent? Where were the brewer's bells? A Puritan and a Friend, working together in the dark of night. What were they up to?

Whatever it was, Caleb didn't wish it to be made known.

"That was odd." James sent the horse forward again. "I wonder what they were doing out at this time of night. 'Twas the brewer driving, was it not?"

"I believe so." Hester wouldn't lie, but she could soften the truth. "In the dark, I may have been mistaken."

James urged the horse to go faster. "'Tis no affair of mine." He shook his head. "'Tis a good time to keep one's head down and mind one's own business, I say."

"Thee are a wise man. I shall endeavor to do the same." She flashed him a grin she hoped seemed genuine. "And our business is to see thy wife and child safely delivered."

"Aye." He slapped the horse with the reins again. "Get up there."

Hester tightened her grip on the seat. But for all her brave words, she couldn't help but wonder what those men were doing, Frances Nurse especially. A man of his age and frail health shouldn't be out in the middle of the night. He must be deep in grief. Why, just that afternoon poor Rebecca had been hanged.

Caleb—the coffins. Of course. They must have brought Rebecca's body home. But why in the dark of night? And why had Caleb shaken his head at her?

They reached the Rupert's farmhouse, and Hester climbed off the cart, taking her basket and canvas bag. Whatever was going on out there this night was none of her concern. For the next few hours, she needed to concentrate on the woman inside and the babe about to be born.

Dawn was still an hour or so away when Theodora awoke, wet and hungry. Hannah Jr. raised her head from the table, her neck stiff from having fallen asleep on her chair. She rubbed the grit from her eyes and stood, scooping the infant from her blanket. "Hungry already?"

"I am." Caleb Jr. entered the kitchen. "Any sign of Pa yet?"

"Not yet." Mother rose from the rocking chair by the hearth. "Go on and start chores. I shall see to breakfast."

Robert and Joseph came into the kitchen, each snatching a thick slice of bread before following Caleb Jr. out the door, both dogs on their heels. Tamson and Verity arrived, looking refreshed after their full night of sleep.

"Verity, will thee roust the little boys and bring them down this morning?" Hannah Jr. asked.

"Is that Theodora?" Verity came and peeked at the child Hannah Jr. was feeding with the reed and nursing cloth.

"Indeed. Thee can hold her after the boys are up and about."

With a grin, the young girl raced up the stairs.

"I believe Theodora will sup from a pap cup before long," Mother said. "She is growing like those weeds in the dill patch." She raised an eyebrow at Tamson.

Her sister hung her head. "I will dig them out this morning."

"Until then"—Mother pointed to the large mixing bowl—"start a batch of biscuits."

They were almost done preparing the meal when the back door opened. The boys had gotten through chores in record time. Hannah Jr. turned to ask if anything was wrong, but it wasn't her brothers standing in the doorway. "Father."

"Caleb?" Mother spun from the hearth, petticoat flaring too close to the fire.

"Have a care, my dear." Father came into the kitchen. "I have returned unharmed and wish not to see thee go up in flames."

Mother folded her hands at her waist, the picture of calm, while inside she must be as weak with relief as Hannah Jr. was. "Did all go well?"

"It did." Father collapsed onto his chair, a weary groan escaping. "But I hope 'tis the only time we must do such a thing."

"What did thee do?" Tamson asked.

"Helped a neighbor." Father yawned, his jaw cracking. "And lost a night of sleep."

"Why do thee not go up to bed?" Mother asked. "Thee can sleep for a couple of hours before we must leave for meeting. I will keep a plate warm for when thee are fully awake."

"Wise advice." He stood and left the kitchen.

Mother watched his exit with a wrinkle on her brow. "Will thee finish breakfast, girls?" At their nods, she followed Father up the stairs.

Would this be the only time Father would need to undertake such an errand? Or was this only the beginning?

Chapter 27

MARTHA WAS YOUNG AND scared but also determined. Hester's heart went out to her. While she administered to the laboring woman, she also prayed that the Lord would give her a perfect peace about being a second wife. Life was hard enough without being in competition with the dead.

"Oh, Midwife, that one was the strongest yet." Martha had one hand on the wall, steadying herself, as Hester supported her on the other side.

"Thee are almost there." Sunlight streamed through the bedroom window, as it had for several hours. The labor had been long, but not overly hard. Until now.

Not for the first time, Hester wished Martha had another to comfort and help distract her, but with no siblings and her own mother long dead, she was at the mercy of friends and neighbors. Hester blamed the hangings on Friday for keeping everyone close to home. One more reason to be angry at what was happening in Salem Town. It didn't stay there. Its evil ripples were scouring the countryside.

Martha bent double, as nearly as she could around the tight bulge of her middle, her groan rising in urgency.

"'Tis time for the birthing chair." Hester ushered her to the corner where she'd set up the apparatus. "Remember how I told thee it would work?"

Martha nodded, her bottom lip caught between her teeth.

"Thee must let thy body relax and not fight the contractions but work with them. 'Tis a rhythm of life. Embrace it as much as thee can."

In a quick motion, Martha grabbed Hester's arm and drew her close, until their foreheads almost touched. "Promise me, Midwife." She groaned and panted through another pain. "Promise me, if the babe be born dead, you will not bury it until I have seen it." The grip on Hester's arm tightened. "Promise me you will not let my husband bury the child until I have held it in my arms."

"Of course not." Hester knelt so she could look Martha directly in the eyes. "I would never do that, not to any woman. But hear me now. There is no reason to think this babe is anything other than alive and healthy and beautiful."

"My neighbor thought the same a few months ago." The words came out filled with anguish. "She fainted at the birth, and when she came around, her husband and the babe were gone. He buried the child alone. I could not abide that, Midwife, I could not."

Hester had done her best to push James Rupert's words out of her mind, ever since he'd mentioned what his neighbor had done. A child who must be her Theodora. But she couldn't dwell on it now.

"As I understand it, that woman had not a midwife with her. Thee do." Hester eased her arm out of Martha's grip and took her hands instead. "I will see thy child safely into this world unless the Lord wills it otherwise."

"Then let us pray that He will not!" The words came on a cry as another contraction gripped Martha.

While it went against her upbringing, Hester prayed out loud, "Lord, we ask Thee to deliver this babe into my hands, a hearty and healthy infant to bring joy to James and Martha."

Martha's cry of "Amen!" was followed by her bearing down.

Within minutes, Hester caught the babe in the receiving blanket. He was wrinkled and red and squalling his protest of the birth for the whole house to hear. She smiled up at Martha. "A boy, and as perfect as any I have seen."

The tears coursing down the young woman's face couldn't mask the joy. "I did it."

"Of course thee did. And a good job of it, too."

Once the babe was cleaned and swaddled and the mother cared for, Hester allowed James in with the three older children for a quick peek. "Now thee must let her rest." She shooed them from the room. Her basket and bag already packed, she followed them out. "I shall walk home so thee can stay with her and the children." She would be too late to join Sunday meeting, but she could be home before Hannah Jr. arrived with Theodora, as she almost certainly would.

"No need, Midwife." James dug coins from a crock on the mantel and passed them to her. "My neighbor has offered to drive you home." He gestured to a man seated on a chair at the table. "This is Jonah Cooke."

The man raised his face to her, and from underneath his broad-brimmed hat, Hester looked into eyes so like Theodora's that she pressed a hand to the pain lancing through her chest.

Hannah Jr. went upstairs to fetch a pair of socks for Jonathan, who had shown up barefoot in the kitchen on a Sunday, the one day they wore shoes in the summer. As she passed her parents' room, Father's voice carried to the hallway.

"Thee could not imagine the scene, nor will I describe it to thee."

It was wrong to listen in on a private conversation, but the door wasn't fully shut. Hannah Jr. stopped, then took a step closer.

"Can we hope that 'twas a one-time thing?" Mother's voice was lower, but still easy to make out.

"Nay." A weary sigh followed. "Thomas is sure the madness has only just begun. He is as worried as we are, for the village, for his family, for the whole colony."

"Thee are still sure we should stay?"

"I am. Especially as I learned from Thomas and Francis that this has spread as far as Boston now, with accused people in the jail there."

"Oh, Caleb. When will it stop?"

Fear pebbled the skin on Hannah Jr.'s arms, her punishment for listening in.

"We must pray daily—many times a day—for the Lord to intervene." The bed ropes creaked. "Which I will do after I get some sleep. Wake me in time to leave for meeting."

Hannah Jr. crept away and shut herself in the room she shared with Benji and Jonathan. Thomas was worried for his family—which included Benjamin. She pressed the backs of her fingers to her mouth. Prayer was the answer, as Father had said, but would those prayers be answered before anyone she loved was accused?

On wooden legs, Hester followed Jonah—undeniably Theodora's father—to the wagon that waited outside. Everything in her had wanted to shout *Nay!* when James had introduced them. But to do so would have brought forth questions she didn't want asked. Questions she didn't want answered.

She climbed onto the wagon before he could offer to help her. His touch might break her resolve to remain silent.

He got on the other side, unwrapped the reins, released the brake, and clicked to the matched pair of sorrel horses. The animals trotted out while the silence wrapped around like a wet cloak, but Hester kept her lips pressed together. That lasted until the farmhouse was out of sight and thick forest banked the road on either side.

"Midwife, you know not who I am."

"I think I do." She refused to look at him directly but caught his grimace from the corner of her eye.

"Then you must think me an awful person."

"'Twould be my preference to think of thee not at all." She was never rude, but this man had thrown his child away. How did that make him anything but a monster?

"I am forever in your debt." Jonah slowed the horses to a walk. "Your reputation is such that I felt you were the right person to leave her with. Everyone speaks so highly of you that had there been time, I would have fetched you to attend the birth."

What was she supposed to say to that?

"I must also apologize for frightening you."

Frightening her? She snapped her head up and faced him. The wide-brimmed hat, so common it could have belonged to any farmer must have been worn by the man who the neighbor had seen watching her. The man who had made her skin crawl with fear.

"Aye. 'Twas me watching from the forest path." He shrugged. "I wanted only to see that the girl was doing well. When there was no public outcry, I knew you had not revealed her..." He didn't finish his thought.

"Her birthmark." The words left Hester in an angry rush. "Thee tossed aside a child for a common *birthmark*."

"I—" He clamped his mouth shut and stared straight ahead.

That was fine. Hester had no desire to hear him justify his decision.

"I wish I had not done so." Jonah's voice took on a more forceful tone.

"Do thee mean to claim her now?" Fear sprang into Hester's throat. "After all these weeks? Will thee wrest her away from me?"

"Nay." He stopped the wagon and faced her, his face awash with emotions she could only guess at. Shame, grief, maybe regret. "My wife is with child again. 'Tis best she never know the truth. 'Twould crush her if she knew what I had done, even though I did it for her, to keep her from facing what the church might do to the babe. Would almost surely have done, under the circumstances. Nay. I do not wish the child back."

"Theodora." Hester said the name clearly. "Her name is Theodora."

That brought a flicker of pain to the man's eyes.

Instead of feeling justified or satisfied, Hester regretted her words. More than her words, her thoughts, her feelings. What right had she to pronounce judgment upon another? Was not the Lord alone the only rightful judge of mankind. Was Hester acting any better than the so-called court in Salem Town? Shame washed over her.

"In fact"—Jonah got the team moving again —"we will move to the Carolinas after this child arrives, to be near my brother and his family, where there can be no way she will ever see the child, even on the street in the village."

"That is good." Hester clutched her basket tighter, needing the feel of something solid and familiar. "Because Theodora looks so much like thee, sooner or later, thy wife might wonder."

The man bowed his head and closed his eyes, covering them with a gloved hand. When he raised his head again, he looked at Hester. "I will not come to see her again. I know she is in the best of hands and getting the best of care. I look forward to the coming child. The Lord has granted me another chance."

"Do not fetch me when thy wife's time comes." The words came from Hester's heart. "Do not make me attend to a woman thee have lied to. In that act, thee have included me in the lie. I am not sure I could keep silent with her. But in the village, to all else, I will not reveal thy secret. Thee have my word on that."

"For that as well, I will forever be in your debt."

"Thee have given me a daughter I otherwise would not have had." What to say next? It wasn't her place to absolve him of guilt any more than it was her place to judge him. But she needed to close the matter for herself. "As far as I am concerned, it more than cancels thy debt."

Above his neckcloth, his Adam's apple bobbed a few times, and then he nodded.

They continued in silence right up to the cottage. When he jumped down to assist her, this time, she allowed it. He dropped her arm once her feet were on the ground.

"Love her well."

"I already do."

With that, he climbed back and slapped the reins on the horses' rumps. The wagon lurched forward, taking a large chunk of Hester's worry and uncertainty with it.

Theodora was hers forever.

Pumpkin's deep-throated *baa* sounded from behind the cottage.

Hester opened the gate and entered the back yard to see Hannah Jr. coming toward her with Theodora in her arms.

"Thee look particularly happy this fine day," Hannah Jr. said. "'Twas a good birthing, then?"

"'Twas." Hester didn't try to lessen the smile that stretched her cheeks. "A fine boy to add to the family, and the young mother doing well."

"Thee must be exhausted after being up all night."

Hester should be, but she wasn't. How could she be when her foremost thoughts were that Theodora was hers forever? When she had the assurance there was no stalker? She was safe enough to stay in her home with her daughter. As safe as anyone could be in Salem Village.

"Come in. I am more hungry than sleepy." She took a closer look at her friend. "But thee have circles under thy eyes. Was Theodora troublesome last night?"

"Nay. She was an angel. There were, however, other things happening last night."

Memory flashed back to the wagon with Thomas, Francis, and Caleb, as well as several others aboard. "Let me make us some tea, and thee can tell me what has happened."

Even if it were vile news, how could it erase her happiness over Theodora?

Chapter 28

H ESTER ROCKED THEODORA. EVEN though the infant was fed and dry and tired, she fussed in the heat. Sweat plastered the gown to her back. With every window thrown open, the cottage was like a bake oven. Hannah Jr.'s report of what had happened in the night only added to the general discomfort.

"My heart grieves for Frances Nurse and for Sarah Good's husband, although I have never met him." Hester gave up the rocking chair and instead paced with Theodora in her arms. "To lose someone in such a dishonest way, for I can call it none other, and then to have their bodies treated so callously—'tis one of the most evil things I have ever heard."

"Mother and Father agree, as do I." Hannah Jr. paused while putting away the remains of their simple Sunday meal. "And as I said, thee must keep this to thyself. Father shared none of it at meeting, nor will he, I think."

"Perhaps thee should not have told me." It had certainly brought her feet back to earth after learning Theodora was to remain hers forever.

"Thee are already involved, since thee approached the doctor for Father."

Involved. Not a word Hester relished when it came to the situation in the village and Salem Town.

Theodora cried again, kicking against Hester in her unhappiness and discomfort, blissfully unaware of the evil happening around them. Oh, to be a babe in all her innocence at a time like this.

"Why do we not take her outside and let her rest in the shade?" Hannah Jr. asked. "There is a bit of a breeze, at least, and she might settle there."

Hester squashed the momentary spike of inadequacy that still plagued her sometimes. The suggestion was both logical and practical, born of years of experience when Hannah Jr.'s siblings were babes.

Hannah Jr. walked out to release the goats for grazing while Hester spread a blanket in the shade near the garden and settled Theodora on her belly where she could reach the grass. Her little fingers grasped the green blades and let them go, repeating in a motion that seemed to soothe her.

Hester walked to the garden's edge, and Hannah Jr. joined her there. "My plants need water." She gazed at the cloudless sky. "But there seems no hope for that today. I shall have to water in the evening, and perhaps again in the morning lest some of these wither and die."

"'Tis the same on the farm. Tamson and Verity and I have been watering most mornings. Except for yesterday, when we went and cleaned house for Pearl Hoffman."

"Thee did?" She wasn't surprised Hannah Jr. would do such a thing, but she was surprised Donald and Pearl had allowed it. Donald because of his deep suspicion of others, and Pearl because she'd worry her youngest daughter's deformity would be discovered.

"Indeed." Hannah Jr. shook her head. "'Twas hard to know where to start, but we got the kitchen and parlor cleaned. I hope to return and tackle the bedrooms, if time allows and if it suits Pearl for us to do so."

"The family needs help, but sometimes 'tis difficult to admit it."

"Aye, but do thee know what I think?" Hannah Jr. turned to face her. "I think Donald is not so much disagreeable as he is protective of his family. I wonder if something happened in their past that made him the way he is."

"Everyone is the product of their upbringing and experiences." Not that Hester was fully convinced about Donald. He was hard working, no doubt, but also gruff—and what had Hannah Jr. called him? Disagreeable. Yes. He was that and more. But perhaps she should consider

Hannah Jr.'s insights as well. There was always more to a person than what one saw on the outside.

"Hello?" The gossipy neighbor waved at them then hurried toward the fence. "I just wished to tell you, my husband and I saw no one around your back gate last evening. We knew you to be gone, so we kept an eye out." She gave a decisive nod.

"Thank thee, but there is no need." Hester smiled, and it came from deep within at the memory of her talk with Jonah Cooke. "I have learned who it was, and he will not be there again."

"Who was he?" Of course the old gossip would ask.

"A nervous soon-to-be father." That much was true. "A Puritan from south of here." Also true. "He wished to reassure himself that I would be a good midwife when the time comes." Not even close, but the woman was like a bloodhound on a trail, and it should throw her off the scent.

She put her hands on her hips. "'Tis just like a man to do something like that, scaring the life out of a person instead of taking the direct route to address the issue."

"Indeed." Hester was about to make some polite excuse to move away, when the neighbor gasped and covered her open mouth with her hand, eyes focused behind Hester.

Hannah Jr.'s breath hissed between her teeth.

Dread climbed from Hester's heels to her heart. She turned as if mired in knee-deep mud.

Seed, the gangly young goat, had joined Theodora as she often did, but to Hester's horror, the animal had pulled Theodora's gown up—

Exposing the birthmark.

"The Lord preserve us."

The neighbor's voice brought Hester out of her trance. "Hannah Jr., will thee take Theodora inside?" Then she whirled back to face the woman and whispered, "'Tis nothing but a common birthmark. I have seen the like many times over the years."

"Aye." The woman dragged her attention away from Hannah Jr. and Theodora and back to Hester, keeping her voice to a whisper as well. "I have seen the same. But in this village? At this time? 'Tis clear why the babe was left as she was."

"Indeed." Fear clawed at Hester, and she cleared her throat. "But I will protect my daughter. If thee must spread the word of her birthmark, at least give me time to get her away, I beg of thee."

"Spread the word?" Eyes flashed wide as the woman took a step back, shaking her head. "Never."

Disbelief must have been written clearly on Hester's face, because the woman came close again, keeping her voice down. "I do not agree with what is happening in this village, what happened to poor Goodie Nurse." The anguish on the woman's face was too deeply etched to be fake. "I will not subject a poor foundling to the same inhumane treatment. Nay. I will not."

Hester reached across the fence, and the neighbor took her hand. "We are in agreement then. We will work together to safeguard the innocent life of this child."

"Indeed. We shall." The fingers around Hester's tightened. "Not even my husband will hear of this, I vow before the Lord."

That was a solemn pledge from a Puritan, one she wouldn't make lightly, one she wouldn't break without having to repent before the Lord and in front of her church. Hester knew enough of their teachings to understand that.

"Many of the Puritans look down on your people, Midwife, but I know the good you have done for the women of the village and the surrounding area. Now I understand even more the selfless risk you are taking to keep this child. I am not blinded by your beliefs, even if they do not match my own. You can trust me."

Could Hester truly trust the woman with Theodora's life? She seemed sincere. But what about the next person who saw the birthmark? How long could Hester keep others from finding out?

Her mind still in turmoil over the events of the previous day, Hannah Jr. leaned against the work table in the dairy and drew a hand across her brow. That anyone knew of Theodora's mark was unsettling enough, but a Puritan woman? How could that not end in a bad way?

And yet, Hester had seemed to come to terms with it, had chosen to believe the woman's pledge to keep the secret.

Hannah Jr. yawned. She would wager her best petticoat that Hester hadn't slept any better than she had. The heavy drizzle outside was a welcome relief from the July heat and the crops needed the water, but the gentle patter would lull her to sleep if she wasn't careful.

"Hello?" Benjamin stepped into the doorway, water dripping from his tricorn hat and cloak.

"Come in, where 'tis dry." She looked over his shoulder. "Did no one greet thee?"

"I expect they did not hear Blaze on the softened ground." He took off his hat and pushed the cloak back over his shoulders. "But I do not mind being able to speak to thee first." She had enough brothers to recognize the mischief in his grin.

"Thee should not make a habit of coming to the dairy alone."

He spread his hands, mischief gone and replaced by studied innocence. "'Twas not my intention, 'tis only how it happened."

Bantering with him about the propriety of the situation would just prolong it. "Have thee thy mother's list? I have other things to do this day." She held out a hand.

Sobering, he passed it over with a sack he withdrew from under his cloak. "I wish I had other things to do."

"Is business slow at the brewery?" She scanned the list, all items she had enough of.

"Nay, business is as brisk as ever." His tone didn't indicate any satisfaction with that.

She glanced up. "What else would thee do?"

"I wish Father would have allowed me to accompany him and your father the other night to retrieve the village women's bodies."

"Nay, Benjamin." The words were out in a rush. "'Twas a dangerous thing they did. I am glad thee were not involved."

His smile bloomed for a moment, then fell away. "I like that you are concerned for me, but I dislike feeling useless when I could be helping to make a difference."

"Thee are. The water for Hester—"

He waved her words away. "I mean, make a difference in the witch hysteria—that is what the doctor calls it. I would do something to help those who are falsely accused." He lifted one shoulder and let it drop. "Which is probably all of them."

"Indeed. But thee are not a village elder like thy father. 'Tis best to leave such things to those in charge."

"Perhaps, but—"

"Benjamin?" Caleb Jr. entered the dairy with Robert and Joseph close behind, crowding the small space. "When did thee arrive?"

"Only just." Benjamin nodded toward Hannah Jr. "Your sister has not yet finished filling my mother's order."

Hannah Jr. turned back to the work table, more to hide the heat flooding her face than to finish filling Sarah's sack, but she help from peeking back over her shoulder.

"The boys and I are planning on fishing this evening," Caleb Jr. said, "at the bend in the river west of here."

"Join us." Robert shouldered past Caleb Jr. "Bring Thomas Jr. too. The fish should be biting after this rain. They often do."

Joseph nodded, his straw-colored hair somewhat contained in a queue. It had grown long enough since he'd been living at the farm to adopt the more mature style.

"My fishing pole is broken," Benjamin said, "and I have not taken the time to fashion a new one."

Caleb Jr. cuffed the taller young man on the shoulder. "Come with me. I have an extra one thee can borrow."

With a wry glance in Hannah Jr.'s direction as he settled his hat on his head, Benjamin followed her brothers back out into the rain.

Hannah Jr. leaned against the work table again. As if she hadn't fears enough with Father going out on dangerous errands and Theodora's birthmark having been revealed to the neighbor, now Benjamin wished to get involved in helping the accused.

Three days had passed, and Hester had hardly drawn a full breath. No knock had come to her door. None had been there except for Hannah Jr. on her usual Tuesday after deliveries. The neighbor had kept her word, allowing Hester to work up the nerve to tend to her garden while it was cool in the early morning. Monday's rain had caused more than the vegetables to grow, and she needed to hoe out the weeds.

With Theodora settled on her blanket and Seed tethered to the fence on the opposite side of the yard, Hester attacked the encroaching grass and sprouting weeds with determination. She was halfway down the first row when the front gate squeaked.

Benjamin came through with a bucket in each hand. He startled at the sight of her, and then smiled.

"Thank thee for the water—again." She should find some more substantial way of expressing her gratitude, but she doubted the young man would want one of her baskets and he certainly didn't need her midwife services. Not yet, anyway.

"'Tis no bother." He poured the first bucket into the one she kept on the porch, and then emptied the other for Pumpkin. He touched his hat with two fingers was retracing his steps to the gate when someone else came through.

The girl, maybe twelve years old, crossed her arms and glared at Benjamin. "What are you doing here at the midwife's, Benjamin Buffington?"

Hester was a little taken aback that the girl could tell one brother from the other so easily, but more so by the belligerence in her voice and stance. What right had she to address anyone in such a way?

"I brought water for the midwife, as I do every morning." He moved to walk around the girl, but she stepped in front of him again. "What business is it of yours?"

"Business enough with witches all around the village." The girl glared at Hester, then noticed Theodora on her blanket. "A babe?"

Fear clawed at Hester like the hoe through weeds. Why had she come outside this morning?

"Aye, a babe." Benjamin moved, but the girl blocked him again. "Let me pass."

"Why would you help a Quaker woman with a babe, I wonder?" The girl's voice took on a tone that raised the hairs on the back of Hester's neck. A tone full of judgment.

"Again, Ann Jr., 'tis none of your business." Benjamin's voice reflected his frustration, but there seemed to be another edge to it. Then the name struck home.

Ann Jr., as in Ann Putnam, Jr. One of the afflicted girls. One of the chief accusers.

Hester dropped the hoe and scooped up Theodora.

Benjamin, having seen her, moved closer as if to protect her.

Oh, no. He shouldn't have done that. Fear kept Hester from saying a word, although she'd no idea what needed to be said, what could change the course of events unfolding before her.

The girl's eyes narrowed into slits. "You must be the babe's father. This Quaker woman must have bewitched you."

Chapter 29

"THEE ARE IN DANGER, as am I." Hester threw whatever she could fit into her two largest baskets and stuffed every last coin she had into the pocket tied at her waist. "I will ask thy father to drive me to the Buffum farm for now, but thee must also seek a place of shelter."

"Ann Jr. is but a young girl."

Hester whirled and faced him. "It has been young girls—including Ann Jr.—who have started this whole muddle. Take her words not lightly. She means thee harm."

His face paled, but he took the two full baskets she handed him. She fitted Theodora into her sling, then grabbed her midwife basket and the canvas sack with the birthing chair. Wherever she wound up, she would be able to ply her trade.

"Come." She headed for the door, his footsteps following. "If thy father will not help, and I will lay no blame at his feet if he declines, I shall stash two baskets in the forest and return for them when I can." Then she stopped, a hand on the open door's frame. "What shall I do with Pumpkin and Seed?"

"Someone will get word to the woman who owns them," Benjamin said. "I will make sure of it."

"Once again, I owe thee a debt." She let out a sigh mingled with frustration and fear. "I have repaid thee by allowing suspicion to be cast upon thee."

"'Twasn't anything you did. 'Twas this village and the vile things happening within it." His words were sincere, but there was an underlying thread of something else. Fear, probably. He'd be a numbwit not to be fearful, and he wasn't that. "'Twas you she accused of witchcraft."

Indeed. While Hester might have stayed and fought the charge that was sure to come against her, how could she? If she were taken to the prison, they would take Theodora with her, as they had taken the babes of other accused and jailed women. Once there, they would find her mark and...

She stepped outside and Benjamin followed, closing the cottage door behind them. The click was so final. The chances of her ever coming back were slim. A knot formed in her throat. All her work to build a life of helping women deliver their babies, a life where she could support herself and her child, was crumbling away beneath her feet.

"Midwife?" She hadn't realized she'd stopped walking, but the question in Benjamin's voice brought her back to her mission—getting them all somewhere safe.

"I am fine. We should take the back way to the brewery, away from the eyes of others." Hester cast one last look into the goats' shelter. She'd have to start boiling oats for Theodora again, but it couldn't be helped. The thick oat broth would be easier for the babe to sup from a pap cup anyway, and she was old enough to start trying that as opposed to the nursing cloths.

They circled the village, avoiding being seen. Benjamin changed direction a couple of times. The young man knew the back ways better than she did, so she followed his lead. The normal three-minute walk down the street to the brewery took them closer to twenty. Hester's arms were aching by the time they reached the house behind the brewery. Benjamin opened the back door and ushered her into the kitchen.

"Benjamin?" Sarah Buffington hearth. "What has happened?" She dropped the spoon she'd been holding into a kettle, the resulting splash sending liquid to sizzle in the fire below. She hustled across the room.

"I do not wish to worry you—" Benjamin began.

"You already have." Sarah cut him off. "Tell me plainly. What has happened?"

With each word from her son, Sarah's face creased deeper into despair until she had both hands pressed to her cheeks, as if to stop the story. "I cannot believe this." She faced Hester and Theodora. "I know this to be a lie, but there are others who will believe anything those girls say. What can we do?"

"Is thy husband home?" Hester asked.

"Indeed." Sarah turned and called toward the doorway, "Abigail?"

A young girl, about the same age as Ann Jr., and looking like a younger version of Sarah, came into the kitchen.

"Fetch your father. Tell him to make haste." Sarah turned back to Hester. "What will you do? Where will you go?"

"Emily, my sister, married a sheep farmer near Milford in Connecticut Colony." The plan had started to come together on the walk around the village. "She is quite a bit older, but she will give Theodora and me shelter until I can get established and on my own again." And she was a long way away, unlike Hester's brothers, who lived too close to Salem Village.

Thomas burst into the kitchen, Abigail behind him, and surveyed the room as he came to his wife's side. "What has happened?"

Benjamin repeated the details while Thomas stiffened beside Sarah, drawing up to his full, imposing height, face like a thundercloud. "She accused you of fathering a foundling child?" His booming voice brought a whimper from Theodora as he turned to Hester. "And you of bewitching our son for doing a good Christian deed?"

Theodora cried, so Hester released her from the sling and brought her to her shoulder.

"Do lower your voice, my dear." Sarah patted her husband's arm. "'Tis frightening the child."

"We all should be frightened." Thomas's words were just as intense, but not as loud. "That a girl—a mere child—could wreak such havoc on our family. And on yours, Midwife. 'Tis the only indecent act here."

"If thee could give me a ride to the Buffum farm, I will find another to help me out of the colony."

"Of course, of course." Thomas pulled a hand down his face. "And we shall have to find somewhere for Benjamin to hide out."

"The Danforth land?" Benjamin asked.

Thomas shook his head. "I do not believe that to be as safe as people think, and I wish to have you closer, if possible."

A thought struck Hester, and yet she resisted speaking up. Had she not caused this family enough heartache? What right had she to meddle any further in their affairs? But it must have shown on her face.

"Midwife?" Sarah took a step closer. "Do you have an idea? A safe place in mind?" The earnest hope on the woman's face tugged at Hester's heart.

"I am not sure where the idea came from." Hester picked her words carefully.

"Often, the Lord gives us wisdom in such a way," Thomas said. "Tell us."

"There is a Puritan family northeast of the village. They have not, I think, been attending the church here. They moved in not too long ago. Donald Hoffman is... is not a trusting sort of man. He keeps to himself."

Thomas's brows drew together. "Then why would he help us?"

"Because he has eight children and the oldest boy is but five years old. He needs help to repair the old place they moved into and to work the farm."

Benjamin straightened beside her. "Would he take me on as a hired hand?"

"I doubt he can afford to pay, but perhaps as an apprentice, he might, even though thee are above the normal age."

"Why would he stick his neck out to help us," Sarah asked, "if he is the sort of man you described?"

A good question, and one Hester couldn't fully answer. "His good-wife, Pearl, has been allowing some of the Friends to come in and assist her. I believe she could sway him."

"Farming is something I have been wishing to learn, but"—Benjamin looked at his mother and then his father—"would it be better for me to stay and face whatever accusations might come? Neither the midwife nor I have been formally accused, after all. Perhaps nothing more will come of Ann Jr.'s words."

"Nay." Sarah grasped her son's arm. "That girl has a tongue that knows no end. 'Tis best you go to a place where none will find you. Since we have not met this Mr. Hoffman, 'tis plain he does not attend church. There would be no reason for anyone in the village to know where you are." She looked up at Thomas. "Is that not true?"

"I like not the thought of my son living with a man I have never met."

"Then I shall introduce thee." Hester jiggled Theodora at her shoulder. If they didn't leave for the farm soon, the babe would start crying from hunger. "If thee will give me a ride to the Buffum farm first, perhaps Caleb would do the introduction. It might be better coming from another man."

"Of course." Thomas turned to her. "I cannot say how much it sorrows me that you have been caught up in this hysteria, and all because you took in a foundling." His normally merry eyes were a murky brown. "I fear it will catch up with more of us before 'tis done. But if you can secure a safe place for my son, I will be forever in your debt." Without giving Hester a chance to reply, he turned to Benjamin. "Pack what you will need for the remainder of the summer. I shall send Thomas Jr. out to hitch the team."

Hester leaned against the wall behind her, almost dizzy with relief. It wasn't what she wished for. If she could, she would remain in the village, but God had provided a way of escape. Although Emily was sixteen years older, her sister would welcome Hester into her home. She would be safe.

And maybe, Lord willing, she and Theodora could return someday.

The dogs barked a warning as the jaunty jingle of the brewery's wagon pulling into the farm lane on a Thursday, bringing a stab of dread to Hannah Jr. She laid aside her hoe and shielded her eyes from the sun.

"'Tis Hester on the wagon with Theodora." Tamson came to Hannah Jr.'s side. "She must be on her way to a birthing."

Then why was Thomas bringing her and not the expectant father? Someone stood up in the back of the wagon, and Hannah Jr. had to suppress a gasp.

Why was Benjamin with them?

"Can we watch Theodora today instead of weeding the garden?" Verity asked.

Hannah Jr. lifted the hem of her petticoats and hurried toward the house, ignoring Verity's question. Tamson followed. They arrived as the wagon stopped, and one look at Hester's face said it all.

Something was horribly wrong.

Mother came out of the house, wiping her hands on her apron. "Hester, what?" Her words cut off when she focused on their friend.

Benjamin leaped over the wagon's side and took Theodora from Hester, handing the babe over to Tamson, who had rushed forward. Then he handed Hester down from the tall seat while Thomas climbed down the other side.

"Is Caleb nearby?" Thomas's normally booming voice was subdued.

"Verity." Mother turned to the girl. "Run to the back pasture and fetch him."

Petticoats in hand, Verity sprinted away.

"Come inside, all of thee." Mother moved aside and gestured toward the door. "'Tis almost the noon hour, and we have plenty to share. Hannah Jr., would thee bring up another wheel of cheese?"

"Of course." Decorum aside, Hannah Jr. mimicked Verity's run as she rushed to the springhouse and brought out a wheel of cheese, then hurried to the house. Father, Caleb Jr., Robert, Joseph, and Verity were coming up from the barn when she reached the back door of the house. But she didn't wait for them. The dread pressing against her was too strong.

Taking a calming breath to still her racing heart, she entered the kitchen. Tamson was feeding Theodora at one end of the table with Benji and Jonathan looking on. Mother sliced a smoked ham and put the slices on a platter. Thomas sat on the other end of the table with Hester across from him. Benjamin stood behind his father.

No one spoke.

Benjamin's eyes caught hers, and the look in them deepened her fears.

Boots stomped on the porch, and then Father entered, followed by the rest, filling the large kitchen. "What has happened?"

"We waited for you to arrive." Thomas stood and faced Father. "I fear 'tis bad news. The worst."

Hannah Jr. pressed her hand to her throat. It had tightened enough to make breathing difficult.

Hester rose and faced Father. "I have been accused by Ann Jr. of bewitching Benjamin."

A gasp went around the room, while the floor tilted beneath Hannah Jr.'s feet. Wind rushed in her ears. She tried to steady herself, but the edges of her vision darkened, and then the floor rose up to meet her. Just before she struck the wood, strong arms caught her, and she was gently lowered to the well-worn boards. A fleeting glimpse of dark curls above her was all she saw before the darkness filled in.

Never would Hester have imagined Hannah Jr. to be the fainting type. Nor would she have imagined Benjamin leaping to the young woman's rescue the way he had, nor the stricken look he'd turned toward Hester as Hannah Jr. went limp. A look both fathers couldn't have missed for what it was—a man very attached to the woman he knelt beside.

Hester and Hannah had shooed Benjamin out of the way, and Hannah Jr. had come back to them almost immediately, embarrassed and distressed. Hester's heart ached for her young friend. The secret was out between the families now, and only time would tell the outcome.

For now, they must work together to secure Benjamin's safety and find a way for her and Theodora to get to Connecticut Colony.

"Well." Thomas pushed his fingers into the curly mass of his uncovered hair. They were all seated around the table, cup of tea dispersed by the younger girls, and Theodora on Hester's lap. "Hester came up with an idea for safeguarding Benjamin. I would know what you think of it, Caleb."

Hester sketched out her idea of apprenticing Benjamin to Donald Hoffman, who lived five miles from the Buffums' farm. Perhaps too close, after what everyone had witnessed.

Caleb rubbed the back of his neck, no more comfortable under the circumstances than Thomas was. "Her idea has merit. The boy would be out of sight and out of the village." If he stressed the word *boy*, it was only slightly, but Hannah Jr., seated between Hester and Hannah, stiffened on her chair.

Hannah turned to Hester. "And of course, thee and Theodora are welcome to stay with us for as long as thee wish or have a need."

"While I appreciate thy offer, I think 'tis best if I go to my sister in Milford in Connecticut Colony."

"Nay." Hannah Jr.'s response was quick and sharp, her emotions obviously still raw. "Thee cannot leave!"

Hester squeezed her arm. "Not because I wish to, but because I must. For Theodora's safety."

Understanding bloomed in the younger woman's eyes, but so did a new layer of grief clouding their usually bright blue.

Hannah took hold of her daughter's hand on the other side. "Hester is right. 'Tis the safest thing for her to do." They were the only two in the house, other than Hester, who knew about the birthmark, but none of the others objected to the plan. For even without a marked babe, leaving the village—leaving the colony—was the safest thing for Hester.

Now that she had joined the ranks of the accused.

Chapter 30

F ATHER HAD NOT BEEN happy when Hannah Jr. had insisted on coming along to the Hoffman farm. She was sure he would have forbidden it but for Mother's intervention. And who better to appeal to Pearl if need be than Hannah Jr.? Had she not forged a bond with the woman while cleaning the house? Had that been just five days past? It seemed a lifetime.

The brewery wagon turned onto the neglected farm lane and bumped along toward the house. As before, Donald was in the field. He dropped his hoe and stalked toward them. He looked as if he wished he had his musket in his hands again.

Hannah Jr. was glad he did not.

This had to work—for Benjamin's sake. To have him safe and still nearby would be a blessing. A relief. And not just for her, but for his family. *Please, Lord, let it work out if it be Your will.*

Donald's strides slowed as he approached and Thomas stopped the horses. "Caleb?" he called the question across the last few rows of corn.

"'Tis I, and the brewer. We would have a word with thee, if thee would allow us the time."

Donald glanced at Pearl, who was approaching from the garden, one of the twins in her arms, and then continued until he stopped beside the wagon. "Have you come for the cows?"

"Nay, for another reason entirely." Father motioned to Thomas. "This is Thomas Buffington."

Donald bobbed his head in a curt form of greeting.

"'Tis a pleasure to meet you, Mr. Hoffman." Thomas touched his hat brim and looked at Pearl. "And you, Goodie Hoffman. Hester Fuller has told me good things about you."

The surprise on Donald's face was there and gone so quickly that, if Hannah Jr. hadn't been staring at him, she'd have missed it. Was he so unused to people saying good things about him and his wife, and why wouldn't he be, when he seemed to go out of his way to be disagreeable? But that was uncharitable of her, and they needed his help. So she smiled and hoped it looked genuine.

"Climb down and we will talk," Donald stepped back from the wagon, giving everyone room. Father and Thomas climbed down from the seat, while Benjamin jumped over the side and then assisted her out of the back, steadying her arm under Father's watchful eyes. Her feet on the ground, Hannah Jr. went to Pearl's side. The woman took her hand and squeezed it.

Donald gave Hannah Jr. a nod when he noticed her, and his expression softened for a moment. That was probably as close to a *thank you* as she'd get from him for her work cleaning his house last week, but it helped to settle her nerves. The man simply must agree to their plan.

The men gathered around Donald, and Thomas started the conversation. "You must have heard of the hullabaloo going on in the village."

"The witch nonsense, you mean." It wasn't a question, it was a statement. And by the twist of Donald's lips, he wasn't in favor of what was happening.

"Exactly that." Thomas cleared his throat. "My son, Benjamin, has been accused of being bewitched by a woman in the village."

Pearl's soft intake of breath couldn't have been heard by anyone else, but Hannah Jr. firmed her grip on the other woman's hand while releasing a breath of relief when he didn't name Hester, who had decided to stay back at the farm and let the men handle things.

"Bewitched how?" Donald's brows drew together.

"I was carrying water in the mornings for the midwife, Hester Fuller, who has need of it."

Hannah Jr. did her best not to cringe.

"She has no husband and has taken in a foundling." Benjamin shrugged. "It seemed the Christian thing to do."

Donald shifted his feet, attention squarely on Benjamin. "And for that, you were accused of being bewitched?"

Benjamin didn't flinch from the direct stare. "After I was first accused of being the babe's father."

"The midwife seemed a proper woman." Donald's eyes narrowed to slits. "Who would level such an accusation?"

"A twelve-year-old girl." Benjamin didn't name her, which was generous of him. She was misguided, for sure, but still just a child.

Hannah Jr.'s appreciation of Benjamin rose even further.

"Bah." Donald shook his head, glancing at the house, perhaps thinking of his ten-year-old daughter. He brought his attention back to their group.

"We must do something to help." Pearl's voice was low but intense. "Hester was a Godsend the night the babes were born, and we owe the Buffums something."

Donald turned to his wife, and his expression softened again. Perhaps he wasn't as unfeeling as Hannah Jr. had assumed, for he faced the men and asked, "How can I help?"

"We had hoped," Thomas didn't allow a breath to pass before speaking up, "that even though he is above the usual age, you might agree to apprentice Benjamin, at least until the witch hysteria has passed."

"I have wished to learn farming for a long time." Benjamin cast an apologetic glance at his father. "While I do not mind working in the brewery, I would like to learn to grow things, especially apples." His earnestness was plain in his voice and the way he all but bounced on the .

Hannah Jr.'s middle was aflutter again. While he was in a tough spot—all for performing a charitable Christian act to please her—he was willing to see the silver lining. Willing to step out on his own. How could she not admire that?

"An apprentice." There was a wealth of doubt in Donald's tone.

"I am a quick learner," Benjamin said, "and very willing."

"I can attest to the boy's desire to farm." Thomas sighed. "I had hoped it was but a boy's passing fancy, but he is nearly twenty years old, so I must confess that 'tis genuine. And"—Thomas held up a hand—"you have no need to clothe him or provide more than a bed and his meals. His mother and I will see to his other needs, and gladly, if you will safeguard him out of sight of those in the village. 'Twould be essential that no one else know he is here."

Donald eyed Benjamin up and down, and Hannah Jr. wouldn't have been too surprised had he looked at his teeth, as one would before purchasing a horse on market day. Whatever he saw, it must have made up his mind, for he nodded. "Aye. I could use a young man with muscles around the place."

Benjamin's grin flashed first to Donald, and then he turned it on Hannah Jr.

Oh, did the fluttering take off then, but she lowered her gaze to the ground and hoped Father hadn't been looking.

"Fine." Thomas's voice boomed, the first time he'd unleashed its volume since he'd received the bad news. "Benjamin, unload the cider and small beer we brought. That can be your first chore."

Donald gave a half-hearted protest about the kegs, but Thomas brushed them off, saying they were a gift of gratitude.

"I can show him where the cellar is." Hannah Jr. and the girls had needed to find it on their cleaning day to retrieve some things to make supper.

Father shot her a look she couldn't interpret, but Donald nodded his consent. As the cellar opening was within sight of the wagon, it wouldn't be improper in the least.

Benjamin followed her, one keg on his shoulder. "I cannot believe he agreed." There was a note of joy in his words.

"I am beyond grateful that thee will be safe."

"And not too far away." His voice had dropped to nearly a whisper.

"Nor too close." She kept her feet moving, almost feeling Father's eyes on her back. "This changes nothing between us, quite the opposite. My untimely collapse brought our fathers' attention onto us." Sorrow compressed her chest. "This is likely our last time together."

"Not if we were to meet halfway, somewhere in the forest."

The idea skittered across her nerves and raised all sorts of emotions she couldn't—or wouldn't—identify. They reached the cellar, and she pulled the door open. "I will not enter with thee, for 'twould not be proper. If this is to be our last few words together, I would have thee know how much thee mean to me, Benjamin Buffington. But I would also have thee know to expect nothing more."

He shifted the keg to his arms in preparation for descending the stairs.

"I would have you know, Hannah Buffum, Jr., that I do not give up so easily." His grin was full of self-confidence, not tinged at all by the accusation hanging over his head. "We shall meet again, mark my words."

She inclined her head, turned, and retraced her steps to the wagon. Each footfall to the ground pounded out the repeat of *mark my words*.

Hester held out her cup, and Hannah filled it, the fragrant blend of tea with mint rising from it.

"Are thee sure?" Hannah set the teapot on a colorful woven pad. "Someone of the Friends could hide thee until the witch trials are over. What about—"

"Nay. If 'twere only me, I would do as thee say, but I must put Theodora's needs above my own desires now."

"Aye." Hannah sat back and sipped her tea. "'Tis the way of a mother and her children. She must protect them, especially when they are so young and helpless." She glanced out the window. "'Tis much more difficult when they are older."

"Thee are thinking of Hannah Jr., are thee not?" None could have missed Benjamin's tender attention to the young woman when she'd fainted.

"Aye. Benjamin's attachment to her was too obvious to be ignored, I fear. I have no idea how Caleb will react to it, much less Thomas." Lines gathered between Hannah's brows. "Those two have established a friendship since the witch hysteria started. I should hate for this to break it apart."

A Friend and a Puritan, two men who had found a way to work together to save Verity and were now working together to save Benjamin. Surely such a bond—forged in the protection of their families—wouldn't be unseated because of an unlikely romance between the daughter of one and the son of the other. Would it?

Hester would miss her twice-weekly visits with Hannah Jr. Aside from Theodora, those had become the high points of her life. She hadn't realized what a lonely life she'd led until the babe had been left on her porch and Hannah Jr. had stepped up to fill the need of a mother's helper. The idea of being alone again didn't appeal to her at all.

For the first time since Ann Jr.'s hateful accusation that morning, Hester allowed herself to imagine moving in with Emily, being part of a family of more than just her and Theodora. Emily would fuss over them for a while, but once things settled, they should get on well together. Perhaps in time, Hester could have her own small house built nearby. Emily's husband, Tobias, was a prosperous sheep farmer with plenty of land. While she hadn't seen either of them in at least ten years, she had only good memories of them both.

The longing to be independent, the need to prove she could support and take care of herself, were no longer important. Theodora was. Getting her away from the witch craziness, away from anyone else who might see the mark on her belly, was Hester's only goal.

The only thing that truly mattered.

The back door banged, followed by Caleb Jr.'s entrance into the kitchen. Caleb had dispatched him and Robert to let Phoebe know about the goats, and then to circle around to David's workshop and inquire about a boat for Hester.

"What did thee learn?" Hannah asked before Hester could summon the question.

"David says there are boats sailing almost daily this time of year, and it should not be difficult to find one stopping in Connecticut Colony. He is traveling to Salem Town on the morrow to pick up musket parts and says thee are welcome to ride along with him. He said to reassure thee that where he goes is far away from where the witch trials are held, so thee should be in no danger."

Relief washed over Hester. "And the goats?"

"Phoebe sent her daughter to fetch them back to their farm."

Another relief. Hester had not only been dependent on Pumpkin, but she'd grown fond of the goat and her kid as well.

"Hester, look." Tamson held Theodora in the crook of her arm, a pap cup in one hand. The oblong-shaped cup, filled with a thickened mixture of cow's milk and oat broth, was held to Theodora's lips.

The babe's smacking sounds were music to Hester's ears. "She figured it out." Hester stood and went to stand beside Tamson. "Thee are a clever girl, showing her how to eat from that contraption."

"'Twill make it easier for thee on the journey, will it not?" Tamson asked.

"Indeed." One more worry off Hester's shoulders.

"She will be taking mashed foods in no time now," Hannah said. "But keep the pap cup. I have no need of it any longer."

Tears brimmed in Hester's eyes, and she had to blink them away.

"I will miss thee." Verity slid her hand into Hester's. "But I am glad thee will be safe away from the village and will be with thy sister. Sisters are important."

Hester knelt and hugged the little girl. "I shall write once I am settled and let thee know that all is well."

"Will thee ever return?" Tamson asked.

Hester took some time to form her thoughts before she said, "I cannot make that decision now. Too many things are outside of my control." It might take every coin in her pocket to secure passage to Milford, and perhaps years to raise enough for a return passage. And her new, tender thoughts about being part of a larger family still filled her heart. "Truly, I know not. But I will miss thee."

She was giving up much to flee to safety, but it was for Theodora, so there was no question that it was the right thing to do. It was as if the Lord had orchestrated all things to work together. How could her heart be heavy when she knew that He was watching over her and her daughter?

Chapter 31

H ANNAH JR. STIRRED THE porridge, her thoughts and emotions in turmoil after an almost sleepless night. Benjamin was safe at the Hoffmans' farm, even having arranged for Thomas Jr. to bring Blaze to him.

Mark my words.

She shook her head to dislodge the cadence of his parting words to her. They'd already robbed her of a night's sleep.

Though, to be fair, she'd not have slept much anyway. Hester and Theodora were leaving right after breakfast. Over the summer, Hester had become more than just a best friend to Hannah Jr., she'd become a mentor and confidante.

She was losing both Benjamin and Hester.

The temptation to give in to anger was very near the surface. Anger at those who cried *witch* and pointed fingers. Anger at the Puritans and Friends who couldn't get along. Anger at facing spinsterhood when it wasn't what she wanted.

"Are thee all right?" Verity's voice jolted Hannah Jr. out of her dark thoughts.

"Of course I am." She fought a twinge of guilt at the outright lie that rolled off her tongue.

Verity wrapped her arms around Hannah Jr.'s middle, cheek pressed against her apron. "'Tis all right to be sad when someone goes away."

The girl who had lost her parents, her brother and sister, and finally her uncle was comforting Hannah Jr. over her friend moving away. Shame washing over her, Hannah Jr. dropped the spoon in the kettle, knelt, and hugged the child who was now her sister. "Thee are right, and I am sad, but I have thee, Tamson, and our brothers to keep me busy, do I not?"

"I love thee."

Tears clogged her throat, but Hannah Jr. smiled. "I love thee as well."

"Because we are sisters now?"

"Aye. We are family, now and always."

Hannah Jr.'s anger melted away and her hurt lessened while holding the precious girl in her arms. It was too easy to count one's losses instead of one's blessings.

Tamson came inside with the basket of eggs from the henhouse. "What is going on here?"

"Hannah Jr. was sad, but now she is not." Verity took the egg basket. "And we are making breakfast."

Tamson came close to Hannah Jr. while Verity sorted the eggs. "Hester is moving away, but Benjamin is just through the forest, not more than three miles as the crow flies."

"I am not a crow, nor likely to become one." Not to mention the river she'd have to ford if she didn't take the road and use the bridge on the longer route. Not that she planned to traverse the distance in any case.

"But thee could see him from time to time."

"Tamson Buffum." Hannah Jr. planted her hands on her hips and faced her sister. "Thee have no business thinking such things, nor saying them to me. 'Twould be entirely improper even for me to consider it."

"But thee love him—"

"Hush." Hannah Jr. shot a glance around the kitchen, but it was only the three of them still. The boys and Father were finishing chores, Mother was upstairs getting the little boys dressed, and Hester hadn't come down with Theodora yet. "I know him not well enough to love him. And even if I did, 'tis none of thy concern."

Tamson leaned closer and whispered, "'Twould be my concern if he were to become another brother."

Matching her whisper and with as much force as Hannah Jr. could put into the words, she said, "Which will likely never happen, so thee had best be prepared to care for an aging spinster sister in the future."

"What are thee whispering about?" Mother stepped into the kitchen, followed by Benji and Jonathan.

Hannah Jr. pinched the underside of Tamson's arm hard enough that the girl squeaked but otherwise kept her mouth shut. "Nothing of importance. Does Hester need a hand this morning?"

Mother eyed her with a doubtful look but let the matter pass. "She said they will be down shortly."

"I am ready to fry the eggs," Verity said. "Hannah Jr. has finished the porridge."

The porridge! Hannah Jr. swung around and moved it further from the fire. The whiff of scorched oats said she hadn't been quick enough, and she'd better not scrape the bottom of the kettle when she dished it up. Could anything else go wrong that morning? Losing her friend, fighting with Tamson, and now burning the porridge.

Verity's gray eyes met her from across the room.

Hannah Jr. took a deep breath. *Help me count my blessings, Lord.*

Hester settled herself on the high wagon seat, and took Theodora from Hannah Jr., thankful that it wasn't their final goodbye—yet. The younger woman climbed into the back of the wagon while Caleb joined Hester on the seat and unwrapped the reins.

Everything Hester had grabbed on her way out of the cottage was in the wagon. She tried not to mourn for the other things she'd had to leave behind. She'd suggested Hannah Jr. should collect them, but Caleb had been against it. He didn't want his daughter seen coming or going from the house of an accused woman. While it was the prudent thing, it still hurt a bit, being associated with the frightful word. *Witch.*

Caleb chirped to the horses, and the wagon started forward. The sun was above the trees, but not by much, and clouds were crowding the horizon to the southwest. David would be waiting for her, and beyond that, she would trust her care to the gunsmith and God.

No one spoke. Only the steady pounding of the horses' hooves and the occasional bird call broke the stillness. Even Theodora remained silent on Hester's lap, facing forward, her head supported by Hester's front, but only when necessary. The babe had gained much strength over the past few weeks.

All too soon, they arrived at David's shop, but there was no wagon out front hitched and waiting.

"Hello?" Caleb called as he set the wagon's brake.

Instead of coming out of the door of the shop, David and his oldest, Matthew, came from the barn, Matthew leading a gray horse.

David reached the wagon. "'Tis a sorry thing." He poked his thumb at the horse. "Izzy threw a shoe in the night. I cannot hitch her until she sees the blacksmith for a new one. Matthew is taking her to Stephen now, but 'twill delay our departure by a couple of hours."

Would Hester miss sailing with the evening tide, then? Would she need to pay for overnight accommodation? She mentally counted the coins in her pocket. There were none to spare.

"I can drive us into town," Caleb said.

"Are thee sure?" David scratched the back of his head. "'Twould make things easier."

"Climb aboard." Caleb nodded toward Dolly. "'Twill be good for Dolly to be away for a while longer, since her filly is old enough to be weaned. Matthew, would thee stop at the farm and let my goodwife know of the change in plans? Under the circumstances, she might worry at our delay."

"I will," the young man said.

David climbed into the wagon's bed and settled on the opposite side from Hannah Jr. "All set. Let us make haste and see Hester on her way, shall we?"

The gunsmith's presence in the wagon seemed to shift the very air around them, to lighten it somehow. Soon, they were chatting and even laughing at the most inconsequential things. Theodora burbled her baby noises until she drifted off to sleep, and the rest of the journey passed in a different mood altogether.

Then they arrived at Salem Town.

A knot formed in Hester's middle. She would not breathe easily again until she stepped off the boat onto Connecticut soil. And even then, she would need to find her way to her sister's house.

"The witch nonsense is happening that way," David pointed, "and so we should take the other direction." He'd taken a wide-legged stance behind Caleb, rocking on his feet to the motion of the wagon as it turned. "I know a dockmaster down by the harbor, an honest man with a love of fowling pieces. I have made two for him so far. He has been after me to make a third, but I have yet to see any coin to back it up. He will, though, when he is ready."

Caleb guided the wagon along the busy street, following David's instructions, until they arrived at the wharves. The overwhelming odors of fish and brine filled the air, which grew heavy as the rain clouds approached. Ships dotted the water beyond, bobbing at anchor as they awaited their turn dockside to load and unload their cargoes. Docks of varying lengths and widths bustled with longshoremen, some toting barrels and bundles on their shoulders, others wheeling their cargo out in barrows.

Two men came down one of the longer docks with a line of a dozen black slaves between them, the men and woman—and children—chained together. Hester's heart broke at their vacant, hopeless expressions. Why did men have to traffic in other human beings? The Friends were very much against the practice of slavery, and for that she was glad. But how long would it be until the other churches—the Puritans, the Church of England, the Methodists, and even the Catholics—would also speak out against it?

"There." David pointed to a rickety shack set among several others, all looking as though they could blow down in the next gale. Salem Town had run a booming shipping business, the chief export being codfish and the chief import sugar from the southern islands, since the colonies had been settled. "Get the wagon as close as thee can, and I shall see what is available. Hester, what is the name of the town in Connecticut where thy sister lives?"

"Milford. 'Tis a seaport town."

"That should make things easier." The spry man vaulted over the edge of the wagon's bed as soon as the wheels had stopped. "I shall return shortly."

Hannah Jr. took his place standing behind the seat, her arms coming around Hester. "I am going to miss thee. But thee will be with thy family, and I pray thee will be happy."

Hester put the hand not securing Theodora over the young woman's. "I shall miss thee as well. I know not how I would have managed becoming a mother to this babe without thy help. 'Twas as if the Lord sent thee to me in my time of need."

"Will thee start working as a midwife again once thee are settled? And making thy baskets?"

Would she? Or would she be content simply to be Theodora's mother? A lot depended on how she found Emily and her husband's situation. "I know not at this point. I shall have to take each day as I find it and trust the Lord to provide."

"'Tis always the best way," Caleb said.

Hester squeezed Hannah Jr.'s hand. "There was a time when I thought all I wanted was my independence, my ability to care for myself. Theodora has changed all that."

"What do thee wish for now?" Hannah Jr.'s tone hinted that the answer meant a great deal to her.

Choosing her words with care, Hester said, "I wish for my daughter to grow up to be the kind of young woman thee are, my friend. 'Twould be my greatest accomplishment, should I be able to guide her to that end."

Thunder rumbled in the distance, and somehow, that seemed fitting, as if the Lord had given his blessing to her answer.

People milled about the street near the docks, mostly dressed in Puritan clothing, a stark contrast to the often garish colors of the sailors' garb. Shouts came from the ships being loaded and unloaded, some words too distinct for Hannah Jr.'s comfort. She might not know the meaning of all of them, but she could infer the intent. Never had she heard Father swear, but she had caught Caleb Jr. at it once. Just the threat of telling Father had kept the boy from repeating his error—at least within Hannah Jr.'s hearing.

The minutes crawled by as they waited for David to reappear. What was taking him so long? Hannah Jr. felt exposed in the high wagon, on display for all to see. In the town where the witch trials were ongoing, it made the skin between her shoulders itch.

"There he is." Father nodded toward where David emerged from the building.

David looked both ways before he darted to the wagon. "They have a ship leaving for Connecticut Colony within minutes, so we must make haste."

"At which port will she dock?" Hester asked.

"New Haven, which is but a dozen miles from Milford, or so I was assured." David reached up, and Hannah Jr. handed him Hester's canvas bag and one of the baskets. "He said 'twould take most of two days to sail there, so thee may need to find lodging for a night in New Haven before hiring a driver to take thee the rest of the way."

"Do I purchase the ticket in that building?" Hester asked.

"'Tis already accounted for." David handed a slip of paper to her.

"I cannot let thee—"

"Be not proud"—Father leaned neared to Hester—"nor rob us of the blessing of helping thee in thy time of need."

Hester hung her head for a moment, then faced Father. "How can I thank thee?"

"By doing as thee said, and raising thy daughter to be the same sort of young woman Hannah Jr. has become."

Hannah Jr. nearly choked on the emotions that flooded her. There was no way Father and Mother hadn't discussed Benjamin and her last night after everything that had happened. And yet, still he said such a thing. Still, he regarded her with that level of respect. Dare she hope...?

"Is that her?" A strident voice cut through the general noise of the street.

Hannah Jr. turned and scanned the crowd until she spotted a trio of girls from Salem Village to her left. The tall one was the doctor's niece. There was another, shorter girl with a finger pointed toward them, and then... she recognized the third as Ann Jr. They were sitting so much higher than the crowd, in plain sight. If Ann Jr. recognized Hester now, she could set up a cry that would prevent her escape.

"Come now." David half-handed and half-hauled Hester from the wagon, causing Theodora to wake with a cry.

"Keep the wagon between thee and the girls," Father said.

"As soon as we are lost in the crowd on the dock," David said, "drive to where we entered the town. I shall make my way there as quickly as I can."

"We will wait."

"Here is the last basket." Hannah Jr. handed it over the side.

Hester grabbed it, her other arm full of Theodora, her face written with words there was no time left to say.

"Write when thee can," Hannah Jr. said.

With a nod, Hester hustled off in front of David, his slight form barely blocking her from sight.

The girls from Salem Village were drawing closer, but having to fight their way through what had become nearly a mob of people, many of them having just disembarked from one of the ships.

Was it enough to keep them away until the ship's gangplank was raised? Until Hester and Theodora were safe?

Chapter 32

A S THE CROWD SURGED around the wagon, Hannah Jr. climbed onto the seat beside Father, keeping low to escape notice and watching the village girls' approach.

Another rumble of thunder rolled over the town. Dolly neighed and half-reared, while Dandy snorted and tried to step away from the mare, jostling the wagon.

"She likes not the coming storm," Hannah Jr. said.

"I think 'tis more that she misses Honey." He crooned to the mare, "Easy now. Thy filly is back at the farm, where we shall go as soon as we can."

The distraught horse was having none of it. Her back hooves lashed out, thudding into the wagon below the kickboard. Hannah Jr. grabbed the seat to steady herself, and lost sight of the village girls. Where had they gone?

Dolly squealed again and lurched backward, forcing Dandy to join her. The wagon jerked to the rear.

Someone screamed, and the horses surged forward again.

Father rose sawed back on the reins to stop them.

Hannah Jr. twisted on the seat.

Behind the wagon, the doctor's niece and Ann Jr. bend over a crumpled figure knocked to the cobblestones by the wagon.

Father set the brake, wrapped the reins firmly around it, and jumped off the wagon, hurrying to Dolly's head and trying to calm her.

Hannah Jr. climbed down, her insides trembling nearly as much as her hands. She glanced at the docks, but there was no sign of Hester or David, who had blended into the foot traffic between the large ships. Hannah Jr. approached the girls.

"I am so sorry. The horse spooked, and my father could not control her."

The doctor's niece, a young woman as tall as Hannah Jr., stood and faced her. "Are you the midwife?"

"What?" Hannah Jr. took a step back. "Nay, I am Hannah Buffum, Jr. My father is the carpenter who made the doctor's furniture."

The other woman swung and shot Father a glare, then frowned and looked to her fallen companion, who was now seated on the cobblestones. "She thought she saw the village midwife on the wagon."

Hannah Jr. spread her hands. "There is only my father and me."

The doctor's niece turned to Ann Jr. "Did you not recognize her too?"

The younger girl shook her head. "My eyesight is not good enough to see that far. 'Tis why I said we must get closer." She helped the shorter girl, the one who had pointed at Hester, sit upright. Blood seeped through her petticoat at the knees.

Hannah Jr. folded her hands at her waist and addressed the wounded girl who had tears in her eyes, but kept mute. "I am so sorry for the accident. I hope thee are not seriously hurt."

The doctor's niece knelt again and examined the bloodied knees, then she looked up at Hannah Jr. "They are badly scraped, nothing more."

A shaft of lightning lit the sky, followed by another deep rumble. *Lord, let me be gracious.* "Can my father and I give thee a ride somewhere?"

Dolly chose that moment to rear again, shaking her head and nearly lifting Father off his feet. She came back to earth and neighed, mouth agape and her sides heaving like a beast possessed.

"Nay. I think not." The doctor's niece went to one side of the injured girl, Ann Jr. the other. "We shall be fine." With that, they walked away, the short girl limping and whimpering between them.

Hannah Jr. joined Father, who had been watching. "I am sorry for not being truthful."

"Thee told the truth, if not all of it." Father glanced at the docks, then motioned for Hannah Jr. to get back in the wagon. He joined her on the seat and unwrapped the reins. "Under the circumstances, I think thee did very well."

His praise brought a flush of warmth as she scoured the docks, looking for one last glimpse of Hester and Theodora before they were lost to her. But she saw nothing of them, nor even David. "Do thee think they made it aboard the ship?"

"Aye. David slipped off the dock and behind the harbor masters' buildings while thee were speaking to the girls. He would not have until Hester was safely aboard and out of sight."

It took all of Father's driving skills to get the upset mare moving in the right direction without bolting and trampling the crowd around them. But within minutes, they had broken free of the mass of people and found themselves on a back street, heading toward where they'd entered the town. Dolly finally relaxed, either from the lack of people or because they were heading home. The team slowed to a walk, a pace that wouldn't draw attention on the quiet town street as raindrops started to fall, speckling the wood of the wagon and dampening their clothing.

"I am proud of thee, daughter." Father's words caught Hannah Jr. off guard. "I meant what I said to Hester. She could have no greater hope than that Theodora grow to be like thee."

"Thank thee. I hardly know what to say."

"Then let me say a few things, and hear me out before thee answer."

The solemness in his voice made her stomach tighten. It was the tone he often slipped into when he told of difficult things, as when he'd spoken to her of the nightmare he and Mother had endured many years before at the hands of the Puritans.

"I know thee have lost a great friend with Hester moving away." He sent her a pointed glance. "Thy mother has also confirmed my suspicions that there is a young man thee are taken with. I had not, however, perceived it to be young Buffington. Not until yesterday, that is."

"I am—"

"Nay. Let me finish."

Hannah Jr. folded her hands in her lap, fingers interlaced tightly enough to make them tingle.

"We are going through troublesome times, as I have no need to explain to thee, and none of us know how 'twill end."

Dolly started to trot, and Father pulled her back into line.

"But end it will, as all such things do, and when that happens, we shall speak again of Benjamin Buffington and thee." He cut her another look she couldn't quite interpret. "Not until then, and with no promises made. I know not what Thomas must be thinking of this, for he saw as much as I did when his son rushed to thy side."

"Yet thee helped Thomas settle Benjamin with Donald Hoffman, to keep him safe." Hannah Jr. released her fingers, which were growing numb.

"Aye, and I will do all within my power to see that the young man stays safe." He shook his head. "But I would ask thee to keep thy distance from the Hoffmans' until all this nonsense blows over. Do I have thy word on that?"

"Thee do." She barely breathed the words, her heart wanting to soar with the hope he'd given her. Guarded, couched with caution, full of uncertainties, but hope all the same, and far above her wildest dreams. When the sky fully opened and let loose the downpour, Hannah Jr. didn't mind in the least.

The ship wasn't the largest or the newest-looking vessel along the dock, but as Hester sat on the narrow cot in the room she'd been shown to, she clutched Theodora in relief. The room had three cots built into the walls. Hers was opposite the narrow door. The rough wool blanket upon which she sat smelled of fish and body odor, but that was nothing.

She'd made her escape.

David had all but shoved her up the gangplank, whispering a short prayer for safety into her ear, which went against the traditions of the Friends. But that was David, always kicking against the goads. She'd miss him along with the rest of the Friends in Salem Village, especially Hannah Jr.

Hester startled when the door opened again, and two women entered. The first was up in age, her hair the color of snow beneath her linen cap. The other was younger and by the roundness of her middle, heavy with child.

"Hello?" The older woman came to an abrupt halt when she noticed Hester. "I did not realize we were to share a cabin."

"Then perhaps we should return to your house," the pregnant woman said.

"What? Nonsense." The woman pointed to the cot beside Hester's. "You take that one, and I shall have this." She plopped a large basket onto the other bed, a small cloud of dust rising from the blanket. Then she turned to Hester. "I am Goodie Minter, and this is my daughter, Goodie Dutton."

"I am Hester Fuller." Hester bit off the rest of her usual introduction of *the village midwife*. That was something she would say to no one aboard the ship—even a pregnant woman. She wanted no one to connect her to Salem Village should anyone be questioned.

The ship tilted, and a scraping sound came from behind her as the ship left the dock. They were underway. In two days, she and Theodora would be safe in Connecticut Colony.

Goodie Dutton lowered herself to her cot, one hand holding onto her belly. It wasn't a good idea for a woman so far along to get aboard a ship.

Goodie Minter collapsed on the other cot, raising more dust as the ship shifted again. "I do wish they would give a warning." She huffed and straightened her petticoat, then turned to Hester. "What a sweet babe you have. How old?"

"She is just over three months."

"Such a precious age." The woman nodded to her daughter. "This will be Alice's first and my first grandchild." The pride in her face shone even in the dim light slanting through the porthole now awash with rain.

A first babe? And she was on a ship in the last weeks, perhaps last days, of her pregnancy? Nothing about that seemed good to Hester, but she kept her opinions to herself and smiled. A change of topic would be good.

"Where are thee headed?"

"Thee?" The woman's eyes narrowed. "Here I thought you were dressed like that for the journey."

"You are a Quaker?" Alice sat forward on her cot as much as her girth allowed. "I have never met one before."

"Indeed, I am." It wasn't worth the effort to tell them she preferred the word *Friend*. She'd tried that many times in the past, only to have it brushed aside.

"To answer your question, we are going to Boston," Alice said. "My husband has been stationed there. He serves in His Majesty's Army. He has secured a house for us now." She shifted, stretching her back in a manner too familiar to Hester, and more than a little unnerving, considering the circumstances. "I had hoped to birth this child first, but Mother decided it best we get out of Salem Town after—"

"I am sure we need not bore"—Goodie Minter looked Hester up and down—"was it Goodie Fuller?"

"Hester is fine." Sometimes she could get the Puritan women to use her given name, sometimes not.

"Hester, of course." To her daughter, she said, "We need not bore her with the details."

"Oh, Mother, 'tisn't a secret. Everyone near Salem Town knows of the witch trials."

Goodie Minter fanned her face with one hand. "My dear, you know how much I dislike the sound of that word."

"I believe we all do," Hester said. "'Tisn't a pleasant subject."

"Indeed, it is not." The mother gave the daughter an *I-told-you-so* look. "Best left behind."

Alice slumped against the wall behind her cot. "If not for that, I would not be on this ship."

"We shall be in Boston before nightfall. The babe will wait until then." How Goodie Minter surmised that, Hester had no idea, but it was obvious that Alice was very close to labor, if not in the initial throes of it.

Theodora began to fuss, and Hester battled a moment of panic. How was she to change the babe with two other women in such close quarters and without exposing her mark?

"Come, my dear." Goodie Minter stood and reached a hand to her daughter, helping her off the other cot. "Let us leave this mother alone to feed her babe. We can walk along below decks and stay out of the rain."

Relief rolled off of Hester until she was sure the women must feel it against their backs as they left and shut the door.

"There he is." Hannah Jr. pointed out David, huddled under the spreading branches of a tree. When he reached the wagon's side, he waved off Hannah Jr.'s offer to move to the back.

"Stay there." He climbed into the back. "Thee might as well keep thy backside dry."

Hannah Jr. laughed.

"That is a good sound to hear." David stood behind the seat, holding onto the raised back to steady himself. "'Tis a relief to have Hester and her babe safely on board the ship and slipping out of the harbor, is it not?"

"Indeed." But Hannah Jr. had much more than that to be relieved about. Father knew of her attachment to Benjamin, and he hadn't forbidden it. He'd forbidden her from going to the Hoffmans' until the witch hysteria passed, but he hadn't forbidden her from her interest in Benjamin. He hadn't said he was disappointed in her. While not a promise of anything in the future, she would bask in what she'd gained this day. She may have lost a friend, but she'd been given hope for a future.

Perhaps a fragile hope, but the Lord would have the final say as He worked in the hearts of two fathers in Salem Village.

Chapter 33

A SHARP INTAKE OF breath woke Hester from her sleep. Not that she'd been sleeping soundly, between the uncertainty of being becalmed at sea—held hostage on the watery depths without waves or wind to move the vessel—and Goodie Minter's snoring.

Hester rose up on her elbow, careful not to disturb Theodora, who slept at her side. There was a hint of pink at the porthole glass, the merest suggestion that dawn was on the horizon. The air in the cabin was hot, damp, and reeked of old wood, brine, and neglect in proper cleaning between passengers.

Another sharp breath was followed by a low moan.

"Alice?" Hester whispered. "Thee are in labor?"

"I believe so." Despite this being her first babe, and the uncomfortable conditions aboard the ship, Alice's voice was amazingly steady.

Hester eased herself off the cot, bolstering Theodora with the blanket before turning to Alice. "I can help. I have delivered babes before."

"You are a midwife?" Dark eyes sought hers in the gloom, perhaps looking for reassurance.

Hester paused, reluctant to claim that title when the charge of bewitching someone might follow her, sending people looking for the midwife of Salem Village. "My father was a doctor." All true. "I assisted him many times." Also true. She would sleep with a clear conscience afterward.

"Thank the Lord." Alice curled around her middle, sucking air through her teeth. "I could not dissuade Mother from this trip, but I knew I was close. Too close. When the ship stopped last evening—"

"Everything will be all right." Hester took her hand and gripped it. "There is no room for thee to walk in here. Would thee be comfortable walking in the aisle belowdecks?"

"Nay." Alice shook her head, dislodging her nightcap. "I will not be a spectacle for those leering, smelly sailors."

What a relief. Hester wouldn't have to leave Theodora with Goodie Minter, even for a moment. She glanced at the cot across the room, just an arm's span away, where the older woman still snored. "Would thee like me to awaken thy mother?"

"Anything but that." Alice finished with another sharp intake of breath.

How long had the woman been masking her pains?

"I need to stand."

Hester helped Alice to her feet. No sooner had her heels connected with the floorboards then she gasped. The telltale splash of liquid said it all.

"At least thee kept the bedding dry," Hester whispered.

A shaky laugh followed. "The babe will be here shortly, am I right?"

"Hard to say. Babes arrive on their own schedule." She glanced at the cot with the sleeping woman. "Thy mother is a sound sleeper."

"Thank the Lord."

"Thee truly do not wish her assistance?"

"You have met her. She will take over and start issuing orders—to both of us." Another sharp breath as Alice leaned forward, hand bracing herself against the wall.

They stood like that for a long time, Hester steadying the younger woman. The light filtering in through the porthole was now bright enough to illuminate the tiny cabin. While the calm seas were delaying them, they also kept the ship still, which would make the birthing process easier. Trying to deliver a babe on a pitching ship was something Hester was happy to avoid.

"Ahhhh..." Alice couldn't suppress the sound as the next contraction gripped her.

Goodie Minter snorted, rousting herself on her cot. "What is going on?" Her nightcap had fallen off, leaving the hair that had escaped her braid in disarray, looking like a bird's nest upon her head.

"Nothing to worry about, Mother." But Alice's words came between pants.

Goodie Minter got to her feet, filling the remaining space in the cabin. "You cannot have the babe here." Her voice rose with each word.

Theodora awoke with a cry at the untimely interruption.

Just what Hester didn't need.

"Goodie Minter." Hester turned her calmest smile on the woman. "Would thee go to the galley and ask the cook for whatever clean cloths he has? Mind thee, they must be freshly laundered and not in salt water."

"Leave my daughter at this time?"

"Go, Mother, please." Alice straightened. "She has delivered babes before. Her father was a doctor."

"Have I not delivered five of my own?" Goodie Minter huffed. "Send the Quaker for the cloths."

The Quaker. Hester bit back the sharp retort that wanted to burst forth. While she had years of experience soothing distraught, frightened, and even combative women during childbirth, tolerating the attending women was always more of a challenge, especially one who was as outright insulting as Goodie Minter.

Alice groaned again, folding almost double.

Theodora's fussing was becoming a full-throated howl for attention.

Hester helped Alice onto the bed, then turned to Goodie Minter. "We need the cloths, and I need to tend to my daughter. Will thee help? Or will thee hinder?"

Goodie Minter puffed herself up like a partridge on a branch. "Well, I never—"

"Go, Mother." Alice's cry was as strident as Theodora's. "I cannot wait for you to bicker. The babe is coming. We need the cloths now."

With a huff and a snort, the older woman disappeared into the hallway beyond, the door slamming shut behind her.

"Let me check thy progress."

"Nay. See to your daughter first." Alice winked at Hester. "I may have misled Mother just a little. But 'tis my first babe, so how would I know?" She sank back against the thin mattress.

Hester scooped up Theodora and quieted her while rummaging for a dry clout, then, turning her back on Alice so that her petticoats would block the other woman's line of sight, Hester quickly changed the babe, pulling the gown down to cover the mark. Theodora still fussed when she lifted her off the cot. She was hungry.

How was Hester to feed her daughter and tend to Alice?

It was mid-July hot in the kitchen, the air wet enough to wring out after yesterday's storm. Hannah Jr. slumped into a chair on the opposite side of the table from Mother. The other girls had taken the young boys outside to play in the shade, so the house was quiet.

"Hester should be halfway to Connecticut Colony by now." Mother took a sip of cider, the day already too hot to drink tea.

Hannah Jr.'s heart squeezed at the loss of her friend. At the same time, she was happy for Hester—happy that she would be reunited with her sister. Although Hester had bravely taken on the responsibility of raising Theodora alone, it would be so much better for her—and the child—to have the support and love of her family close at hand. More than anything, Hannah Jr. was relieved that her friend was far away from the dangers of the witch trials. She was relieved that Theodora would have a chance to grow up, loved and safe, away from any suspicion caused by her birthmark.

Mother set her cup down and got right to the point. "Thy father spoke to me last evening of thee and Benjamin."

All it took anymore was the mention of his name to alert the flutter inside of Hannah Jr. "He did not try to dissuade me, nor was he disappointed in me."

"Of course he was not. Neither of us is. We are proud of all of our children—in the best sense of the word."

"I must admit, for a time, I was sure I would disappoint thee both."

"Oh, my dear girl." Mother reached across the wide table and hooked Hannah Jr.'s fingers in her own. "Thee could never do that."

Hannah Jr. made a wry face. "We both know I could, if I made decisions against what thee believe, against what the Bible teaches."

"Thee would never do such a thing." There was a wealth of certainty in Mother's voice that Hannah Jr. appreciated, even if she didn't feel it as strongly herself.

After all, where Benjamin was concerned, she seemed to lose the ability to think clearly. Or did she? She rethought their conversations and her reactions to them. Perhaps Mother was right. Perhaps, in the end, Hannah Jr. would deny herself and turn away from Benjamin no matter what he said, to honor her parents' wishes.

But how lovely it was not to have to make that choice! At least, not yet.

How lovely it was to be able to dream of a future with Benjamin. A dream, not a certainty. Nothing could be certain with the threat of accusations ever-present and hovering over them, Benjamin hidden away from the accusation that he'd been bewitched by Hester.

All they needed to do was survive the witch trials.

"Goodie Minter." Hester looked up from where she knelt beside Alice's cot. "We could use more boiled water. Would thee fetch it from the cook?"

"Really, I do not see why I should be running back and forth like a—"

"Please, Mother?" Alice turned her face toward her mother, agony written across her features.

"Oh, very well." The woman bustled out the door and showed her restraint by not slamming it.

Alice turned her sweaty face back toward Hester. "I did not have to fake much of that this time." She gritted her teeth against another pain. "Pray this babe comes before she returns."

"'Twould not surprise me." Hester glanced at her cot, where Theodora gazed back at her, eyes wide and uncertain. At least Hester had managed to get her to eat a half cup of the premixed pap of thickened oat broth, enough to keep the babe happy and quiet.

"Your little girl is well-behaved for one so young. I hope my babe will be the same."

But without the mark that had sent Hester and Theodora running. Yet the nearer they came to Emily, the more Hester looked forward to seeing her sister. Odd that it had taken a witch trial and a babe left on her porch to get her to see the truth. Family was the most important thing—after the Lord.

"Oooh." Alice grabbed onto Hester's hands and squeezed. "I think this is it."

Hester's quick check confirmed it. She grabbed a blanket from her canvas sack and talked Alice through the pains that followed, encouraging, supporting, and directing, until the babe was securely wrapped in the blanket.

The cabin's door opened. "That odious man made me wait. He refused to bring the water to the cabin himself. If I never—" Goodie Minter's words cut off when Hester lifted the precious bundle.

"The babe is here already?" The older woman set the kettle of water on the floor, her demeanor changing faster than the flash of a firefly. "May I see? A boy or a girl?"

Hester glanced at Alice, who gave a weary nod.

"Thee have a granddaughter. Can thee hold her while I attend to the cord?" Hester half expected the woman to blanch and step away, but to her surprise, Goodie Minter took the child with infinite gentleness and held her still while Hester finished the task.

"She is beautiful, my dear." Goodie Minter turned to her daughter. "The very image of you when you were born."

The ship's floor rose beneath them, the snap of canvas audible even in the confines of the cabin.

Hester looked out through the porthole. "We are moving again."

"The Lord knew I needed it calm to give birth." Alice took the babe from her mother, then met Hester's eyes. "As He knew I needed you this very night as well. I cannot imagine what would have happened had you not shared this cabin with us. Truly, you were sent by God."

When ye thought evil against me, God disposed it to good. Never had that verse meant as much to Hester as it did at that moment. She'd always been taught that God wished good things for those who believed in Him, even while He allowed bad things to happen, that sometimes the bad things were part of a greater plan to move His believers in the direction of His will for them.

Hester gazed out the porthole at the sunshine glinting off the water. She'd been unsure about continuing as a midwife, but not anymore. God had put her here, on this ship, in this very cabin, to show her that her skills were still needed. With a certainty she couldn't deny, Hester knew it to be true.

After she was settled with Emily and had the support of her family, Hester would gladly step back into the role for which she'd been born.

In the comparative cool of the evening, Hannah Jr. lifted her petticoat and waded into the pond, willing to ignore the pesky mosquitoes for a chance to refresh herself.

"So what did Pa say?" Caleb Jr. leaned close, the two of them keeping an eye on the younger boys. "About Benjamin?"

Hannah Jr. had to snap her mouth shut before she found the words to reply. "How did thee know?"

Her brother's low chuckle was covered by the little boys' noisy splashing. "Everyone knows. Benjamin practically announced it in the kitchen when thee keeled over." Caleb Jr. straightened and stepped back, the water lapping around his bare legs. "Did thee do that on purpose?"

"I did not." Hannah Jr. lowered her voice. "I was overwrought. It happens."

"Never happened to thee before."

"I have never been in—" She caught herself.

Not fast enough, because Caleb Jr. grinned like an opossum. "I knew it. I told Robert and Joseph—"

"Thee did what?" So much for the cool of the water. Heat soared from under Hannah Jr.'s collar and raced across her cheeks.

"Worry not, they both had already come to the same conclusion."

"I would like to take a switch to the lot of thee." She let her petticoat go, not caring that it landed in the water and would weigh down her walk to the house. "'Tis none of thy business, any of thee."

"Whoa now, that is not so." Caleb Jr. held both hands out, palms toward her as if she might charge into him.

Which might not be too far from the truth.

"If thee take up with Benjamin, we would all have a Puritan broth-er-in-law."

That hadn't occurred to her before. "Would that distress thee?"

"Nay, sister. Put thy mind at ease." His grin was as reassuring as his tone. "We all like Benjamin and would welcome him gladly into our family if Pa—and Thomas—will allow it. And this whole witch nonsense works in thy favor, if thee ask me."

She gaped at him, equal parts outraged and mystified.

"Do thee not see? Thee cannot do anything about Benjamin, nor he about thee, until the witch trials cease, which they will in due time. During this delay, Pa and Thomas will grow accustomed to the idea. 'Twill make it all the easier for Benjamin to present his case to Thomas and Pa when the time comes."

Her brother had a point. The same brother who had teased her too many times to count. The same brother who had several times helped her escape from Isaac. Her irritating, wonderful eldest brother had a good point. But he was so very... dry.

With a laugh, she launched herself into him and shut her eyes as water rushed over them both.

Benji and Jonathan were watching with mouths agape when she surfaced again. Caleb Jr. rose from behind her and pulled her back under. When they resurfaced together, laughter mingling, she waded to the shore and grabbed one of Benji's hands and one of Jonathan's.

"Come on, boys, 'tis time to go home and ready ourselves for bed." She grinned as Caleb Jr. shook himself like Rags or Button would have, water spraying them all. "Tomorrow is a whole new day."

Witch trials or not, she had the love and support of her family—even in regards to Benjamin.

Epilogue

A FTER THE DELAY ABOARD ship, followed by three days in New Haven waiting for the weather to clear, Hester was almost to Milford. She'd hired a driver, the eldest son of the boarding house owner where she and Theodora had waited out the rain. If Caleb and David hadn't paid for ticket aboard the ship, she'd not have been able to afford either.

Her driver claimed to know where the Wade farm was. Tucked into a buggy with a cover for shade, they'd left New Haven at first light. While the buggy's cover kept the sun off their heads, nothing could ease the stifling August humidity. Theodora fussed and whimpered, unhappy in her sweaty clothing and unable to sleep.

But nothing could dampen Hester's anticipation of her reunion with Emily. It had built to an almost physical pressure beneath her ribs. It'd been so long since she'd seen her sister and Tobias, the man Emily married when Hester had been a young girl.

Theodora let out a long howl of protest. She was likely hungry again, and there might be more than sweat bothering her.

"Almost there." The boy glanced at Theodora before pointing to a bend in the road ahead. "Just around that corner."

"She can wait that long." Hester moved her daughter from her shoulder to her lap. Holding her so she faced forward, she said, "Look ahead, little one. Our new life awaits."

They were six days out of Salem Town. Six days of praying, waiting, and praying some more. Everything hinged on Emily's reaction to her poor relations showing up unannounced on her doorstep.

The pressure of anticipation was joined by a battalion of butterflies in her middle as the buggy rounded the curve in the road. Maple and oak trees blocked their view, but mixed in with them were soaring red pines. The perfect tree for her pine needle baskets. Hester pulled in a deep breath, appreciating the familiar scents of the forest.

The horse perked its ears and nickered.

In a few hoofbeats, a farm came into view. It was flanked by more of the forest, but one side grew fields of corn and wheat while the other side had pastures dotted with sheep. The house itself looked like most farmhouses around Salem Village. It had a wide porch, long windows with squares of glass, and two chimneys, one at each end. Two barns stood behind the house. One of a pair of heavy workhorses tied outside a barn answered the buggy horse. Chickens scratched in the dirt near several outbuildings, a flock of geese started honking as they approached, and a large red hound rose from the porch and bayed.

A man stepped out of the barn and raised a hand to shield his eyes. When a woman emerged from the house, Hester's heart nearly skipped a beat.

Emily.

Her sister came to the edge of the porch and waited, drying her hands on a piece of toweling. Then, before they were even close enough to call out a greeting, she tossed the towel aside and raced down the steps.

"Hester?"

Throat too tight to answer, and tears blurring the face of the woman approaching, Hester nodded.

"Odds bodkins!" Emily came to a halt just beyond arm's reach, her hands flying to cover her mouth. As well she should, since most Friends considered that oath to be the same as cursing.

Tobias reached her side, taking her elbow. "What has upset thee?"

"Nothing." Emily pulled away and came to where Hester was still seated on the buggy. "I cannot believe thee are here."

"Who?" asked Tobias.

"Oh!" Emily focused on Theodora. "Thee have a child?"

Hester cleared her throat and managed to say, "Theodora." Who chose that moment to scrunch up her face and howl again.

"My dear," Emily said over her shoulder, "bring Hester's things into the house." Then she scooped Theodora off Hester's lap and stepped back to give Hester room to leave the buggy. "Come inside. I hope thee are prepared for a long stay."

"Well, about that—"

"Come inside." Emily walked away with Theodora, who had quieted upon being picked up. "We shall talk out of the sun."

Hester thanked the driver and grabbed the basket with Theodora's remaining dry clouts and a corked jug of oat broth. She smiled at Tobias before hurrying after her sister.

The kitchen smelled of herbs, several bundles of which hung upside down to dry before the hearth. Hester put her basket on the long table.

"I did not even know thee had married. Thee should have written me." Emily lifted Theodora until they were nose to nose and made a silly face at the babe. "Such a beautiful child."

Another odor encroached on the drying herbs and had Hester reaching into the basket for a fresh clout. "She will need changing."

"Of course, allow me." Emily held out a hand for a clout.

Fear spiked through Hester. Changing Theodora would mean her sister would see the mark. But then, she couldn't keep such a secret from the one she hoped to take shelter with. That wouldn't be right. They were a long way from Salem Town, away from the witch hysteria. But months of guarding the secret made her hesitate.

"What is it, Hester?" Emily cocked her head. "Thee look just like Mother when she was in a quandary."

Quandary. The perfect word. Hester handed over the clout. It was time to trust.

"Theodora was a foundling left on my back porch."

Emily gasped.

"Thee will see the reason." Hester pointed to her daughter's belly as Emily eased up the gown and exposed the large red birthmark.

Boots thumped in the doorway. "Where should I put these things?" Tobias asked as he arrived with Hester's belongings.

"In the girls' old room." Emily efficiently swapped out the soiled clout for a fresh one. "Tobias, thee do remember my sister Hester, do thee not?"

"I could not have picked thee out of a crowd," he smiled at Hester, "but I can see thee favor thy mother."

"Indeed, she does." Emily finished tying off the babe's wrappings and lifted her to her shoulder. "This is Theodora. They shall be staying with us for..." She glanced at Hester.

Hester looked at Tobias, then back to Emily before clearing her throat. "Until I can establish a place of my own, if thee will have me for that long."

Emily's mouth dropped open. "A place of thy own? When we have this big old house to ourselves since our youngest son married in the spring?" She shook her head. "We would not hear of it, would we, Tobias?"

Face wrinkling into a grin, he gave Hester a wink. "She might have been willing to see thee walk out the door, but now that she has thy babe in her arms, thee has not a chance of escaping."

Relief made Hester's knees weak, so she sank onto a chair. "But thee should understand, the babe is marked."

"A birthmark." Emily scoffed. "Our second son has one not unlike it upon his shoulder. 'Tis nothing to worry over."

"But in Salem Village—"

"Have no worries, little sister." Tobias's voice grew solemn. "We know of the happenings in Salem Town. Word has traveled this far, but we do not hold to their superstitions. There are no witches in Milford, and none have arrived this day. Fear not. Thee are family and welcome here." He winked at Theodora. "Especially the little one." He left the room, carrying all of Hester's worldly belongings.

"I hardly know what to say." Hester blinked back another round of threatening tears.

Emily took a chair next to hers. "I have been fearful for thee, and our brothers and their families, in light of the reports from up north. 'Tis a wonderful relief to have thee here with us. I meant what I said, this is thy home now, for as long as thee desires." She bounced Theodora on her knee. "And I hope thee desires it for a long, long time, so we can share in and enjoy this one's growing-up years."

Peace descended on Hester in such a way that she knew it was from the Lord. The answer to her prayers. She had a home and a family who accepted not only her, but Theodora as well—mark and all. Without the witch trials, she never would have made the trek to Milford, yet already she felt at home, at ease, as if she belonged. What man had meant for evil, the Lord had used for her good.

Author's Historical Notes

Fictional Hester Fuller has reason to be worried about the accusation of witchcraft. Margaret Jones was a midwife, and in 1648, she was the first person in the American Colonies to be convicted of witchcraft and hanged.

While *The Ragpicker* and *The Carpenter* dealt only with women accused of witchcraft because that was how the event in Salem started, as time went on, several men were also accused. John Proctor, who spoke out against the accusations from the beginning, claiming the young accusers were lying, was accused himself in April of 1692. Even though more than fifty men from the villages of Ipswich, Topsfield, and Salem signed a petition claiming they did not believe the accusation against Proctor, not only was the man arrested, but his wife, Elizabeth, was accused and arrested as well. Elizabeth was pregnant, and it was determined that they would not hang her until after the baby's birth. John Proctor, on the other hand was hanged on August 19, 1692. Elizabeth gave birth to a boy, John Proctor III, in January of 1693. The witch hysteria had calmed down by then, and she was one of the many who were released from jail.

In early Colonial America, diapers were called either clouts or napkins. I chose to call them clouts as napkins have such a drastically different connotation in our modern times.

Raising a child on the broth of boiled oatmeal is something I took from my own memories. Back in the 1980s and 1990s, when we lived near Owosso, Michigan, I knew a woman we all called Grandma Kurney. Since her mother died at her birth, she was given to a neighbor to raise. That was December of 1920, and times were hard. The neighbor had no milk, and so she raised young Marie on oat broth. Marie Kurney passed away in 2022, just a couple of months shy of 102 years old. A testimony to the nutritional value of oat broth!

The birth of a child in Colonial America was both exciting and frightening. So many women and babies did not survive the ordeal. Experts estimate around forty percent of babies didn't survive to their second year. Lack of knowledge about sanitation was a large part of that, along with lack of antibiotics, lack of medical skill in general, and sometimes superstitions and old wives' tales that did more harm than good. A typical birthing included the midwife in attendance with the woman's mother, sisters, older daughters, neighbors, friends, or whoever could be on hand. They would talk to distract and encourage the woman. After the birth, the new mother was allowed a three- or four-week lying-in period. The same women would help during this period by cleaning, doing laundry, tending the garden, preparing meals, and watching any other young children. At the end of her lying-in, the new mother would prepare a feast, called a "groaning," and invite all those who has assisted her. The meal got its name from both the groaning during birth and the groaning of the table because it would be so laden with food.

Flax could be purchased in a "brick" or bundle that was already prepared to be spun. It was more expensive than growing one's own flax from seed, but not everyone had enough garden space to do that. The fibers were extracted from the flax plant, the woody outer husk having been "retted" (a wet process that literally rotted it off), then the fibers were put through a "brake" to remove the last hard bits. Finally, the fibers would be combed over a "heckle" to separate them into long, strong linen fibers. After purchasing the brick, the goodwife would "dress" her distaff with the linen strands in final preparation for spinning.

Thomas Danforth owned roughly 15,000 acres of land southwest of Boston. He was not a believer in the witch trials, and he turned a blind eye to the people who took refuge in it. Those who hid there did not associate together, instead keeping their camps separate, because they didn't know whom they could trust. The place came to be known as Salem's End.

Roger Toothaker died in jail of natural causes. By all records, he was a poor husband who had abandoned his wife and twelve children years before the witch trials. Little is known of why he was accused of witchcraft. He did have a son named after him, a doctor, but whether or not any of his family claimed his body, I do not know.

Several of the accused women had young children at the time they were jailed, and at least one gave birth while incarcerated. The children were taken into the jail with their mothers, most likely because there was no one else willing or able to look after them—perhaps due to the perceived taint of witchcraft. At least one of the children died under those conditions. Another, Dorcus Good, was eventually released, but her mind had been scarred by the ordeal, and she was considered insane for the rest of her life.

Ann Putnam Jr. was only twelve years old when the witch trials started, but she became one of the foremost accusers, having "called out" sixty-two people during the course of the trials. Of those, seventeen were executed. Many believe that her father, Thomas Putnam, a prominent and powerful man in the village, encouraged her in her role as accuser, but we will never know for sure. Her parents died in 1699, leaving her, the eldest, to raise her seven siblings. She never married and never moved away from Salem Village. She did, however, recant her accusations seven years after the fact, the only one of the afflicted girls to do so. She died at age thirty-seven. The cause of death was never recorded.

The scene where the men rescue the dead from Salem Town is based on actual history. Caleb Buffum helped the families recover and bury their dead, at great personal risk to himself had he been discovered in the act. That's as much information as I could recover in my research. I don't know if anyone went with him, but it would have been a very difficult job for a man alone, so it's more than plausible he had help.

Historically, no Quakers were accused of witchcraft during the Salem Witch Trials, but as this story progressed, it seemed plausible that my fictional Quaker midwife would have been suspected, at least. It was a twist even I didn't see coming until nearly the end of this story. For the sake of historical accuracy, she was never formally charged.

If you've read my novella, *In Sheep's Clothing*, you may have recognized the town of Milford, Connecticut, and the surname of Wade. While you didn't meet Hester Fuller's sister in that book, her husband was mentioned as the knowledgeable sheep farmer who was out of town when Yarrow Fenn needed his assistance, causing Peter Maltby to step up to the task. It's always fun to weave my stories together in small ways when I can.

Reviews are Golden

Reviews are the lifeblood of authors. Leaving a review on **Amazon**, **Goodreads**, and/or **BookBub** means that more readers will find our books! Reviews can be long or short—your honest opinion of the book. Shout-outs on any social media platforms also help!

About Pegg Thomas

A LIFELONG HISTORY GEEK, Pegg Thomas lives in Michigan's Upper Peninsula with Michael, her husband of *mumble* years. She creates American stories with real history and fictional characters inspired by her ancestors who immigrated here in the early 1600s. When not working or writing, Pegg can be found in her garden, her kitchen, or sitting at one of her antique spinning wheels creating yarn to turn into her signature wool shawls.

Pegg won the 2019 FHL Readers' Choice Award for novellas, was a double-finalist for the 2019 ACFW Carol Award for novellas, and a finalist for the 2019 ACFW Editor of the Year. She was a finalist in the 2021 FHL Readers' Choice Award for novellas. Pegg won the 2022 Selah Award for historical romance and placed 2nd with her second entry. She was also a finalist for the 2023 Selah Award, placed 2nd for the 2024 Selah Award, and won two 2024 Will Roger's Medallion Awards. Pegg spent 3 ½ years as the managing editor of Smitten Historical Romance.

PeggThomas.com
Facebook
Goodreads
BookBub
Amazon
https://www.subscribepage.com/PeggThomas
(newsletter signup)

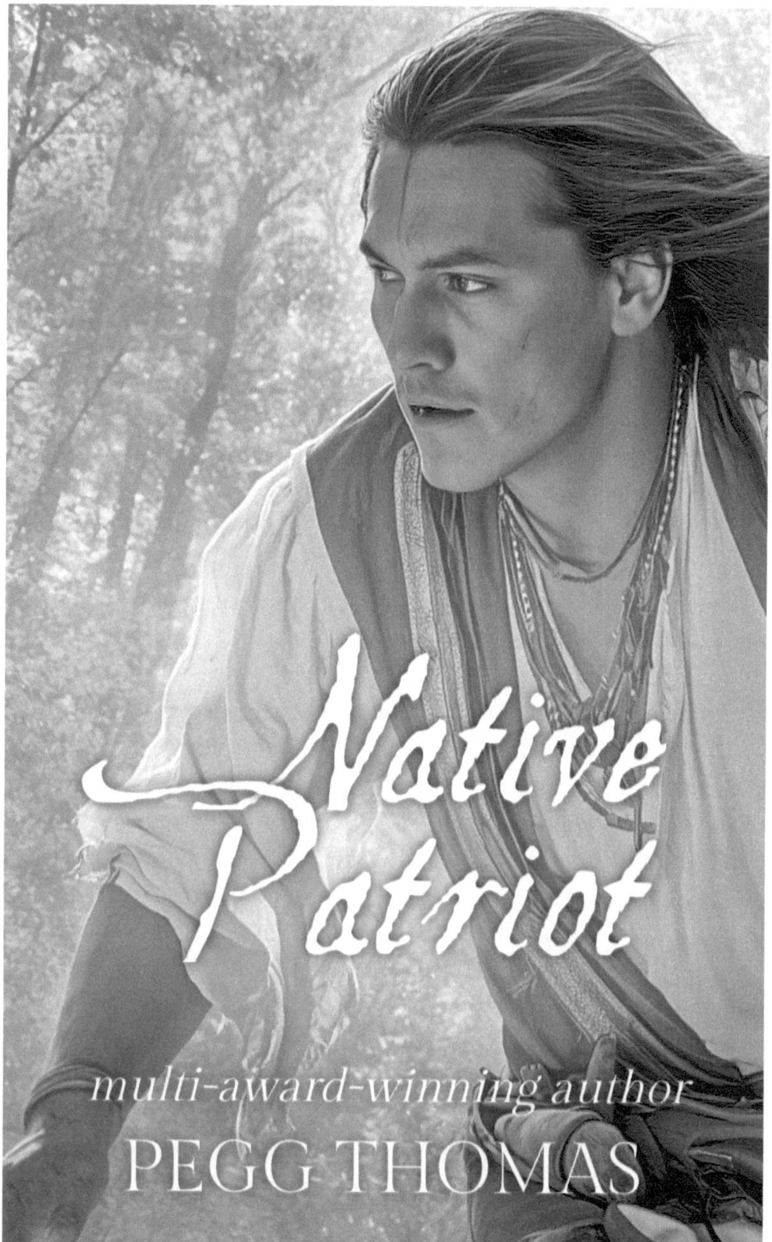
Native Patriot
multi-award-winning author
PEGG THOMAS

Native Patriot

HAIR AS BLACK AS midnight, he flowed into the tiny forest clearing in front of Grace as if materialized by her scream. Long and lanky despite the breadth of his shoulders, his crouch matched that of the panther on its rocky perch before them, both illuminated by the lingering glow after the sunset. He grasped a musket in one hand but did not raise it.

"Walk backward." His voice was soothing and low, cultured, with not a tremor of unease or uncertainty.

Grace's foot obeyed his directions, her mind clogged with the fear that had held her throat shut since her scream.

"Do not turn and run, only walk backward."

Grace forced her other foot to move, then the first again.

The man shadowed her movements without a glance in her direction, his attention on the large cat. His shoulders now blocked her view of the animal's yellowed teeth and amber eyes. She reached behind her, feeling for anything that might block her retreat.

They'd traveled at least seven rods in distance into the trees, leaving the panther behind. When a branch caught her linen cap and tore it from her head, it dislodged the pins that secured her hair. She snatched the cloth before it hit the ground, taking another step back as her hair spilled across her face. She'd made no sound, but the man turned.

Eyes barely a shade lighter than his hair met hers in the shadowed depths of the forest. The strong plains of his face were free of wrinkles, his wide mouth a straight line across his tanned skin. A dark mark divided his brow left from right, perhaps a scar. Shoulder-length hair free of a tie framed him against the deep green shadows. If not for his common hunter's clothing—a white linen shirt under a buckskin hunting jack and buff breeches—he might have been an Indian.

"Are thee hurt?" The cultured flow of his words belied his wild countenance.

Grace smoothed the front of her apron with trembling hands while she found her voice. "I think not."

He cocked his head. "I do not believe we have met."

"Nay. I have only just arrived. With the army." Washington's army had marched in earlier that day. She should have been with the rest of the camp followers, who'd set up along a tributary of Brandywine Creek. She'd been a fool to stray so far into the forest, but it kept her out of reach of—

"'Tis best to stay close to a fire in the evening."

His words were warming, reassuring, not the least threatening, but still she tensed. How often had she turned away invitations to share a man's fire... and more.

"The forest predators respect fire and avoid it."

This man might speak of panthers, but they weren't the only predators. Despite the sultry air, she wrapped her arms around her ribs.

He took a step closer. "Pray accept my pardon, 'twas not my intention to frighten thee." His brows drew together along the dark line, his eyes impossible to read.

A frog croaked in the distance, and crickets took up their evening chorus. A shiver worked the length of her back. Where was the camp? How had she allowed herself to be caught out alone with a strange man? The cultured voice meant nothing. Hadn't her mother warned her of that? Hadn't John Perkins' relentless pursuit proved it? Her throat threatened to close off again.

He retreated a step. "I would be honored to escort thee to the army's camp, should thee wish it."

Did she wish it? Nay, but what choice was left to her? Her own foolishness had caught her out.

"I would be most grateful." Had he noticed how thready her voice was? Would he pounce on her weakness as surely as the panther? Had she exchanged one dangerous beast for another?

Yet he spoke with the Quaker *thee*. Mother had installed her with Major General Greene's camp followers because of that man's Quaker beliefs. Quakers didn't walk the backstreets of Philadelphia, at least, not the backstreets where she'd grown up. That must mean something.

"Where were thee heading, miss...?" He paused, a slight tilt to his head, strands of straight black hair feathering in the breeze.

"Miss Grace. Everyone calls me Miss Grace." Because that was all the name she owned, but he didn't need to know that.